The Tamar Black Saga - Book One

BY NICOLA RHODES

In the same series

Reality Bites
Tempus Fugitive
The Day Before Tomorrow
Faerie Tale
Anything But Ordinary
Rise of the Nephilim
Pantheon

IBSN: 978-0-9561495-0-3

~FOREWORD~

The author accepts no liability for the opinions expressed by the characters in this work (who are all insane anyway). Nor can any responsibility be taken for the possible mind bending effects (or terminal boredom) produced by the reading of this work.

This is a work of fiction and any similarity to persons living, non-living or back from the dead is purely coincidental – as I will explain to my father when he is speaking to me again. (Sorry Dad)

No animals were harmed in the production of this work, but several members of the authors' family will never be the same again. This book is dedicated to them.

For Mum with thanks.
And for Claudia with love.
And for Dad, thanks for bringing round carrier bags full of inspiration, and for talking endless nonsense with me.

~ Prologue ~

IN THE BEGINNING, there was the word. (Actually, there were two words.)

And the words were "System Ready" because it was.

And the programmers saw that it was good. Not as good as it could have been, because the bosses upstairs had only given them a week to build the program. So the universe was something of a rush job in the end, but deadlines were deadlines and it would just have to do. So they pushed "Enter" and the screen flashed up "Mainframe universal systems online"

And underneath that > "Which file?"

So, the programmers accessed the stellar matrix and switched on the stars.

And the void was filled.

And the programmers saw that it was good.

So they switched on all systems and checked the files.

There were files for all things that were and all things that would ever be. And there were some files for things that would never be, but this was dismissed as a system error. They could sort it out later. After all, it had been a rush job, and they could use the overtime.

And so, the planets spun and the stars burned. Mainframe was up and running.

And the programmers saw that it was good.

So they left mainframe, which could pretty much run itself now anyway, and went home for their tea. After all, it was Sunday, and the bosses had temporarily vetoed the file for time and a half on weekends.

And it was on the weekends that some pretty interesting new files were created that the programmers completely missed. A good example of this was the "magic" or "virtual reality" files. By the time the programmers realized what had happened within mainframe, the error was too large to correct. Magic was an integral part of the system, which could not be shut down from within. And the paradox, of course, was that once mainframe was up and running, the programmers who created it, were a part of the system, and always had been, so, when they tried to delete the files, the programmers found that they could not do it. All that could be done now was to try to modify the files from within to minimise the problems for the future. Many subroutines were written to exercise some control over the many and various types of magic that had been created.

One of the worst type of magic files that had been created were the Djinn files. In order to try to sort this one out the programmers demanded, and got, their time and a half weekend pay. Even management could see that they would have to back down on this one.

Even so, the problem was only partly resolved in the end. However, the programmers felt that they had it under control.

There were around twelve hundred Djinn files to be amended. That is a lot of work in anyone's book. Perhaps it's no wonder that they missed one.

In the beginning, there was the word. And the word was "Error" And that explains a lot, doesn't it?

~ Chapter One ~

HAVE YOU EVER pondered on what you would do if you were omnipotent for a day?

Would it be world peace, an end to famine, the total eradication of all forms of county music? For one day? Obviously, what you do is, you make yourself omnipotent *forever*. Obviously! You are omnipotent, aren't you?

Okay, suppose you are offered three wishes. What should you wish for? Anybody who has given this any serious thought surely knows that the first thing to do is to wish for more wishes; which makes sense, don't you think? Wrong. If it ever happens to you, I suggest you think seriously before uttering the words 'I wish ...'

The people in myths, fairytales and the "Arabian Nights" are notoriously lackadaisical about this. Take, for example, a humble fisherman who takes pity on a small and suspiciously glittering fish, or a poor, fatherless, teenage troublemaker who accidentally releases a Genie from a lamp not to mention every heroine who has ever been startled out of their hysterical fit by a Fairy Godmother. What they all have in common is that they all choose their wishes from the standard wish catalogue (aka wishes with hidden consequences). Favourites include.

Wealth beyond the dreams of avarice (but you cause the economic collapse of several small countries and end up in prison for tax fraud).

Becoming a Prince (and then spending years croaking on a lily pad or wearing a monster suit because you offended a witch). Personal beauty (Beauty fades).

True love and of course, a new frock and a glass coach so that you won't miss the big celeb bash after all (the downside to this one should be obvious).

And this, of course, is only the fortunate few who do not waste at least two wishes on a thoughtless slip of the tongue, i.e. 'I wish you'd shut up and let me think.' Genies in particular are obnoxiously talkative; it is all part of their plan to confuse you. All that *they* want is for you to make your wishes quickly and set them free (at least until the next time they get trapped in a lamp by some cunning sod). Then there is the absolutely fatal, 'I wish I'd never opened that damned bottle/lamp in the first place.' Genies do not like this one for obvious reasons.

So, what would *you* wish for? The thing to remember is that all wishes come with a hidden catch, a trap for the unwary (and that all Genies are evil, devious, conniving swine). Better not to wish at all really, but let's face it, how many of us would have the courage to say no?

* * *

Tamaria was bored. Picnics by the river with her sisters were a regular penance. Although it was hard to imagine anything else to do in ancient Greece on a hot, sunny day, except go shopping, which was what she wanted to be doing. Xanthe, who was a year older than herself, was dull and scholarly and always spent the whole day reading under a tree, leaving her to look after Lydia who was only four and usually fractious. What she really wanted, was to be at the Agora with her friends, buying silks and jewellery and staring at young men, who would almost certainly not stare back. Tamaria was nineteen years old.

The sun was burning down on her head; the wine was warm, and the food starting to smell bad.

Xanthe, as usual, had not touched a bite, she was not interested in food or indeed in anything but literature, nor was she interested in anyone who was not interested in literature. She liked to think of herself as an intellectual, not being aware that there is a significant difference between intelligence and academia. In fact, Tamaria, who could not have quoted Aristotle if you had paid her, was far more intelligent than her elder sister (who, nevertheless, looked down on her) and she had, in addition, a store of natural cunning that she was not afraid to make full use of.

And now Lydia was starting to yell, because no one was taking any notice of her. Tamaria longed to slap her. 'Kids!' she thought. Her head was aching, and she longed for some peace.

She made a decision. 'Xan, watch Liddy for me,' she called out, 'I won't be long.'

Although her sister showed no sign of having heard, Tamaria nevertheless started to walk away, leaving Lydia howling unheeded in a muddy puddle.

Once the sound had faded away, Tamaria sat under a tree, slipped off her sandals and dangled her feet in the cool water.

'Ahhh – OUCH!' She jumped up. Something extremely solid and heavy had crashed into her ankle. 'By Zeus!' she cursed and then clapped her hand over her mouth and waited for the thunderbolt. Her mother had warned her about blasphemy. 'You can't be too careful,' she had said, 'seems as if there's a god behind every tree these days.'

When nothing happened to her, she said it again; then she bent over the water; rather like Narcissus, she thought, although with, she had to admit, little chance of the same result; her own face having what is charitably called an "unfortunate aspect".

She fished out what turned out to be a large, unusual looking bottle (unusual to Tamaria that is – in the Far East, where it had come from; it was a perfectly ordinary oil bottle such as you would find a dozen of in every household). To Tamaria, however, it was an intriguing curiosity. She turned it over a few times, shook it and pulled out the cork.

BANG! (In point of fact, "BANG!" is a bit of an understatement when describing a noise that would make a nuclear explosion sound no louder than an Aerosmith concert, and when accompanied by the kind of special-effect that would have George Lucas throwing in the towel and going into radio).

After the dust had settled and she had stopped seeing stars, Tamaria looked up and saw a ...a ...*god*? It *had* to be a god of course. Tamaria was basing this assumption on the manner of its arrival and the fact that it was twelve feet tall; apart from that, indeed, anything less godlike was hard to imagine (although Tamaria had never actually *seen* a god). For the most part, it just looked exceedingly odd. It had a large black, shiny face with teeth like tombstones in its grinning mouth. It was wearing a small, pointed beard with large black mustachios and enough bangles, earrings and chains to make The King of Thebes appear underdressed. On its head, it looked to have a large and colourful bandage fastened with a large jewel. Its chest was bare, apparently because the creature was so large that it needed two togas, one for each of its legs. Despite this, it had managed to find footwear that was much too large and had, therefore, curled up rather amusingly at the toes. Its first comment was 'A HA, HA, HA, HA, HAR!' which was not calculated to be remotely soothing or encouraging.

Remembering her earlier blasphemy, Tamaria fell on her knees, trembling, but the apparition was speaking.

'O' My Mistress,' it was saying, bowing low as it did so; 'I am Askphrit the Black and you have released me from my long imprisonment. My wish is your command – curse it - I mean *your* wish is *my* command.'

'I implore your forgiveness my Lord ... sorry, what?' Tamaria shook her head to clear it. Her ears were still ringing from the louder than BANG! Evidently, she decided, she had misheard; what it was undoubtedly saying was, 'COWER IMPUDENT MORTAL ...' etc. etc.

The thing brought its face close to hers and repeated. 'Your wish is my command.'

' ...?' Tamaria gaped and followed this up with a pretty long silence.

And then, again. 'What?' Tamaria was emboldened by the total lack of smiting that had so far occurred, although she was still feeling highly suspicious.

This god (she wondered which one it was and was leaning towards Hephaestus as the most likely suspect, since all the other gods were reputed to be handsome). Be that as it may, *this* god apparently wanted her to make a wish, and Tamaria did not like it. Since, she reasoned, the gods knew her every thought, it had to be a trap to make her say something to offend them. The only question was, why bother?

Gods, as she understood the concept, did not need much of an excuse to start the smiting or indeed any excuse at all, and they had no conscience to speak of. Still, it was probably safer to say nothing.

The putative god tried again. 'I said your wish ...'

'Yes, but ... why?' Tamaria interrupted. 'My Lord,' she added hastily, 'I am but your lowly humble servant and as such surely not worthy of such kind attention, not that it is for me to decide my Lord.'

Abasement, as her mother had often told her, was seldom out of place around a god. 'The lower you can put your face the better really', was what she had said.

Tamaria agreed with this sentiment wholeheartedly, what she wanted more than anything at this moment, was to be several leagues underground.

The "god" sighed. 'Not this again,' he said wearily, 'look, get up you silly girl.' He glowered at her, and Tamaria scrambled to her feet so fast that she dug a small trench, tripped over it and got up again, much slower this time. The "god", to her horror, was changing form. He now looked reasonably human, if far too handsome to be real, and at least he was now a normal height.

'Better?' he asked.

'Gnnng,' said Tamaria.

'Hmmm – no?' said the "god" changing again. This time it looked like what you or I would recognise as a dragon, but Tamaria had never seen a dragon, nor did she know what one was.

'AAAAGH!' was the only comment, therefore, that she could come up with on short notice, not the most constructive criticism perhaps, but to the point.

The dragon was immediately replaced by a venerable old man who looked rather like Zeus did in his paintings, but perhaps a little less muscular and fierce than the famed Thunder God.

'How about this?' asked the "god".

Tamaria fell on her knees again. 'Mighty Lord ...' she began.

'By Allah!' cursed the "god" and disappeared.

'...?' said Tamaria and looked around her in a slightly comical way rather like a cat chasing its tail. And then, because she was hot and tired and had been badly frightened she sat down and began to cry, she was, after all only young and had, up to this point, led a rather dull life and excitement apparently, was not all it was cracked up to be.

'Huh, more weeping women – just what I need,' said a voice from above her head crossly and mysteriously as far as Tamaria was concerned.

'So how's this?' it added inconsequentially. She looked up, and saw ... the best way to describe his appearance was, what in a modern American teen movie, would be the school nerd, bad clothes, pimples and a gormless expression.

Tamaria smirked automatically; no it was more of a sneer really. She could not help it. She was, after all only nineteen and was popular among her peers by virtue of being from a well off family as well as being naturally bossy, which more than made up for her lack of personal attractions.

She had also long since learned to hide her shrewd intellect, intelligence being anathema to popularity among the rich and brainless. Had she been beautiful, she would have been, on the surface anyway, the perfect airhead.

'Ah, thought so,' said the "god", 'good.'

Tamaria was now more confused than ever. The voice was the same, but surely no god would choose to look so... so... Well, *ordinary* was only the half of it.

'LOOK,' she said, finally losing her nerve, 'if you're going to smite me, just get on with it, will you? I don't have all day you know.' This, she could not help thinking, was the stupidest thing she had ever said, on so many levels.

'Smite?' said the "god" looking confused.

Then his brow cleared. 'Oh, its suicide then, is it? That was a wish then?'

'No,' Tamaria was alarmed. 'No, please, I don't *want* you to smite me – please!'

'Someone else then?' said the "god" equably. 'Who'd you have in mind? Your wish – you know – is my command.'

Finally, Tamaria opened her ears. 'It is?' she asked in wonder.

'Yes,' he told her patiently.

'*Really*?'

'Of course.'

'Oh.'

'By Allah!' The "god" exclaimed suddenly.

'Who's Allah?

'Who's ...? Look; you really don't understand do you?' he said kindly. 'Let me try to explain. I am a Djinn, Genie or Ifrit ...'

'Well, which is it? And what are those anyway?'

'Shut up.'

'Sorry.'

'As I was saying, I am a Djinn, sometimes known as a Genie or Ifrit. I am the slave of the bottle. You opened the bottle; therefore, you are now my mistress – until I have granted you three wishes. Then I will be free. They call me Askphrit the Black,' he added, feeling sure that she had not been listening to him when he had told her this earlier.

'Why?' she asked.

Askphrit shrugged. 'I don't know,' he admitted. 'They just do – the other Djinn I mean.'

'*Other* Djinn?'

Tamaria thought about all this, and then realized that she could not think about this, not yet, so instead she asked. 'And who is Allah?

'That's not relevant right now,' said the Djinn impatiently.

'So, who is the mistress here,' she said tartly, 'and who is the slave again hmm?' You can see that she was getting comfortable with the role already.

'Oh all right then,' said the Djinn, giving in. 'Allah is the Lord of all creation, the one true God,' he said, making Tamaria wish she had not asked. She looked around nervously. Back where I started from, she thought.

'Is that another name for Zeus then?' she wondered aloud.

'Zeus!' barked the Djinn contemptuously. 'Bit player. No real power at all, except over mortals and the local weather. So, I'm in Greece, am I? I was wondering. It's hard to keep track in the sea, one shark looks remarkably like another you know.'

Tamaria ignored this digression and seized on the rest.

'So the gods ...?'

'Temporary,' the Djinn assured her, 'in fact, they've already been phased out in some parts of the world.'

Tamaria digested this. It was not as surprising to her as you might have expected. She had already entertained certain suspicions. After all, if even half the stories were true, then the gods had never behaved exactly divinely.

'So what are *you*?' she asked.

'I *told* you; I am a Djinn, Genie or ...'

'Yes, but what does that *mean*?'

The Djinn bit his enormous lip. 'It's complicated, but what it means to you is that you can make any three wishes that you want, and I will grant them for you. You *have* heard of magic I take it?'

'Anything?'

'Yup.'

'Anything *at all*?'

'Yes!'

'But only the gods have that power.'

The Djinn sighed 'There you go again. Look, it's like I said, it's complicated, but basically, I have more power than all of your tin pot deities put together. I have the greatest power in the universe - under Allah.'

'Gosh.'

'I can boil the seas, change the seasons, blot out the sun ...' said the Djinn, apparently quite carried away.

'But only if my master or mistress wishes it,' he ended sadly.

'Gosh,' again.

'You see,' he explained, 'when mortals turned up on the Earth, we were enslaved to prevent us from harming them or destroying the world or whatever. Now you mortals are the only beings capable of that, "Your wish..." etc. etc.'

'Take your gods now,' he carried on in a lecturing tone, 'the only reason they exist at all is because you mortals believe in them and they can only do such damage, as you believe they can. Even mortals, it seems, need someone to blame.'

'But if you were set free...?'

'Oh don't worry about that. *I* won't do any harm. I like mortals, I mean everybody needs somebody to look down on, and I like the world the way it is anyway. But it would be agreeable to be my own boss for a while – um *change* I mean.

'So, three wishes,' he carried on, anxious now to get to the point. 'What's it going to be then? Inexhaustible wealth, great beauty (pointedly) true love?'

'Um, about the smiting, can you honestly? Only I can think of a few people ...' she trailed off thoughtfully.

'Oh yes. No problem, just point me in the right direction. Show me your enemies, sort of thing.'

'So you can even smite gods?'

'Well yes I dare say I could, but what would be the point? They'll all be gone soon anyway, lack of belief. Still, if it's what you want …'

'No,' said Tamaria with what she fondly believed to be great shrewdness, 'this is an important decision, three wishes. I mean this looks like the opportunity of a lifetime to me. I can see that this sort of thing wants a lot of thinking about. So can you just go back in the bottle or whatever, until I'm ready?'

'*Oh marvellous,*' thought the Djinn with more than a *soupçon* of irony, 'this is just what I need, another one trying to beat the system! Why do I always get them? This could take forever.'

But – 'Of course O' My Mistress, I am at your service,' is what he actually said (abasement is in the Djinn Charter) and he turned to smoke and wafted back into the bottle.

Damn!

~ Chapter Two ~

ASKPHRIT SAT ruminating in the bottle. If, he was thinking, he was smart about this, it might be worth the wait.

This one, he decided, was too clever for her own good, and he might be able to turn that to his advantage; if he could just lead her in the direction he wanted her to go.

He had a feeling that she was halfway there already – which made things easy. Not that he had not tried this before; most wishers were selfish, stupid or power mad. Oh, not all of them of course, some were hopelessly idealistic save the world types - like that strange girl who had wished that the sun would never go down (for the sake of the flowers apparently). Fortunately, it had not lasted long; there's always another Djinn whose master/mistress is out to destroy the world and when old Jham Bhutti's master at the time wished for an eternal night it had evened things out.

For "power mad" see Ashota, a Grand Vizier who, rather predictably, wished to rule the world (Grand Viziers all tend to think like this). Praise Allah that he had died from overwork before anyone noticed.

But, although all these types had possibilities, no one so far had had the right combination of sheer arrogance, stupidity and ambition to serve Askphrit's needs.

This girl, however, he judged, was all of these things and furthermore fancied herself cunning into the bargain – perfect.

He was relieved to be away from his last master, whose first wish had been, somewhat inevitably, more wishes (that happened a lot; somebody ought to review the Charter) Askphrit sincerely hoped that she did not catch on to that one, she was undoubtedly the type. But, in truth, that was a *good* thing. Yes, he was confident that she would only need a slight nudge in the right direction. After old Ibn Kadlin … but the less said about *him* the better. Total lack of ambition, not a chance there of entrapping *him*; his idea of a fabulous wish had been a new net (he had been a fisherman) mending the holes in his boat, food on the table every day, that kind of thing. And the smell! Askphrit had never wanted to be anywhere near another fish ever again, so it had been particularly disagreeable luck indeed to have spent the best part of the last fifty years at the bottom of the sea. It had made him more than usually determined to escape once and for all.

If Askphrit had only known it, he was closer than he could have ever dreamed. Tamaria, when talking of smiting had been struck by a thought. The exact thought that Askphrit wanted to plant in her head, in point of fact.

At first it had seemed just too outrageous, but the more she thought it over, the more it seemed not only feasible but even, quite possibly not really enough. If Tamaria had had such a hackneyed thing as a motto, it would have been along the lines of "Enough is never enough" or even "Too much is never enough"

The thought germinated, grew and evolved, wild fantasies gnawed at her. Soon it would not so much be a case of giving her a nudge, as of holding her back.

The thought had started as this,

'What if I could do my *own* smiting? I bet he could do that, give me that power.'

Then she had moved on to, '... or another power, not smiting! Or another power *and* smiting power. Or even smiting, plus another *two* powers; three wishes, three powers, of *course*! But what?' What powers?'

It was at this point that she had told Askphrit to get back in the bottle. You can see where this is going of course, so let's jump ahead to the following morning when Tamaria had contrived to be alone in her bedroom by means of an invented headache. The other obvious advantage to this was that, for once, it was Xanthe and not herself who was taking care of Lydia, who had cried and cried when she heard the news. (Tamaria was not particularly kind to Lydia of course, but Xanthe was worse.) And, in this way, she could also avoid the suspicious questions of the latter, who had badgered her for an hour after she had returned to the picnic party about where she had been - assuming that Tamaria had sneaked off to see her friends. Xanthe had no friends, and naturally resented the fact that Tamaria had plenty. At least she had not spotted the bottle, hidden carefully among Tamaria's clothes.

Having finally shaken herself free of her worried mother and her offers of possets and spices and various other dubious "cures" and having promised to rest, she settled down to open the bottle. An *actual* headache was, naturally, out of the question she felt exhilarated and her hands were shaking, but there was a strange pounding at her temples, which was rather worrying. She decided not to worry about it; if this worked it would mean that she would never have to worry about anything ever again.

She took a deep breath and pulled out the cork. BANG!

Curse it! She had forgotten about the noise. Her mother came running across the courtyard. 'Tammy, Tammy, are you all right? I heard the most terrible noise. What happened?'

Tamaria panicked; also she hated being called "Tammy" naturally. 'Think,' she muttered, 'think!' Her mother was almost at the door.

'Of *course* I'm all right mother,' she said imperiously. 'Don't be silly. It must have come from the street. Please go away, so I can sleep,' she held her breath and heard

'Oh, a - all right dear, um if you're sure.'

'I'm sure.'

'Yes, well… I could fetch you some ...'

'No Mother, please.'

'Yes well, I'll um ... pop in later to see if you're feeling better.'

Tamaria un-gritted her teeth as she heard her mother's footsteps fade away. Phew! As they say.

Askphrit was disappointed, a perfect opportunity for a wasted wish. Gone! This one was obviously way smarter than she looked. He was trying, with a conspicuous lack of success, to hide behind a pot-plant. Just as if he could not turn himself into anything he liked – an ant for instance – or even make himself invisible. He was hoping that she would not think to wonder why he had not.

Apparently, it never crossed her mind. She looked at him acidly 'You can come out now,' she said dryly.

'O' My Mistress ...' he began.

'Yes, yes,' she said testily. 'Now then,' she took a deep breath, 'I wish ...'

* * *

Askphrit could not believe it – literally. As a purveyor of human misery by the dispensing of countless 'free lunches' over the centuries, he could not help looking for the catch. There had to be one. It just could not be that easy; it never is. Nobody knows this better than a Djinn. Thousands of years of luring humanity into believing that they could have it all for nothing had made a confirmed sceptic of him. See the gift horse? All I want to look at are its teeth.

On the other hand, he had waited years for an opportunity like this, and experience told him that it would never happen again. Besides, what could go wrong? No, do not go there. Because, he realized, it was too late, she had made the wish.

'Very well,' he shrugged, 'here goes nothing.' He smirked maliciously.

'Your wish is my command.' And he snapped his fingers. There was a special-effect that would have made a couple of amateur filmmakers, working in their dads' garage with plasticine and a camcorder, feel ashamed.

'I don't feel any different, said Tamaria pettishly. 'Are you sure it worked?'

'Oh yes, it worked,' he held up his wrists, and the shackles that Tamaria had not even noticed, broke apart and fell off and to her everlasting horror, materialised on her own wrists.

'What the ...?' she shrieked.

Askphrit laughed

'What have you done?'

'What you asked me to,' he told her complacently.

'NO!'

'But yes. You wished to be omnipotent, omniscient and immortal. That's three, so I'm free. The catch is ... there's *always* a catch; you knew that didn't you? Oh you didn't? Well there is. In this case, the *only* beings who possess all those powers are The Djinn. So, you're a Djinn now. You asked for it!'

'But, what about the gods?' she asked plaintively.

'Oh no, haven't you been *listening*? They're on the way out. And as for omniscience, most of them couldn't locate their backsides with a map, as the saying goes.'

'But,' she grasped at a straw, 'all I have to do is grant three wishes and then I'll be free too, right?'

'Not exactly, you'll only be free for as long as you can stay out of the bottle, and trust me, some cunning swine always manages to get you back in there – eventually.'

'What bottle?'

Askphrit pointed.

'But that's *your* bottle.'

'Not any more little girl,' the former Djinn sneered, 'I'm free now, and since *you've* replaced me, it's *your* bottle now.

Nobody's ever putting me back in *there*. Can't!' He laughed and laughed and laughed and… Well you get the idea.

He stopped suddenly. Tamaria's face was such a picture of misery that he felt suddenly sorry for her.

'Look,' he said, consolingly, 'it's not that bad. You're a bright girl. You'll be free – for a while at least – pretty soon, and if you're smart, you can make it a long time. Then again, maybe you can pull the same stunt on some other poor sap.'

Tamaria brightened up slightly.

'Look,' he continued, 'I'm sorry I did it to you, (well really, you did it to yourself) but I've waited a long time to be free. Really free, I mean, permanently.'

'How long?' Tamaria whispered.

'Oh um – never mind. The point is *you* know how it's done. I didn't. I had to figure it out for myself, didn't I? And in the meantime you have all these amazing powers.'

'Not much use to me in a bottle, are they?' said Tamaria bitterly.

'Yes, well. How would it be if I set you up with your first sucker? I mean client.'

'No, you had it right the first time. I certainly feel like a right sucker. You νόθος.' * she added feelingly.

'Well, there's gratitude for you. I'll just let you get on with it shall I?'

'No! Please, I mean you *did* get me into this mess, the least you could do is…'

'All right, all right, point taken. I suppose I can spare you some time. After all, I do have an eternity now.'

'Don't rub it in.'

'Right; well first you'll want to see what you can do. Try this.' And he changed back into the very handsome man she had seen the previous day. Tamaria concentrated and changed.

'Er yes, very good,' he said trying to suppress a laugh. 'Now how about trying something a *little* more feminine? Let me see, what have you always wanted to look like?'

---

* An extremely rude Greek word that I have no intention of translating, use your imagination

She tried again.

'Take a look. No, don't *walk* to the mirror, teleport – just sort of move yourself there with your mind. Always impresses the suckers.'

She did it, and there in the mirror was Aphrodite herself, as seen in various paintings and sculptures that Tamaria had seen all her life. Gone was the limp, mousy hair that never dressed properly, the too small eyes, the prominent slightly hooked nose and pale lips. In their place was a cascade of golden hair, large blue eyes and a button nose and rosebud mouth set off by a peaches and cream complexion. She appeared to be taller too.

'Wow, that's me?'

'Yup.'

'By Allah – why did I just say that?'

'Oh, er it's a Djinn thing.' He said this rather cagily, but Tamaria did not notice.

'You can take on any appearance you can think of now,' he told her, 'but I have to admit I like that one.'

'So do I,' breathed Tamaria. 'Maybe darker hair, what do you think?'

'Try it?'

She watched in fascination as the golden hair became a glossy raven black. 'Wow.'

As you can probably imagine, this went on for quite some time; so let's skip over the makeover scene to the point when Tamaria was finally satisfied with her appearance, and Askphrit was thoroughly fed up. Eternity's a long time, but there's no point wasting it. Hadn't he wasted enough of it?

Although, he had to admit, the final result was breathtaking. Aphrodite, pah! Eat your heart out. Tamaria had obviously been thinking about this for a long time.

She then learned to fly, to teleport all over the globe (she was surprised to learn that it *was* a globe) and to manifest and transmogrify. Of course, she did not actually have to *learn*. It was a question, as Askphrit explained it, of "think it and it happens" – easy. 'Want to move a mountain, dry up an ocean?

No problem. Although, you'll find you can't do the really big stuff like that unless a mortal wishes for it.'

He manifested a copy of the Djinn Charter. 'Read it in the bottle,' he advised. 'It gets boring in there after you've redecorated for the millionth time. Although I flatter myself that I've made it quite cosy in there. You might not like it though,' he said, doubtfully, looking around her room.

'If it's so damn cosy, why don't you get back in there?' said Tamaria with some asperity, as the reality of her situation came back to boot her in the face.

'No fear.'

'Worth a try,' she said ruefully. The convivial atmosphere had dissipated faster than new Government's election promises, leaving behind nothing but an awkward silence.

Askphrit had never expected to feel so guilty about this; he had never truly expected it to happen at all.

'That's the spirit,' he said heartily, 'don't despair.' He was suddenly desperate to cheer her up.

'There are two ways to free yourself permanently,' he advised. 'One is the way I used on you. You fool some suck... some mortal into taking your place. The other is for the client to wish you free.

'Don't hope to hard for that one,' he added sagely. 'They're a selfish lot. Anyway the downside to that one is that you'll become human again.' He stopped, realising that this line of encouragement was not helpful.

They both looked at the bottle.

'Need I get in right now?' she asked woefully.

'Yes I'm afraid so, the rules are pretty clear. I tried to get around it once, well I tried everything. It was nasty.'

'What ...?' she began to ask, but he held up a hand.

'Pray you never find out.'

She sighed. 'I suppose there's no getting out of it.'

'No, sorry.'

'So – what will *you* do now?'

'Oh, I don't know, you know how it is. You make all these plans for your retirement then, when it finally comes, you just don't know what to do with yourself. I mean, I'm still a Djinn, if you know what I mean, but then again I'm not. I expect I'll figure it out. After all, I've got plenty of time.'

'What do you usually do with your time off?' she asked, not because she cared, she was stalling for time.

'Oh, you know this and that. They were just holidays you know, and I couldn't use all of my powers then. I can now.'

There was another awkward silence.

'Well thanks,' said Tamaria thrusting out a hand, 'for, you know, starting me off and everything. I don't suppose you had to.'

'Least I could do.'

'Well yes!'

'Right,' Askphrit clapped his hands and rubbed them together like a nervous substitute teacher on his first day trying to take refuge in a business-like manner.

'Better get in. I'll drop you off with a decent first mark. Nice callow youth to start you off, should be no problem for you, not looking like *that*.

Tamaria said nothing.

Askphrit held out the bottle. 'Er, by the way,' he said 'what's your name? You never did tell me.'

'Tamar...' she began.

Askphrit cut her off. 'Of what House?' he asked with a twinkle in his eye.

'Of the house of Menelaus,' she said proudly.

Askphrit grinned. 'Not anymore,' he told her. 'Now you are "Tamar The Black" Oh and one more thing, I should have told you before. Don't know what's happened to my memory. When you do get out, keep an eye on your bottle. Once a mortal gets hold of it, you're his, even if you're not actually in it at the time.'

'Oh terrific,' she moaned, 'Look, just do it will you, the suspense is killing me.'

'Djinn home,' he said, and Tamar the Black felt her body dissolve with a horrible feeling of destiny. When she re-materialised she found herself in a nasty, untidy room with a faint smell of oil permeating the brown walls. She could not see out, which was a surprise; surely glass was transparent?

And the light seemed to be coming from within the bottle not from outside as she had expected. She surveyed her surroundings.

'Cosy!' she snorted disparagingly, 'huh! What a dump. Oh well better get on with it. This could take some time.'

Thirty seconds later she was standing in an exact facsimile of the temple of Artemis that she had visited with her mother. Her – mother… she waited for the pang that she knew, in the deep recesses of her conscience, that she should be feeling about her, about the fact that she would never see her, or any of her family, ever again. It did not come. In fact, suddenly they seemed quite far away and insignificant. She had forgotten for the moment that she was not human anymore and, as such, could no longer experience human feelings of any kind. She shrugged and added a bed to the furnishings, picked up the Charter and then Tamar the Black settled down to read and wait.

* * *

Later on, Tamar's (former) mother came bustling into the room. She was muttering under her breath in the way that mothers do. 'I don't know, these girls what a mess it is in here, look at this, scrolls strewn everywhere. I do wish Xanthe would go out more, make some friends or something. If only she had a sister more her own age than poor little Lydia. Someone she could *talk* to.

~ Chapter Three ~

TAMAR WAS BORED. She had spent the best part of several millennia feeling bored actually; Askphrit certainly had not been wrong about that.

She had considered choosing a surname, just for something to do, and to help her fit in. Suddenly everybody had a surname; it was the latest thing she assumed. She was not really sure when it had started. The truth was, she had never fitted in anywhere, even in her own family, and she just could not think of one that she liked anyway. Not that it would have mattered for long if she had. Surnames, she assumed were just another human fad. She had seen many of them come and go over the centuries. Family names had been popular before - in China for instance and ancient Rome (but only for the nobility) but these usually had some significance. Modern surnames seemed, primarily to be for distinguishing one Julie or Alan from another. The same objective could be achieved by assigning everyone a number. Indeed, since the twentieth century, this seemed to be the way things were going, with everybody having a myriad of numbers attached to their name.

National insurance or social security numbers, bank accounts, medical cards and video club card numbers and so on. It would not be terribly long, Tamar surmised, before names were phased out entirely as unnecessary. In fact, give it another century or two, and people would just be given a barcode at birth, and that too would just be another fad as far as Tamar was concerned.

What humans liked best, as far as she could see, was not sex or fighting each other or making money. These were just the things they *thought* they liked doing best. What they *really* liked was organising the world, categorising people, listing them and putting them in order so that they could always lay their hands on them. Making up a huge ledger of humanity to keep everything and everyone in their place. They seemed to find doing this reassuring; all trying fervently to make order out of what was essentially chaos. It had never changed, and it was very different from what they believed they wanted. But when a man wishes for power, what he actually wants is to be the one at the top of the list, the person who draws up the ledger and organises all the rest. Those without power console themselves with organising their CD collection. It is the reason that parents interfere with their children's marriages.

It had been, up to a point, an interesting life, which contrasts sharply I know with what was said earlier about boredom. But, in fact, although there had been enough interest and excitement to fill one ordinary lifetime, Tamar had now been around for the equivalent of several hundred lifetimes; hence boredom most of the time.

She considered that she had got off to a particularly unfortunate start. The callow youth had turned out to be a nasty cunning weasel whose first wish had been for unlimited wishes for the rest of his life, which had meant that she had been stuck with him for the next sixty odd years. Praise Allah he had not thought to ask for immortality. He had never married; there had been no need with Tamar on hand to provide hot and cold running girls day and night, and Tamar herself to perform all domestic requirements. So this meant, at least, that he had had no heir to leave the bottle to, and when he finally died, Tamar set off with the intention of hunting down Askphrit – the νόθος' and giving him a piece of her mind.

To date she still had not found him, and sometimes she wondered if he had left the planet, which was entirely possible (she herself had run a few trips to the outer rings of Saturn.) She hoped not, because now what she wanted was a lot more than a sharp word.

After the cunning weasel had died Tamar became a mermaid for a while. She had harboured this fantasy for a long time, ever since she had been a small girl. Unfortunately, the reality, as is usual in such cases, was a bit if a disappoinment and she only stuck it for a decade or so. At first it had been wonderful, the freedom of the ocean was intoxicating, and it was so beautiful down there. More importantly, she felt sure that nobody would force her into her bottle in the sea. The other mermaids (whose existence had surprised her at first) were magical creatures in their own right and not interested in wish-fulfilment. They had recognised her as Djinn straight away (something about the eyes apparently) but had made her welcome anyway. And it had been fun for a while, but eventually, as with everything else, it became tedious. Mermaids, in common with Rhine Maidens, who she met later on, are not known for their intellectually stimulating conversation. Perhaps having a short attention span is an evolutionary advantage in such a repetitive environment, stopping them from going insane with frustrated boredom. But the real problem in the end for Tamar, was the neighbours. Not the sharks, barracudas or stingrays, any Djinn (or mermaid for that matter) can deal with that. No, it was the cursed Sirens.

A mermaids' main MO is to sit prettily on a rock, singing sweetly to lure sailors to their doom.

Likewise, the job description of a Siren, as laid out by Circe, is to sit prettily on a rock, singing sweetly to lure sailors to their doom, in their case, straight into the clutches of Circe, a sorceress who was seriously overreacting to being dumped by her boyfriend.

What began as a bitter rivalry had degenerated over time into the feudin' an' a fightin' normally reserved for those clans who live in the backwoods and marry their cousins. What had started out with the marine equivalent of tipping the rubbish bins over the fence into next doors' garden had escalated into sneaking about in the middle of the night, rearranging shark nets or breaking into the menagerie and letting out all of Circe's pet sailors (some of which were dangerous animals) causing no end of chaos.

By the time Odysseus arrived, a big muscular chap with destiny written all over him, and the whole thing had degenerated into a bloody free for all with the Sirens winning, Tamar had had enough. She put herself back in the bottle and hitched a ride with the hero. It was either that or join the sirens – she felt she would have made a good siren, she was alluring and she had no morals, but, unfortunately, she had no singing voice to speak of. Besides which, she did not like them.

* * *

The three wishes of Odysseus were: -

One, 'Get that damn song out of my head.'

Two, 'Get my ship safely past that monster and the whirlpool from hell' (Scylla and Charibdis)

Three, 'Help me to string this blasted bow; my arthritis is playing me up.' (Well he had been at sea for ten years.)

It was all far too easy and, sooner than she could have believed, she was free again; though somewhat disappointed. Anybody, she thought, manifesting destiny all over the place like that, should have had more ambition. She had sincerely hoped that he might be the one; it was the only reason she had not turned herself into a seagull and got the hell away from there.

"The one", the ultimate sucker, had proved frustratingly elusive. Nobody, it seemed was prepared to be as stupid and greedy as *she* had been. How many times had she wheedled, 'You could have all the power that you want, if you knew what to ask for,' to those who had seemed amenable? Mainly those who had started off by wishing for more wishes and there were a depressingly large number of these. But they never did get the point. It is forbidden in the Djinn Charter to directly suggest a wish to a client, but nobody could say that she had not done her best. Enlarging on the amazing powers that she possessed, just as Askphrit had done to her (the νόθος). But they were all either too stupid or too wary to fall for it. Even the foolish Prince, who had come so close and then had inadvertently wished for impotence. She had always felt that it served him right. His first wish had been to become King, and his father had immediately died.

And always, always she ended up back in the bottle; Askphrit had been right about that too. Djinn genetics dictated a fatal flaw, a tendency to get suckered back into the bottle by even the most obtuse of humans, or even – and she had done this herself once or twice – a penchant for saying to themselves. 'I'll just get back in for a while to get away from it all.' And of course, once inside it takes a mortal to get them out – another thing Askphrit had failed to mention. There is a strong link between a Djinn and her or his prison. It calls to them as irresistibly as any Siren to a boatload of sex starved jolly tars. There is no escape; it's probably psychological.

Tamar, on making her first escape had, quite predictably, smashed the bottle. She had not really expected it to work; nothing's ever that easy. It had not; she had smashed it three times and every time she turned round, there it was. And every time she turned around for evermore, there it would be.

She had watched the world change; intermittently naturally, she had missed bits and had had to catch up later. Although, being a clever girl, she had spent more time out than in. She had been all over the world and had been slaved to many different types of people. She had spent time with the Vikings and the Hun and other assorted warrior types until they all began to look the same, fierce, drunk and waving a bloodstained sword. With Kings, not so many of these, royalty tend to have people to open bottles for them. Sorcerers, although they seemed to have become extinct now. Come to think of it, she had not seen a dragon for a hell of a long time either.

Mostly though, she had met ordinary people, some of whom had become Kings or Sorcerers (and even one dragon, but he had been killed shortly afterwards by a chap named George, she seemed to remember) soon after they met her.

She had seen history being made, then changed, and then forgotten as the centuries piled up, and now she had arrived in the twenty first century; a time when technology was threatening to make magic redundant, something she had never thought she would see.

Technically, she was not seeing it now, since she was once again back in the bottle. (Since nineteen ninety-two, in fact, when her last master had refused to use his last wish saying he was saving it for an emergency. He had then had inconsiderately gone and died on her, leaving her trapped) more than ten years and she was bored.

She tended these days (that is for the last two centuries or so) to spend her time in the bottle, in between redecorating and experimenting with her appearance, (even a million years would not see her tire of this) thinking about how to make the world a better place for human beings.

Because, unlikely as it seems, she had become quite fond of them. Something she had never been when she had been one. Even the worst human always had some redeeming quality (even politicians, who were there, apparently to give the rest of the population someone to blame now that the gods were gone)

Until *she* turned up, that was. Getting rid of all the Djinn, she had decided would be a good start. But so far nobody had thought to wish for that and she could not suggest it (rule seventeen) but if she were only free... As it was only humans are free and have the power to change the world – shame.

The elimination of all evil was not the answer. It is never that simple, there has to be balance. Without evil, there cannot be good – a cliché but true nevertheless, like all clichés. Getting rid of the Djinn, however, would definitely be a step in the right direction. It would stop them from popping out of bottles, barging in on some poor mortal's life and downright buggering it up; like *she* always did. Sometimes she hated herself, but she could not help it, it was not as if she could pop out of the bottle and say 'Your wish is my command – but I wouldn't recommend it.' And even if she did, no one would listen. If mortals have a fatal flaw, it is wanting something for nothing. Not one of them so far had resisted temptation; she could not blame them; that is the whole point of the Djinn/Master set up.

She had been over this a thousand times (at least). It was only increasing her frustration. She was trapped; all she could do was carry on trying to get free at someone else's expense. She wished (ha) that there were another way. But if she ever *did* escape… ha, if!

In the meantime – there was only boredom.

There was a familiar rush of air above her head, and her body started to dissolve. *Here we go again!*

~ Chapter Four ~

DENIS SANGER WAS in a good mood, Denny to his frie … as he was known informally; to his boss, for example, although his boss also variously called him Pete, Mike, John and even sometimes just "Hey man".

Also to the Landlord of the "Fiddler's Elbow", and to Barry, Mosh and Skinner who he sometimes met in the aforementioned Fiddler's Elbow; he did not, however, regard these last mentioned as his friends. The last person he had regarded as a friend had been Timmy White in Junior School. (He had had "cronies" at high school, of course, of the Barry, Mosh and Skinner types, who had tolerated him for his "wicked" sense of humour. A sense of humour which had included, wearing his school tie around his head instead of his neck, filling his mouth with maggots in biology class and leaping around on tables playing air guitar.) Since his definition of a friend was a person with whom one had interests in common and who was unlikely to kick your head in if he inadvertently offended them, Denny now had no friends that he considered worthy of the name.

So far, however, Denny's head remained intact and Barry, Mosh and Skinner were useful contacts whose housebreaking proclivities had provided Denny with some interesting items of cult memorabilia, the true value of which they were entirely unaware.

Not that he approved of their methods of course, but he did not want to offend them by saying so. So he pretended to believe what they told him, that they were in the "house clearance" business, which, in a manner of speaking, was true. They just did not bother to get the owner's permission first.

For their part, he knew, they regarded him as an easy mark, to offload all the "geek rubbish" onto, or rather, they now targeted stuff that they knew he would be willing to buy. He could think of no way to dissuade them from doing this without losing his kneecaps.

Denny's cheerful mood today was on account of their latest acquisition. A mint condition original Millennium Falcon still in the packaging. And the fact that he had once again got away with his arms and legs still attached.

Of course, he had, as usual, had to buy a whole box load of rubbish along with it, in what Barry referred to as a "job lot". But it did not matter; he had still paid far less than it was worth. The lads were delivering it to his flat for him, while he was at work. They did not have a key, well they did not need one and Denny knew for a fact that when he got home, a small but significant amount of minor items would be missing and he would have to re-stock the fridge with beer. It was a small price to pay.

He wandered back to work, singing "Don't Fear The Reaper" under his breath, and made a mental note to call in at the off license on his way home.

* * *

The box was on his kitchen table, or rather it was in the space where his kitchen table had once been. He sighed, but he knew it would be returned eventually. Denny was regarded as a good customer, and Barry would certainly be annoyed that the lads had taken something like that from him. Denny could almost feel sorry for them when he found out.

He noticed, as he traversed the hallway, that the photograph of his mother was also missing. He had kept this picture, not out of sentiment, but rather because of a sense of dread that the old battleaxe would come back to haunt him for a lack of respect if he did not. Which was why it had been tastefully framed in solid silver (this was presumably why the lads had taken it and not for the sake of the picture it held therein) and draped in black, like the pictures of war heroes – she would have liked that. He felt a sense of relief; it was gone; no longer would it watch him disapprovingly every time he walked to and from the bedroom, and he could not be in any way blamed for its absence – he had been robbed.

He put the beer down on the floor, there being no other surface available, and knelt down to dismember the box. He did not expect there to be anything else of interest in it, but, he thought, you never knew. Sometimes Barry included items that he thought might be useful. Denny had the feeling that Barry quite liked him really, and even felt rather sorry for him. Or maybe he just could not believe that all that "geek junk" was going to keep Denny interested in buying from him.

Whatever the reason, he had, in the past included in his parcels a toaster, a set of tools, which Denny had sent to his brother as a Christmas present. It served him right for being better looking and more successful than him, in Denny's opinion, as well as being the most complete and total git that had ever stalked the earth. Also, on one memorable occasion, Barry had stuck in a state of the art ten CD changer mini system stereo which Denny, never technically minded, though he would have loved to be, promptly broke, to his great dismay. He could only assume that its inclusion had been an error, or an example of Barry's pity. He could not find out, because Barry never mentioned it, and Denny was afraid to, in case he asked for it back.

He carried the box, staggering a little under its not great weight (Denny had the muscle tone of an elastic band) into the bedroom and plonked it down on the bed, the better to facilitate its dismemberment in the absence of his table.

The contents were a little disappointing, (Millennium Falcon notwithstanding) including some ragged bath towels, two ancient LP's (one of which he already had, but would have denied having even under torture) and what appeared to be a dead cat, but which, on closer inspection, when taken out with great trepidation, turned out to be a Davy Crockett hat.

What sort of person did they hit? Denny wondered. He must have been a right weirdo. Denny conveniently glossed over the fact that he had coveted at least one item that this person had previously owned and already owned another. His own bath towels would not have stood up to close scrutiny either. Only the coonskin hat did not fit in, and Denny *had* once bought a deerstalker on impulse, though he had never worn it in public. He just knew he was not cool enough to pull it off without being beaten up on every street corner.

The dismemberment over, he inventoried his haul, a broken telephone, and a stack of dirty magazines, which he filed under the bed, a box of curtain hooks and a cracked figurine of a shepherdess. He dumped this on top of the rest of the junk back in the box and went to get a beer.

When he got back and picked up the box to dump it on the floor, so that he could lie on the bed to watch TV, the bottom dropped out of it. Cursing he kicked out at one of the tatty towels; his feet were bare, and he did not want a broken toe, but the towel felt oddly solid. It rolled away from him, which was unexpected. Then, it unrolled across the floor, revealing, rather like Cleopatra's carpet trick, something that had been wrapped up in it.

Curiously he went to went to pick it up. It turned out, to his disappointment, to be an old and dirty looking bottle, made out of some opaque type of glass. He sighed and put it on the mantelpiece. He could not have said why he did this, instead of putting it in the box with the rest of the junk. He drew the curtains against the glare and settled down to watch TV.

Djinnx'd

There was nothing on the TV and he could not settle. The bottle on the mantelpiece kept drawing his attention. He wondered what was in it; it had felt unusually heavy. He tried to ignore it, it was just an old bottle, but he kept finding his eyes drawn to it. It was making him fidgety. Eventually he gave up. He switched off the TV with a snarl and flung himself off the bed and grabbed the bottle intending to hurl it into the box, which he would then take out to the bin. But once he had it in his hand curiosity overcame him. It was very heavy for such a small bottle. It could not hurt just to have a look inside, maybe there was something valuable in it. Its previous owner had been something of a kook in Denny's opinion; anything was possible. He pulled out the cork.

~ Chapter Five ~

TAMAR FOUND HERSELF in a dank looking bedroom; the light was of the murky twilight quality that is found when the curtains are drawn during the day. The place looked tidy, but not clean. The wallpaper was peeling, the carpet stained and the place smelled of mildew. Aside from the fact that it had the stark tidiness that comes from having no possessions at all, it reminded Tamar of the way Askphrit – the νόθος' had left the bottle for her.

Staring at her, from under a shaggy fringe of dusty blond hair, with an expression of acute horror in his deep blue eyes, was a skinny young man. His expression puzzled her, bewilderment she had seen, wonder and frank admiration, but never before, horror. It was annoying, particularly as she knew she was looking her best.

She was. What he saw was this, a tall, slender girl of about his own age, icily beautiful with jet hair that shone like glass and looked as if it might reach her feet if it were let down, and sparkling dark blue eyes, like a midnight sea. (Really, he was getting quite poetical in his musings) She had a clear cut ivory

face, and a beautiful Grecian nose, the lines of her face were all strong angles and planes, heroic in concept, yet somehow severe. For all its amazing beauty, it was the face of a woman who had seen too much of the world. The face of a fighter. *
And her skin was so pale she seemed almost luminous, like the moon – Tamar never could get used to the idea of a suntan being attractive. Although not a connoisseur of female figures, he could see that hers was magnificent, and her carriage perfect, as if she had a plumb line from her crown to her feet. She terrified him that was the truth of it. Even moderately attractive women scared him, but this vision… not that she was real of course, he knew that.

Denny was quite understandably under the impression that he was having a nervous breakdown, either that, or the bottle had contained some mind altering substance that created remarkably realistic and yet totally impossible hallucinations. In that case, though, why was she fully clothed, and looking bad temperedly at him? He tried to ignore her; perhaps if he went for a lie down. But somehow he could not, not with her in the room, it would seem rude. Then quite suddenly he knew. He knew she was real, and he was not crazy or tripping or anything. He just did not have the imagination to create her. Somehow, this realisation did not make him feel any better.

Tamar surveyed him intently. This is what she saw:

A pale, pointed face, the features finely drawn and sharply defined with prominent cheekbones set above cadaverously hollowed cheeks, an aquiline nose (his only classically attractive feature) and a fascinating overbite. His hair was too long and too fine and would have been the colour of corn had it been cleaner. He was tallish but not over tall, about her own height and very thin, yet it was a thinness that seemed to be natural to him and due no illness. The face was boyish, and yet the eyes that looked out of this face seemed to have seen a lifetime of unpleasant experience. This gave him a curiously

---

* Although Tamar had chosen her own face, somehow certain aspects of her personality had been stamped on it despite herself. Or perhaps the face she had chosen, was representative of what she was inside, if so, it was unconsciously done

ageless quality. He could have been anywhere between twelve and thirty years old. All this, however, Tamar felt, was only what he *looked* like.

He was interesting. He did not belong here; she could see that. Perhaps this was not his room; he looked wrong in it. Despite the scruffy clothes, longish, unkempt hair, unshaven chin and pasty complexion, he just did not belong here. Technically he looked like a drug addict, in perfect synch with his surroundings, but intuitively he looked like a ... a. She gave it up, it would come to her; maybe she had met one of his ancestors in a very different set of circumstances. That might account for it. She became aware that she was staring at him, that they were, in fact, staring at each other. He at least had some excuse for his surprise.

She decided to get on with it. 'What do you want then?' she asked abruptly.

'Huh?' Denny was understandably confused by this remark. Surely, he thought, in the circumstances, that ought to be *his* line.

Tamar watched the confusion spread over his face and pulled herself together. She began the customary spiel.

'O' My Master, I am the Djinn of the bottle whom you have released into your service ...'

She had found it better, since the eighteenth century, to explain the situation fully, and even then most people took a lot of persuading to believe it.

'You may have of me, any three wishes of your choosing. Your wish is ... my ...' She trailed off, embarrassed. He was giving her the most peculiar look that she had ever seen. It was a look that she really should have recognised. She had felt it on her own face often enough. He looked bored; disinterested might be a better word, and slightly wary.

'No thanks,' he said.

'S – Sorry?'

'I said, no thanks, I'm not interested. Thank you all the same.'

'I'm not sure you understand,' said Tamar. 'Three wishes, anything you want, your heart's desire, anything! I'm a Djinn, you know, a Genie, a real one.'

'Yes, I understand, but I don't want anything thank you. Can you leave the way you came in?' He sounded like a man talking to a double glazing salesman.

'No I can't leave, you're my master.'

'Oh – well, you can stay if you like. Would you like a cup of tea?'

'A – ? Oh well, yes all right then, thank you,' said Tamar, trying to pull her scattered wits together. She did not want a cup of tea; she just wanted him to stop looking at her as if she was a peculiar type of wildlife specimen instead of a stunning and all-powerful being.

Well, may as well get acquainted, she thought. 'What's your name?' she asked the back of his head as he rattled cups. She would not have been surprised to hear that his name was Heathcliff or Tyrone or perhaps Dante. It was those curiously intense eyes, and perhaps the floppy hair.

So it was a bit of a disappointment when he told her, 'Denis Sanger.'

'Is that all?' she blurted out then bit her lip. He did not seem to notice.

It was such an ordinary name for someone with those eyes, deep melancholy eyes, the eyes of a man with the soul of a poet. She shook herself mentally; what was she thinking?

She waited for him to ask for *her* name. To show some interest in her, after all she had to be the most intriguing visitor he had ever had, she thought petulantly.

He said, 'Here's your tea.'

She tried again, 'Denis is a nice name,' she said, untruthfully.

'Call me Denny.' He would not look at her.

'I'm not really sure about mine, it's pretty old fashioned.' She waited. But he did not seem to have heard her. He looked as if he wished she would just go.

She realized, with a shock, that she was probably irritating him.

'Mirror,' she said, and one materialised in her hand. No, still as perfectly beautiful as it was possible to be. Maybe he was ... maybe she should have been male, but somehow she did not think that was it, and even if it was, there was still the whole "Being of infinite power" thing. Perhaps he did not believe in her; perhaps beautiful girls appeared in his room with a flash and a bang as a matter of course. (They did – often, but not in real life.)

Tamar was getting impatient. Perhaps he thought he was dreaming. That had happened before.

Denny knew he was not dreaming; he only wished he were. He thought all this was terrible. He had read about things like this happening, and it always ended badly. He wondered how he could get rid of her. Like Tamar before him, he was finding out that excitement was not all it was cracked up to be. The difference was he had always known this. At least, not when it happened to people like him. People like him who encountered excitement, usually ended up, at best, in hospital.

Tamar gave it one last try. 'One thing I do hate is being called 'Djinn',' she said. (This, by the way, was not true, Tamar could not have cared less if she had been called 'Sideshow Dickie' as long as she got her wishes)

'After all, I *do* have a name you know,' she said very pointedly.

'Sorry,' said Denny, and unexpectedly smiled. He could not have stopped himself for a "Han Solo" collector's edition in its original box.

It was the most beautiful, heart-breaking smile Tamar had ever seen. She would have gone weak at the knees. If she had had real knees.

'I didn't mean to be rude. What is your name?' suddenly he did want to know, she was the only person he had ever met who seemed more miserable than him. Besides she seemed terribly upset at his apparent indifference. This was a complete reversal of the reaction he was used to getting from girls. He knew how she felt.

'Huh! Much you care,' sniffed Tamar, turning away pettishly.

He took her hand. 'Please,' he gave her that heart-breaking smile again.

What was wrong with her? She wondered. He was not even handsome; so pale and thin and scruffy. He looked as if he slept in his clothes – in a skip.

'Tamar,' she croaked.

'What, *just* Tamar? Like 'Cher' or 'Madonna'?' he said, grinning.

Tamar smiled at his way of putting it. Only the famous and society's outcasts had no need of a last name. How was that for irony?

'Not *exactly* like that,' she said.

'But you don't have a last name?' he persisted.

'No, I don't need one. I don't have an address either, unless you count the bottle.'

'I think you should have one.'

Tamar sighed. More human nonsense, she had been down this road, and whatever he came up with was bound to be bloody awful.

'Maybe I'll give you one,' he continued, as she had known he would. 'Let me think about it. What goes with …?' He hesitated

'Tamar.' She repeated patiently.

'Tamar, yeah; that's unusual.' He was covering his embarrassment at having forgotten her name, which he felt truly terrible about, having been called "er Derek" more times than he cared to remember.

'Tamar, Tamar?' he mused, 'That sounds familiar somehow.' Then he opened his eyes wide. 'Are you a goddess then?'

Tamar was amused by this, remembering her first encounter with Askphrit. – the νόθος'. He was no, doubt, thinking of

Tanith, she decided, since she knew of no gods with her name – none that she could think of anyway.

'No, no, *just* a Djinn' she said with heavy irony, which was completely lost on Denny, of course.

'It is an unusual name, though,' said Denny again.

'Yes, I suppose so.' she replied. 'It wasn't when I was named, but that was a long time ago I suppose. It was thousands of years ago. It was the name of a queen of Persia who killed her husband, apparently by talking him to death, my parent's idea of a joke. They called my sister Xanthe, which means "yellow", because she was so sallow. That was when I was human of course.' I'm babbling, she thought. Why am I babbling? He must think I'm an idiot. I *am* an idiot. Just look at him. He's only a mortal, pull yourself together.

She had never told a mortal so much about herself before; it was unnerving.

He was frowning, puzzled. She wanted to reach out and smooth the crease in his brow. Just reach out...

'Human?' he broke into her thoughts abruptly.

Oh hell! If he asked, she would *have* to tell him, he was her master. And then bang goes any chance of suckering him, she thought. But then, she would not; or would she? Not him, not this one.

Then she realized sadly that she would, given half a chance, even him. *So that's what I've become.*

She crossed all available fingers and toes. Please, please just go back to being uninterested.

He asked – it was inevitable – so she told him.

* * *

'It was a long time ago,' she finished. 'You might say I've learned my lesson.'

He was staring at her in horror (again) 'What a rotten thing to do,' he said eventually

'I've always thought so,' she agreed, 'Askphrit got me good – the νόθος.' *

---

* Denny did not need a translation here; it was pretty clear what she meant

'Isn't there anything anyone can do?'

'No,' she said briskly. She was not ready to give up her power yet, besides which she was not allowed to suggest it (rule seventeen – subsection a)

'What about you?' she asked. 'Why don't you want your wishes? I've never heard *that* one before.'

'Oh – well, there's nothing I want that much,' he said airily. 'I mean it's a risk isn't it? There's always a catch: *you* should know that better than anyone. No such thing as a free lunch is there?'

'How do you know about the catch?'

'I've read stuff, the 'Arabian Nights' stuff like that. There's always a catch.'

'Arabian Nights?' thought Tamar crossly, 'damn that Scherezade.' But who would have thought that anyone would believe it.

'And you *believed* it?' she asked aloud, still incredulous this turn of events.

'Well – no, obviously not, not at the time, not until you turned up. And then I thought, if Djinn are real then I'd better be careful, if the stories are true. Just wait and see what happens. That's why I was a bit standoffish with you at first, and now, well, I was right wasn't I?

'Very clever,' Tamar snarled, 'looks as if I've been well and truly snookered, doesn't it? Again!'

'Don't be like that.'

'That's what *he* said. Oh well, at least you haven't screwed me over with malice aforethought. Not that it helps.'

'Look at it this way, even if I made my wishes, and set you free, the way you tell it, you'd be back in the bottle again in no time, and for God knows how long. At least this way…'

'I can live in this grotty pigsty, seeing no one but you and the people you know until one of us dies? I'm supposed to be immortal, but in this damp hole – who knows?'

Denny looked around, as if he were seeing the place for the first time. 'Oh – well, I suppose it is a bit … I hadn't really noticed.'

'Of course you hadn't. You're a man. I suppose I could do something with it.'

'No wishing involved,' she added hastily, seeing his face.

'It's not that; it's just, well ... I'm the master right?'

'Right.'

'Right, so no pink OK, and no frilly cushions or pot pourii or pictures of cats.'

Tamar looked disgusted. 'What do you think I am?'

'You're a girl aren't you?'

'Technically, no, not for a long time.'

'You know what I mean.'

'Yes – well you obviously know nothing about *women*,' she said, stressing the last word pointedly.

Denny silently conceded to this.

'I suppose I shouldn't have called you a girl,' he said.

Tamar looked puzzled at this divergence. 'Why not?' she said finally.

'Well, you know, it's not very PC,' he said.

Tamar wondered briefly if he had gone mad. 'What's that?' she said, deciding to humour him.

'Politically Correct, you know?' he caught her blank expression. 'You don't know,' he surmised.

'Suppose you tell me then,' she said.

Denny's brow furrowed as he tried to explain the concept to her; he realized as he did so, that he himself did not have any clear idea of what it meant either. It had something, he knew, to do with not using insulting terms to describe or categorise people. In Denny's mind, he had always vaguely classified this behaviour as CC (Common Courtesy).

Or, as in the case of not calling a six foot four black man a "spade", CS (Common Sense).

However, Tamar got the idea. She sighed. 'I see,' she said eventually; and added 'how ridiculous.'

This was to be the beginning of many diatribes on human behaviour that Denny was to be treated to over the ensuing months. 'I mean,' she continued. 'Where does it end? If you can no longer call an Indian an Indian,' she plucked an example out from Denny's ramblings, 'but he now has to be a Native American, how long before the term "Native American" becomes an insult in itself? Surely, it's just a matter of familiarity? You calling me a girl as opposed to a woman, isn't insulting in itself, it only becomes so by implication. Ha! Pretty soon, you'll have to call women "persons of the female persuasion" at least until the term "female" also becomes insulting. Which is preposterous, what's wrong with being a girl?'

'Well, nothing I suppose.'

'Right, but saying that you *shouldn't* call me a girl is to imply that there is. Same with anything; so what was once a mere description now becomes an insult by implication, you see?'

'I – I think so.'

'I agree that some terms are definitely insulting of course and deliberately so.' She gave examples. 'But this idea just creates new and interesting ways to insult people. Typical human thinking,' she sighed. 'Why do you do it?'

Denny shrugged. 'I didn't do it,' he said.

'Well, not you personally,' she agreed. 'I suppose it grew out of the idea that people will use anything they can against each other,' she said reflectively. 'But that's just people, you can't change that. Some people will always find a way to be prejudiced. I've met people who can make the word "You" sound like an insult.'

Denny nodded. His father had been one of them; Denny had been a "You" quite often in his youth.

'Anyway,' she changed back to the previous topic suddenly, having made her point; 'I hate pink, and frills, and why would *anyone* want pictures of cats? I just thought I could do something about the damp and put in some actual furniture.'

Denny's thoughts skidded to catch up.

'There's a bed,' he announced eventually. This seemed to fit the new topic.

'*One* bed, where am I supposed to sleep, on the ceiling?

'Do Djinn need to sleep?'

'Yes – no, not really. I like it, though. It wastes time. I miss dreaming though; I keep hoping I'll start again.'

'You don't dream? You know what, being a Djinn sounds awful.'

Tamar heard the note in his voice and saw it in his face. He was feeling sorry for her.

Pity! How had it come to this? Pitied by a mortal! Envied, yes; feared, worshipped, held in awe – but *pitied*? How had she sunk so low? It was humiliating.

Wasn't he right, though? Was it really more humiliating than being at the beck and call of any fool who happened to pick up her little glass prison, than being on the run all the time in between?

A dream is just a way of making a wish and the Djinn do not get to make wishes. Yes, my life is pitiable; it's utterly terrible. He's right to feel sorry for me; it's just that no one ever had the perception to see it before. It's because he doesn't want anything from me.

Tamar had many faults, but self-pity had never been one of them, so she did not give in to it.

'Anyway,' she said, rallying. 'What I had in mind was something like this.'

She snapped her fingers, and they found themselves in a smart New York style warehouse conversion. Not Tamar's style really, but it had the advantage of not being remotely feminine and providing a lot of space, so they would not be on top of each other the whole time. *Do not* think about that. She had chosen the style because she thought he would probably approve of the Spartan aspect of it; if the way he was currently living was anything to judge by anyway.

As it happened, the style was not the feature that concerned him. 'It's bigger,' he said, shocked 'How did you do that?'

'Magic – see I knew you didn't truly believe.'

'Uh huh, well look, you'll have to change it back if the landlord comes round or he'll be charging me more rent.'

'And that's it?' she spluttered furiously, 'no oohs and ahs? Not even a "thank you"? Don't you like it? Isn't it smart, stylish, spacious, *clean*?'

'It's okay; I didn't mind it before. You were the one who wanted it changed not me.'

He caught her eye. 'Okay, okay, I'm sorry, it's great – thank you. Um the big window is ... It lets in a lot of light.'

'Too little, too late,' she snapped and sank down floating cross-legged a few feet off the floor, her head in her hands.

'This is never going to work, is it?' she sighed. 'Why don't you just make three small wishes? Silly stuff that doesn't really matter; otherwise we're going to be stuck with each other for the rest of your life. We could end up hating each other. What catch could possibly be worse than that?'

'Nice try,' said Denny. 'But no. I'm sure I'll cope. So you'll be with me all the time, will you?'

'Yes.'

'Dressed like that?'

Tamar looked down. 'Oh.'

She was a gauzy cloud of turquoise chiffon trimmed with gold braid and looked, she knew, utterly ridiculous, like something out of the harem of the richest Sultan in the world and glittering with more bangles and baubles than the entire Tiffany's chain. The fact was, that although Tamar kept up with human fashions as much as she was able, she had found that, on her first meeting with a new client, the full on traditional "Arabian Nights" rig went a long way toward establishing her *Bona Fides*. After all, who is going to believe in a Djinn dressed just like everyone else?

'So, I take it you can – ?' Denny gestured to the transformed room.

For answer, she snapped the fingers of both hands and changed into jeans and a black shirt. Her elaborately beaded hairstyle unwound itself into a shining black curtain that fell to her ankles. She left her feet bare, and the only jewellery left was a pair of diamond studs in her ears. She now looked like a perfectly ordinary – supermodel (on her day off) although

Denny did not fail to notice that her wrists were still bound by the silvery manacles that she had been wearing when she appeared; now the only outward sign of her true nature and condition, that of a slave.

The next moment she could have kicked herself. A perfectly reasonable opportunity for a wish – wasted. Still, it probably would not have worked anyway. She could just hear him saying 'If you want to look ridiculous, that's your problem.'

'Why do you live here anyway?' she asked.

'It's called "being poor",' he answered tetchily.

'I could ...'

'NO!'

'Hmm, no need to snap.'

No answer.

'I could,' she was thinking, ' always drive him so crazy that he would agree to anything to get rid of me.' She was not sure that this would work. She had never met anyone so infuriatingly calm (and she had been around a long time) It was far more likely that any such plan would drive her mad with frustration long before it even *began* to bother him.

Anyway, she was not sure that she actually wanted to leave him. Why? Why? It did not make any sense. He was annoying and boring and not at all handsome, although why that should matter... Djinn were unaffected by human beauty – in theory. Oh well at least she could take refuge in the bottle if it got too much, and she had not told him that either. Why not? Why was she acting like this? What was she feeling? Why did he make her stomach flutter, and not with revulsion either. Tamar had heard of these symptoms before and knew what they usually meant, but she refused to believe it. Djinn were immune to love.

She had been wooed by lots of mortals in her time, many of them far more handsome and interesting than this one, and had felt nothing.

It was not unheard of for a mortal to fall in love with a Djinn, and it had happened to Tamar several times. But no

Djinn *ever* fell in love, especially with a mortal, and *this* one for God's sake. No, it had to be something else. All the same, it might be prudent to get herself out of here.

Perhaps he had not fully considered what she could do for him. He must want something; everybody had dreams; everybody wanted something.

Fame was favourite. Nearly all the mortals she had encountered since the beginning of the twentieth century had wanted to be famous. It was a strange phenomenon as far as Tamar was concerned but easy to do. She and other Djinn, had created many movie and rock stars over the last century (think hard and you might be able to guess which ones) Why they wanted it was a mystery. There was no real advantage to it and it made most of them miserable in the end. But there it was. In the early years of the century, the wishes had been fairly specific. Movie star being favourite – followed by singing star, Broadway and occasionally an author, the most pointless one of all as far as Tamar was concerned and not hugely popular. But more recently they just asked for fame. It did not seem to matter how they got it. A few times she had naively asked 'Famous for what?' But the blank stares that this question engendered soon cured her of that. She had never quite figured out the phenomenon of fame or its attraction. Back when she had been mortal, the only famous people had been the gods, and they were fictional as it turned out. Or were they? Her observations of fame in the twentieth century had led her to form the hypothesis that people became fictional *after* they became famous; but that they had been real enough before that. Fame, therefore, was surely a bad thing. As the poet said, "Fame is an empty purse, count it and go poor, eat it and go hungry, seek it and go mad." Tamar agreed. Still he *might* want to be famous, actually he looked the type; well she could but try. And if not that, what else? Not money apparently, true love? She shuddered, still it would be OK, she would not have to stay around and watch. There I go again, she chided herself. Good looks? No, he's perfect as he is. 'AAAAGH.' Still, *he* might not think so; most humans were unhappy with the way they looked, *she* certainly had been.

Then again, maybe he was the idealistic type – world peace? It never worked of course; you could not stop humans with free will from making war if they wanted to, but she would be long gone before he realized.

Whatever he wanted, she realized, she would have to find out. It occurred to her that she did not have the faintest idea how to do this. Usually, they just told her – were only too eager to tell her. What none of them had ever bothered to do was to find out anything about her. Denny, on the other hand, had found out a surprising amount about her. How had he done that? And more importantly why?

'I've got it,' he announced suddenly, startling her out of her reverie. 'What about Black?'

'In respect of what?' she asked puzzled at where his train of thought had been going.

'Your name of course,' he said. 'Tamar Black.'

Tamar stared. 'How did you know?'

~ Chapter Six ~

DENNY WAS GETTING used to having Tamar around. He was slightly surprised at how quickly he had adjusted to the idea of having his own personal Djinn, or the idea that such things even existed. Despite his love of all things sci-fi and fantasy related, he had never believed that stuff was real. But, once faced with incontrovertible proof, he had taken it in his stride in a way he would never have believed possible before it had happened. He did not try to analyse the reason for this, but he was dimly aware that others must have had the same type of experience and accepted it, as he had done. Humans, he decided, therefore, must be more mentally tractable than is generally realized.

He had been wary around her at first, but now he had stopped worrying about bad things happening. After all, it had been three weeks, and, so far, everything was fine. As long as he did not make any wishes, he decided, nothing could go wrong. And, as his initial anxieties faded, he found that he was enjoying her company. She had a lot of entertaining stories to tell. She could talk virtually non-stop, in fact, which saved him the bother of trying to think of something interesting to say himself. The only thing he found mildly irritating was her habit of sneakily trying to make him wish for stuff. But he could not blame her for that really, in fact, he felt kind of sorry for her situation, stuck here with him for the rest of his life. Denny had no illusions about himself; he could well imagine that she would rather be off somewhere else, doing her own thing instead of putting up with him. He felt a little sad about this. Despite the fact that they had no real interests in common, he had begun to think of her as a friend. At least she had shown no signs of wanting to kick his head in.

He tried to cheer her up by playing some of his songs for her, but it did not seem to help. He wished – no scratch that – he *would have liked* to have been able to help her out. However, without wishing – and there was no way he was going to risk that – what could he do?

* * *

After three weeks, the recently re-named Tamar Black was not getting very far with her new quarry. Although she was getting used to her new name. (Technically it was actually her old name – in a manner of speaking). Denny seemed to think it appropriate in some way that was beyond her comprehension. She did not like it much, but a glance around his room at some of the posters made her realise that she had had a narrow escape. It could have been "Skywalker".

She had found out that he worked in a record store, had little love for personal possessions, few friends and no family except for an estranged brother who may or may not be married. He cared deeply about music, and would pick out dreadful tunes on a battered guitar until Tamar felt as if she were going to scream. It was at this point that she played the fame card, but to no avail. He was not to be caught.

He wrote songs too; she had suspected this of him but what she had not suspected was that they would be so awful. It was a shame really, because he had an incredible voice (or was she being doting again?) It was melting, deep and sexy, but still, that was not enough to redeem the terrible tunes and lyrics he came up with. However, she did like to hear him singing in the shower, when he would sing (unaccompanied, thank Allah) a selection of Elvis songs or the odd rock ballad.

He was a loner, not by choice but from social awkwardness. He seemed happy enough to have her around, even though he rarely talked to her. He had few girlfriends – no one serious, and this did not seem to bother him. *

He truly did not seem to want anything from her except her company, which of course he could keep for longer by not wishing for anything else.

She had, therefore, resorted to stalking him – hence the listening to him in the shower – in the hope of catching him out in a "slip of the tongue" wish, a tried and tested method. Unfortunately for her, either he had thought of this and was being especially careful, or it was just not something he usually said. He did not, in any case, say much at any time.

One evening, though, Denny suddenly wanted to talk. He put down his guitar (thank God for small mercies) and said out of the blue. 'So what would you do if you were free? Really free I mean – like that other one. Whatisname – Ashpit?'

'Askphrit... Save the world from itself,' said Tamar, surprising herself. She had spoken without thinking.

Denny looked sceptical for a moment and then said 'You mean it don't you?'

I *do* mean it, she thought.

'It could do with it,' Denny observed. 'So how would you do it?'

'I was thinking of getting rid of all the Djinn and taking it from there.'

'Are there many?'

'Just so's you'd notice,' she said sarcastically. 'And they're a plague and a rotten confounded nuisance nothing but trouble.'

---

* Denny was not quite as unpopular with the opposite sex as he thought he was. Some girls like a man who seems to need looking after. Denny had dated a few nurses, who had first met him in casualty with a broken nose or similar. They soon left him, though, when it became apparent that he did not *want* to be looked after.

'You're not.'

'Only because of you, I've often thought that the only sensible master is a silent master (on the subject of wishing I mean). I suppose I shouldn't have said that.'

'I'm glad you did. I thought you hated me.'

'Of course I don't. Why would you think that?'

'Well, you *are* stuck here because of me. I do feel bad about it.'

'I don't mind really.'

'Oh? And you were being so honest.'

Tamar smiled sheepishly. 'It could be worse – it *has* been,' she said, remembering the cunning weasel. Sixty seven years of pure purgatory.

'Still, they say suffering is good for the soul,' she quipped.

'I think you've suffered enough,' he said. 'I want to help you. You deserve your freedom, and I've got a plan.'

Now I understand, she thought, why he's different, why he doesn't belong in this place.

Unlikely as it seemed, and despite the lack of muscles and charisma, she realized that it was because he was a Hero.

She was looking at him through eyes that were shining with tears. Then to his tremendous embarrassment, and later her own, she did what she now realized she had wanted to do since first setting eyes on him. She flung her arms around him and kissed him passionately.

After hesitating for a few seconds, he kissed her back. And then he fainted.

~ Chapter Seven ~

THE PLAN WAS a good one. Tamar was impressed when he finally came round and explained it to her. It had taken half an hour of frantic patting on the face and pouring water on him to rouse him, and she had been terrified at what she had done.

There was a reason why Djinn should not have intimate contact with mortals (rule two-seven-two). It should be rule *one*, she thought furiously. Any longer and I could have killed him. She was pouring cheap whisky down his throat (he did not have any brandy).

The whole incident was tactfully ignored, although they both realized it would have to be dealt with eventually.

The plan he had come up with would not harm the innocent and involved punishing the guilty. Just what you would expect from a Hero, thought Tamar fondly. And it was brilliantly simple. That is to say, it was a simple plan, in that it was not complicated. But it was not going to be easy.

It involved finding Askphrit (The guilty) and Denny refused to use a wish to do so.

'But he could be anywhere,' protested Tamar. 'He may not even be on the planet – you *have* to wish. How else are we going to find him?'

'No, if something goes wrong, we'll need all my wishes. We'll just have to look.'

'Look where? Where do we even start?'

'Here.' He slapped down a copy of the Yellow Pages.

'You've got to be kidding. What are we looking for, G for Git?'

'Very funny! No, C for clairvoyant. All we need is something that belonged to him – the bottle.'

'You're out of your mind – *clairvoyants*, that's not real magic.'

'How do you know? Look, I'll admit I used to think they were all frauds, but then I didn't believe in the Djinn either, until you dropped into my life. It'll only need one to be genuine. I'll go through every clairvoyant, seer and psychic in the country if I have to… that's a good point, look up P for psychic too.'

Tamar was fluttering. His forcefulness was bringing out a hitherto unsuspected *liking* for being dominated (as opposed to just putting up with it) and his grim determination to help her was gratifying, but she knew in her heart that this was not the way. They would have to access the magic underground and consult a witch or a sorcerer. She was badly out of touch with this world. These kinds of people used to work out in the open of course but had been driven underground some time ago (a long time ago in human terms). That they still existed, she had no doubt, but finding them would be difficult (there's no such thing as a wizard pride parade) and dangerous, not to mention costly. Not forgetting too, that the people they would be searching for were dangerous in themselves. Not to her of course, but it would be difficult to protect Denny if he refused to use his wishes.

She tried to explain all of this to him. 'I don't want you to get hurt because of me. It's not worth it. Maybe we should just forget it.'

Denny laughed. 'Don't be silly. Of course I'm not going to forget it; I think it's worth it. It's sweet of you to be worried about me …'

Sweet!

'… but what about you?' he finished.

'Oh, I'm all right, it could be worse.'

'It could be a lot better too – I wish ...'

Tamar put a finger, hurriedly, to his lips. 'Don't,' she said.

'I couldn't live with myself if I didn't try,' he finished lamely.

'Spoken like a true Hero.'

'Like a *what*?'

'Oh you are you know. I should know. I've been around for a long time, and I'm a smart girl. Only the Hero comes to the rescue of the damsel in distress, you know.'

'Don't be silly. I'm not a Hero; I'm damn scared if you want the truth, how heroic is that?'

'Maybe I should do this part on my own.'

'Oh yes, what kind of Hero lets the damsel go off and do the dangerous part on her own?'

'Discretion is the better part of valour.'

'What's that supposed to mean?'

'I won't be in any danger – I'm immortal, and I'd probably get on better if I didn't have to worry about you.'

'I suppose you have a point, even if you are eviscerating my male ego as you make it. But still, I don't know. You may need me for something; you never know.'

'I *do* need you for something, and you don't have a male ego. Look, I need you to be alive and well when I find him. If it makes you feel any better, I'm no ordinary damsel.'

'I know.' He looked at her steadily, in such a way that it made her heart pound. 'And it's not because you're Djinn either.

'No, I'm not letting you out of my sight, he reiterated. 'I can't sit at home twiddling my thumbs and worrying myself sick about you. I'm coming too, and that's final. You can't stop me anyway; I'm the master – for the time being – right?'

Tamar sighed. 'Right.'
'Good, so where do we start?'
'At the coast.'

~ Chapter Eight ~

'I PROBABLY SHOULD have mentioned before' said Denny, –
'I can't swim.'

'It's okay,' Tamar grinned, 'you couldn't follow me where
I'm going even if you could. Just don't fall in.'

'I get seasick too – I just found out.'

'You didn't *have* to come.'

He did look bad though. He was hanging over the side of
the boat looking distinctly green. Tamar had always believed
this to be a mere figure of speech – live and learn. The water
was choppy, but not too bad. To Denny it felt like being in the
middle of a tornado.

'How do you know they're here?' he asked.

They were in Ireland, having been to several other parts of
the coast in England and Wales.

'I just know,' she told him 'I can sense it; right, let's go
back to shore and drop you off. I'll swim out, and you can stay
on nice, dry land.'

Denny did not have the will to argue. He was feeling like a
burden, although Tamar was being terribly nice about it.

* * *

Back on terra firma he watched in fascination as Tamar leaped off a rock transforming in mid-air into a mermaid.

'My God!'

She dived gracefully into the water and with a flick of her tail she was gone, leaving Denny to gnaw at his fingernails.

Tamar had decided to start with the mermaids because they were the only magical creatures that she felt fairly confident of finding quite easily. Also, mermaids tended to be frivolous and thoughtless and would chatter away quite unwarily. If they knew anything, Tamar felt sure she would get it out of them. *If* they knew anything.

About ten miles out, she began to feel the magic, another five, (and pretty deep now) she saw them, silvery flickers of light flashing through the water. She began to wonder just what she was doing, what would she say to them? Then again, if it came to that, if they *could* point her in the direction of a witch or a sorcerer, what then, what did she expect *them* to do? How would a witch, for example, help her to find Askphrit – the νόθος'? And, even if she could, why would she? Hmm, she thought, got to find one first, one thing at a time.

Without warning, she was surrounded by twittering, giggling mermaids.

It should be pointed out here, that "mermaids" is a bit of a misnomer. There is nothing human about them at all for one thing. They are less half fish, half woman, and more all fish that has evolved to look partly human. A pale, silvery colour all over, although, in some, the "tail" part is darker, the scales continue all the way up the "torso", and no mermaid ever wore a boob tube of any kind. The faces are more or less human like, with features that are pale and pointed, except that their ear are inset into the skull and their eyes are dark and liquid with no whites showing, rather like shark's eyes, giving them, to modern eyes, a rather Roswellian look. The fabled long, golden hair of the mermaid is, in fact, a mass of tendrils interspersed with silvery almost invisible filaments which stretch out for around fifty feet and are of the same nature as those of the sea creature, Cyanea capillata, known to sailors as the "lion's mane" or "fearful stinger". These filaments are deadly in the extreme, and the pain of them stops the heart; death is slow and torturous. Mermaids may look pretty and indeed, be vapid and vacuous, but they are also as deadly as many other sea creatures.

'Look girls,' cooed one, 'a new one.'

'Who are you?'

'Oooh! Isn't she pretty?'

'Let's comb her hair.'

'New seashells for her ears.'

'Oh darling, isn't she dull? Try this,' tittered one, draping her in bioluminescent seaweed like a feather boa.

'*Much* better.'

'Do you sing? Not that sailors just aren't what they used to be sweetie. But we do our best darling, don't you know?'

'I remember Captain Nemo, *such* a darling.'

'I remember Sinbad.'

'No, you don't.'

'Where do you hail from?'

'I ...'

'What are the sailors like there?'

'Um ...'

'Are you all by yourself?'

'I ...'

Either mermaids had grown even more foolish than they used to be, or else it was so dim in this part of the sea that they could not see her properly. In either case, they obviously had not realized that she was not a real mermaid. And, despite the questions, they did not seem particularly interested in whence she came. (In any case, not one of them had waited for an answer) So much the better.

'I'm from Greece,' she announced.

'Grease? – Sounds horrible. Is it called that because of that, like, pollution thingy?'

'Not grease silly,' said another, 'Greece – it's a country.'

'Land?' said the first one, looking puzzled.

'Bor-ing.' said yet another, and the subject looked like being dropped.

Tamar, however, was not giving up that easily.

'So, you won't have heard of Circe then?' she ventured, she was making it up as she went, and this seemed as legitimate a way as any to introduce the subject of witches. It felt like the whole ocean erupted in squeals.

'I'll take that as a yes, shall I? Anyone seen her lately?'

'No didn't she die? I think she died, wasn't she a ...' the voice sunk to a whisper, 'a witch?'

'Sorceress, yes.'

'Didn't she run that Siren outfit?'

'That's right.'

'Lousy rotten impostors.'

'And turn all our choicest sailors into a petting zoo?'

'So I heard.'

'The bad old days, huh?'

'So, why do you ask?'

'What? Oh I was just ... Oh all right, I'll come clean girls. There's a new sorceress in town. At least that's what I heard.'

'What's a town?'

'I mean hanging – swimming around. I don't suppose you girls have seen anything.'

'The only witches I know of are on land, they hang around in ovens.'

'Ovens? That you cook in?' Tamar was perplexed.

'Don't they get pushed into them by children?' said another frowning prettily.

Tamar suddenly saw daylight. 'Actually, I think you mean covens,' she said

'Yeah, groups of three or more, safety in numbers you see. If the humans catch them, they burn them.'

'In the ovens?' said the dim one.

'It's not ovens stupid; it's covens,' snapped the knowledgeable one.

'Oooh, pardon me.'

'Shut up.'

'Oooh ...'

'Shut up! Yeah, I was saying, covens for safety. They give them code names for cover, so the humans won't find out about them.'

Tamar was listening with her mouth open, hanging on every word with open fascination. The mermaid preened, and prattled on; obviously proud of her knowledge 'Yeah code names like the WI whatever that means and the Women's Liberation Front.'

'Huh, I always thought that lot were a bunch of witches,' thought Tamar inconsequentially. Mind, you, it made sense in a way, just another way of gaining influence in human lives. Cunning too: giving 'em what they did not even know they wanted.

'But I haven't seen any out here,' the mermaid continued. 'Just let them try it! We're not having any more of *their* nonsense. Setting up on islands – Sirens! Sailors are getting pretty thin on the seabed as it is.'

But Tamar had lost interest, she slipped away unnoticed and headed for shore.

There was a shark behind her, unusual for these waters, but not a problem.

Then she sensed it; it was *not* a shark. There was a power there such as she had never felt before. It gripped her, and she panicked. What had power like that, stronger than Djinn magic? Nothing that she knew of, but the world had changed. It had her; she could not move; she had never felt such fear. *I'm going to die.* She closed her eyes. Then, abruptly it let her go, and she shot toward the surface, but only for a second. Still shark shaped it opened its jaws and bit down on her "tail". She screamed and thrashed, but she could not get free. Her head broke water, and she began to scream in earnest.

'HELP, HELP, HELP! DENNY!' She was only a few yards from the shore. Denny looked up and saw her struggling in the water, bloody surf foaming around her. He ran waist deep into the water as she was pulled back under; he reached down not without some reservations, into the water and grabbed her hand. The jaws melted away; the thing was gone. Denny lifted her awkwardly; he was pretty weedy and the tail was large and heavy. He laid her down on the sand gently and sat beside her helplessly.

'Oh my God … Oh my God …' he kept repeating.

She grabbed his hand. 'I'm OK, thanks to you.' She sighed, 'thank God you were there.' She had stopped saying "Praise Allah" some time ago. Although she sometimes still *thought* it.

'What was that?' he choked, 'I thought you were invulnerable. What ... My God Tamar, I thought ... I thought...'

'It – I don't know what it was,' she stammered. 'It looked like a shark – felt like one too.'

He looked at her tail. 'You're bleeding, it looks quite serious. Can you change back? What can make a Djinn bleed?

'I don't know; I can't make it stop.'

She changed back to a human form; there was a huge gash in her right leg, exactly like a shark bite. Denny gathered her up into his arms. 'I'll take you to a hospital.'

'Denny, you *can't*, I'm not human, they'll probably notice.'

'So, what can I do?'

'Just take me back to the hotel, I'll be okay. – And Denny.'

'Yes?'

'You were right, I needed you. I'm glad you came.'

'So am I.' He answered fervently.

* * *

Although Tamar had used teleportation for the long journeys – to save on airfares, Denny had insisted on hiring a car for local travel, to avoid being conspicuous, which was fortunate now since Tamar's powers were severely weakened.

Tamar was healing fast; it had been so many years since she had felt any pain that the sensation was not entirely unpleasant. But Denny was agitated.

'Don't be silly darling,' she said (the effect of the mermaids' chatter was taking longer to wear off than the pain) 'This just means that we're on the right track. That was probably old Askphrit – the νόθος – himself. Maybe we got him worried. If we keep it up, maybe he'll come to us. Now do sit down, you're making me dizzy.'

Denny sat on the bed, averting his eyes from the large bloodstain on the sheets. There was going to be trouble later on from the landlady, a jolly bustling type, with all the sympathy and compassion of a barracuda, a reveller in the misery of others carefully disguised as concern for their welfare.

Getting Tamar past this Job's comforter, limping badly, with blood pouring down her leg had been a feat of ingenuity worthy of the organisers of the under tens /over sixty fives annual potholing expedition.

'Maybe we should just pack it in after all,' he said, glancing meaningfully at the bloody eiderdown. The fact that the bed had on it, an eiderdown, should tell you all that you need to know about the place where they were staying.

'Oh – yes,' she said and waved her arm vaguely at it. The stain disappeared.

'See? Good as new. - And look,' she extended her leg, now fully healed.

'Not even a scar. Besides I've got you to protect me from that and I can protect you from everything else. Now, are you going to help me find these covens or what?

Unless ...' she bit her lip, 'you really have changed your mind? I mean, you know, it's up to you. Like I said I'm fine really, I don't mean to push. I just got a bit gung-ho, but ...'

'Oh shut up. You're babbling again; I said I'd help you and I mean to do it. It's just that I think that maybe we should be more careful. I can't see that being free is going to be much use to you if you're dead.'

'I'm immortal.'

'*Are* you? Are you *sure*?' He gestured to her leg.

'Even Askphrit can't *kill* me.'

'If it *was* him.'

'Makes sense, I'm pretty sure he was waiting for me. Who else has a reason? Besides he was scared off by you and the only thing that scares a Djinn is a potential master, like you.'

'Potential ...?'

'*You* have the bottle, *and* the power to put him back in it.'

Denny sighed. 'Okay, so what do you mean – covens?'

Tamar explained.

'... So it was worth it, you see,' she ended. 'The only problem is that there are so many of these women's groups. Most of them by now will be splinter groups formed in imitation by ordinary women. So we have to find the right one, looks like it's back to the Yellow Pages after all.'

* * *

In the event, they used the Internet, the computer easily provided with a snap of the fingers (along with a satellite TV).

'They don't even have MTV in this dump.' Denny maintained that he could think better with some background music.

Tamar, however, was proved to be correct in her assessment of their difficulties. The websites provided names and addresses of meeting halls, but, unsurprisingly, failed to highlight those groups with supernatural affiliation.

Tamar was starting her search with the W.I. in the hope that she would not have to resort to the other option. Let's face it; it would take a whole lot more than suffrage to liberate *her*.

Anyway, she ended up zapping in and out of meetings until she was dizzy; just one example of this should suffice to illustrate.

She would materialise in the car-park or driveway of the hall or house and first try to sense the magic

That she did not, did not necessarily mean anything. Witch magic was different from other kinds and difficult to quantify (witches learn their craft over many years and tend to use potions a lot). Also, they would undoubtedly be shielding. Witches traditionally do not like magical competition.

Then there was the problem of actually infiltrating the meetings.

Tamar considered simply appearing in a puff of smoke – "KA–BOOM!", and judging the reactions of the women. Any heart attacks or seizures or just plain fainting fits or other signs of shock such as gibbering and pointing would definitely eliminate the group. But Denny had vetoed this as far too risky, besides, 'No harming the innocent, remember?'

Tamar argued about this. In her view, there was no such thing as an innocent person. 'Everybody's guilty of *something*, even if it's just rubbish singing or the wanton infliction of hideous pullovers on undeserving sons in law.'

Denny would not have it, though. 'They haven't done anything to *you*,' he insisted.

So that just left entering the normal way and trying the magic code signs to see if she got a response, a slow and tedious method at the best of times. But worse than that, it had in the present circumstances, the potential to be highly embarrassing since the codes included:

Surreptitiously revealing a pentangle tattooed onto a normally inaccessible part of the body. (Not a wise thing to do in the presence of a gang of middle aged housewives.)

Producing fire from the palm of your hand (anybody with a box of matches can theoretically do this these days) or making the sign of the goddess Hecaté, a gesture that could be interpreted as a rude sign by ordinary folk.

And there were others, which were, if anything, worse. Whichever she decided on would almost certainly offend the old biddies, or else she would come across as a complete lunatic. Risking the latter seemed the better option given her choices. She decided to go with a verbal code, although these were not much better really, involving words or phrases that sounded either insulting or like complete gibberish, see options a and b above. Option c was to simply walk into the meeting and say 'Any witches in here? No? Good I'll be on my way then.' She would still be accounted insane but at least it would be over quickly. So that is what she did and was met with blank stares, which could mean anything (witches are nothing if not cagey) so she caved and gave the sign of the goddess and was promptly pelted with Victoria sponges, and threatened with Mr. Triplow's dog.

'You ill-mannered young hussy, how dare you?' said one.

'Somebody put you up to it didn't they?' said another. 'One of your silly friends, I'll be bound.'

'Young people today, no respect,' chimed in another.

She beat a hasty retreat. There can be few more terrifying sights, even to an ancient Djinn who had spent time with Caligula and Attila, than a phalanx of infuriated golden agers advancing on you with walking sticks and knitting needles raised like lances.

Denny had laughed like a drain when she had appeared back in the room covered in jam and butter cream. It had taken Tamar longer to see the joke. Jokes like 'They shouldn't have "trifled" with you.' And 'They sure "creamed" you.'

I did not say they were *good* jokes. Denny's sense of humour was roughly equivalent to the average men's club compere.

* * *

Tamar tried variations on this for a while, always with similar results. So we will gloss over this part and jump forward to her arrival in Basingstoke of all places.

She felt the magic as soon as she arrived. Hmm, she thought grumpily, all that trouble for nothing.

Tamar clapped her hands together producing a gratifyingly large explosion.

'Well ladies, now you know what I am and, make no mistake, I know what *you* are, so let's talk. Unlikely as it may seem, I need your help.'

An elderly witch stepped forward. 'We know who you are Tamar Black,' she said.

'I see good news travels fast,' said Tamar, sourly. She had had her new surname less than a month.

Another one stepped in. 'And we are aware of what you want.'

A third spoke up. 'We know all, we can see much.'

Tamar lost patience. 'What are you, "the three fates"? If you know what I want so much the better, now give me any hassle and my master will wish you all into chickens. I'd hate to do it but ...' She shrugged, 'a wish is a wish.'

The terrified witches tried hard but had to admit defeat in the end. A finding spell was tried, but only succeeded in finding a mountain of lost pencils, keys, odd socks and teaspoons. Quite a bit of lost weight (causing much distress) one lost cat and one witch's lost virginity. Since everything that had been found, so far, had been lost in the vicinity of the community centre where they were standing (also used as a slimming club as you will have realized) this caused some curious looks. Then they found the bottle, which created some excitement for a few minutes until Tamar explained, before they gave it up.

At this point, one of the younger witches started to have hysterics. Be careful what you get into. Witchcraft may seem cool and glamorous, but it is a lot more than dressing in black and chanting at the moon. (Sometimes actual magic happens.) Lucinda, for that was her name, left the order soon afterwards and after a short spell in a facility became an accountant – thus avoiding excitement of any kind for the rest of her life.

As it happened, Tamar could not have made good on her threat even if she had wanted to (and you can be sure that she did want to, very much) she knew Denny would never have agreed to wish for any such thing. So she shrugged 'Well, you did your best ladies, back to the drawing board.'

And she was about to leave when another youngish witch piped up. 'You need a sorcerer, a powerful one.'

'Really?' snapped Tamar. 'I never would have thought of that. And where do you suggest I find one? Look one up in the Yellow *Mages*?'

'You could go to Kelon,' said the witch. (She pronounced it Kay-lone.)

'Kelon?' Tamar intercepted the black looks the witch was getting from the whole group.

'You girls been holding out on me? Speak up or it's chickens to the lot of you. Or maybe ducks, how do you feel about penguins?'

The witches looked at each other nervously. Obviously being changed into ungainly birds held less terror for them than whatever this Kelon would do to them.

'Look girls,' she wheedled, 'don't worry, I won't tell him you sent me, he'll never know.'

'She,' interrupted one.

'*She* then, look help me out and there might be a little something in your Christmas stockings, you never know.'

'She's bad,' piped up an elderly witch with a face like a wrinkled cushion. (Vain in the extreme, Tamar could not understand any witch allowing herself to look like that when a simple glamour would take care of it easily. And so much cheaper than plastic surgery)

'She's a bad woman.'

The other witches nodded sagely.

'Terrible – evil,' chipped in another. They all nodded again.

'Worst one we've seen in a long time. Eat you alive as soon as look at you. You stay away from her dear.' There was more nodding.

'I can handle her,' said Tamar. The synchronized nodding was getting on her nerves.

'Where is she? Don't nod any of you or I'll make you stay that way. Do any of you fancy a career sitting in the back of a mini-van?'

The witches did a remarkable imitation of a group of garden gnomes.

'We don't know where to find her, just sort of *how* to find her, if you understand me, sort of a quest sort of thing.'

'She's hidden herself with spells, enchantments you know? In a sort of maze, well no not a maze. But you need clues, only people who have the clues can find her.'

'And you have the clues?'

'No, just the one; she doesn't let anyone have them all.'

'Who has the others?'

'We don't know, we've never looked for her. One clue leads you to another you see, at least I think so.'

'Like a treasure hunt?'

'Yes I suppose so, a quest.'

'Good, then she'll never know if you start me off, will she?'

'She'll know, besides she's bad news, you don't want to go getting mixed up with her.'

'Don't nod, any of you.' snapped Tamar, before they could start.

The witches froze in mid nod.

'Okay, that's better. Now the clue, Kelon's my problem – when I find her.'

The witches looked at each other. She could see them thinking. "Just give her the damn clue and get rid of her. It's her funeral". They nodded then stopped suddenly, self-consciously. But Tamar was smiling.

'That's better,' she said.

~ Chapter Nine~

'I THINK THOSE witches were pulling my chain,' said Tamar. 'Are you sure you don't want to wish them into chickens, I'd really enjoy that. – Or puffins.'

Technically this was breaking rule seventeen. Well, this was, in fact, *actually* breaking rule seventeen and Askphrit – the νόθος' had warned her never to break the rules for fear of terrible consequences. What consequences he had not said. But so what? She did not care anymore; besides, nothing had happened so far, even though she had said it at least twelve times, probably, she thought, because there was no chance of Denny agreeing to it, and she knew it. Or maybe, there *were* no terrible consequences; she had never risked it before, although it had occurred to her that Askphrit had made up the Charter out of sheer spitefulness. He was an evil νόθος.

Denny did not bother to answer this time, the truth was that he was tempted – perhaps Tamar was having a bad effect on his morals. In any case, he was not sure that she was not right. They had come home with the clue two weeks ago and still could make neither head nor tail of it.

It was not, as Tamar had expected, a cryptic rhyme or an interestingly shaped amulet that would turn out to be a key, even an ordinary key would have been something. Nor was it an ugly but significant statue that they could have referenced or an elaborately carved box or in short any of the usual clues to a quest. Not a jewelled chaplet or a sword, not even a paper knife. It was, in fact, a cigarette.

Benson and Hedges. Denny had wondered if the brand name had any significance, but a trip to the factory had proved both fruitless and tedious. Denny did not smoke – too expensive, and a Djinn can smoke without cigarettes.

It appeared to be a perfectly ordinary cigarette too; they had undone it - naturally, and run a hot iron over the paper for hidden messages – nothing. They had had the ingredients tested for – for, well for something, but it contained only what it said on the packet, well more or less, but neither Tamar nor Denny thought it likely that sawdust or bits of cork were significant in any way.

It seemed that the only thing left to do was smoke it and what would that prove? They already knew what was in it.

Of course, the name "Benson and Hedges" might mean something, but trying to work out what would be a mental exercise on a par with doing the 'Times' crossword in Chinese – without clues, or trying to figure out the point of line dancing.

'I'm going to work,' said Denny, 'be good.'

For answer, Tamar transformed herself into a horned beast, complete with cloven hooves and a tri-pronged tail and stuck out her tongue (black) at him. They both laughed, but after he had gone she became depressed. It was over – already. They had run smack into a brick wall.

She had, of course gone back to Basingstoke to ask for an explanation, to beat it out of them if necessary, but the witches had, quite predictably packed up and gone. She could have hunted them down, but it was not worth the bother. If they had shafted her, there was not a damn thing she could do about it without Denny, and he was relentlessly moralistic about that sort of thing. Omniscient my πίσω πλευρά! She thought. But, of course "All Seeing" is not the same thing as "All Knowing" (fine print) not to mention that she could only do it if her master wished. Who would have thought that someone so weedy looking could be so stubborn?

'Benson?' she mused – too vague. There must be thousands of Bensons. Hedges ditto. A man named Benson with a hedge? 'Oh this is ridiculous.' An anagram? This looked promising for a while, but in the end, all she could come up with was: 'hens do ban edges' which was, if anything, worse than ever.

'How about Ben's son?' No, again too vague. Cigarette, ciggie, fag, smoke – *smoke*! 'What else smokes? Chimneys, fires, dragons?' Then it hit her; it was so obvious, why hadn't she seen it before?

The cigarette was not the point at all – how could it have been? It was nonsense, and *that* was the point. Of course, she still was not much further forward yet, but she felt sure she was on the right track now.

Nonsense, *that* was the point. She had been thinking the most ridiculous things ever since she had got the clue. Hold that thought – follow it through. Denny would be better at this really; Tamar did not have a strong sense of the ridiculous. You could not have if you spent your existence popping out of a bottle and saying 'Your wish is my command' and still managing to take yourself seriously.

But she had the train of thought now. Could she get him to understand?

So – nonsense? Things that make no sense; but what constitutes nonsense? Jabberwocky, Soap operas, Baby talk, Elvis movies, Chris Evans? No, this was not the way; it had to be something obvious. 'Oh hell!' Maybe she was on the wrong track after all. Of course, magic makes no sense; at least, it was not logical, "smoke and mirrors" that is what humans called it. Smoke and mirrors...

* * *

'Ready?'

Place two mirrors facing each other with magic in the middle and it magnifies as it repeats back and forth in the reflections. This is dangerous in the extreme as it can create distortions in the fabric of reality, a doorway through time and space or both. It was almost certainly not an ordinary cigarette; it probably had a strong finding spell on it – very clever.

They had set up the mirrors with the cigarette in the middle, in an ashtray stolen from the pub.

So she had been wrong; the cigarette *had* been the point. She could hardly believe it had taken her so long to figure it out, she was getting slow in her old age. Thank God Denny had not asked her how she had done it.

'Ready?' she repeated.

Denny gulped. 'As I'll ever be,' he affirmed.

Tamar touched his hand briefly (very briefly – she did not want him going dizzy on her). 'We don't have to – not if you're not sure.'

'No, I'm sure, we can't stop now.'

'It's dangerous.'

'You already said – just light the cursed thing – or do you want me to do it?'

Tamar picked up a match, which lit itself, and said 'Last chance.'

'Oh, for God's sake.'

She smiled and lit the cigarette placing it back in the ashtray, and then they waited.

The smoke swirled as smoke will, reflected in the mirrors, giving a peculiar effect. Instead of dissipating, it looked thick – solid almost, and it was starting to swirl in circles, faster and faster and denser and denser, until it filled the space between the mirrors. Denny looked concerned.

'Should it be doing that?' he asked.

'Probably – it's the magic.'

The smoke was now almost completely solid. It stopped swirling and started to shimmer like the surface of a murky pond. They could not see through it, but they could see movement behind it, just under the surface.

'What the hell is that?'

'A doorway,' she grinned, – 'coming?'

'A doorway to where?'

'Or when?'

'Oh God!'

'Yes – this is where the fun really starts – coming?'

'Okay what the hell. Who wants to live forever?'

'Exactly – take it from me, it's not all it's cracked up to be.'

'Okay then.'

'Hold your breath – you don't want to breathe in any smoke.'

'I should think that's going to be the least of my problems.'

He drew in his breath, and they walked through.

~ Chapter Ten ~

ON THE OTHER side, it was hard to tell at first whether or not they had got anywhere at all. The smokiness lingered; well, it was either that, or they were in a very smoky room. The silence was deafening.

'Hello?' Denny's voice was deadened, like he was speaking into a pillow.

A shape loomed out of the fug and revealed itself to be an old man of the type usually described as venerable.

'Ah,' he said with a twinkle, 'victims.'

This was not at all encouraging, but Tamar snapped. 'Cut out the Wizard of Oz σκουπίδια,* nobody's impressed – and get rid of all this smoke.'

The old man sagged; he waved a hand and the smoke cleared. They could now see that they were in a bare room, rather like a police interview room. The old man sat on a single wooden chair in the middle of the floor. There were no doors.

---

* "rubbish" – and that is putting it politely

'No expense spared I see,' commented Denny, caustically.'

'You can't blame me for trying to liven things up a bit,' whined the old man. 'Gets boring this job – bit of atmosphere impresses the suckers no end.'

'But I can see that you're no sucker,' he added hastily, seeing Tamar's face darken. 'Now, what's next? – lost the script. It's been so long since anyone came.'

'The clue perhaps,' asked Denny.

'Ah yes, but first – the warning.'

'Stuff the warning,' snapped Tamar, 'and just get on with it.'

'You don't want the warning?' asked the old man, surprised. 'It's good you know, very portentous.'

'Pretentious you mean – No.'

'Maybe we should ...' Denny began.

'They're all the same,' said Tamar. 'Lots of mystic mumbo-jumbo about disturbing the dark forces and taking heed. Did you think he was joking about the script – it's standard.'

'Well I could just give you the short version,' said the old man hopefully.

Tamar sighed. 'Go on then.'

'It's very dangerous – be warned.'

'Oh thank you! – Now ...'

'I have to give you the speech about the seven ...'

'No!'

'Show you the mirror of ...'

'The clue old man – or else.'

The old man shrugged and said. 'Go to the 'Pink Parrot'

'That's it?'

But the room was fading leaving them standing in an alley complete with dustbins and graffiti. They heard a voice on the air. 'I don't know, you wait six hundred years, and they don't even want to see the mirror of futures.'

'The mirror of futures?' said Denny. 'That might have been useful – why did you have to be so ...?'

'It wouldn't have been,' she said testily. 'It would have been a trick, only showed you a part of the future to mislead you. I know that game. Anyway, it's better not to know the future. Trust me; you'd be too afraid to take a pee if you did. You think no one's ever asked for that?'

'Okay, so what about the speech? The seven what?'

'Deadly sins, for all I know – dwarfs – brides for brothers. Who cares? All of that's just mumbo-jumbo; it's just for show, you don't want to take any notice of it, it wouldn't have been relevant – trust me. I mean just look at what the clue turned out to be. The "Pink Parrot" sounds like a night-club.'

'Yes, run by the Mafia.'

'Or Queens.'

'Aren't they usually called the Blue – something?'

'Anyway – back to the Yellow Pages again.'

Then they heard a scream. They looked at each other and without exchanging a word both began to run down the alley in the direction of the screaming. As they reached the end of the alley, they saw them, lit by a window above. Two men, one was holding down a struggling girl on the ground, his intentions, not hard to imagine. The other was holding a gun in a nervous hand, pointing it shakily towards the street in the direction that Denny and Tamar had just arrived by. Fast as thought, Tamar pulled Denny into the shadows against the wall.

'Now,' she whispered, 'how would you have felt if you'd known *this* was going to happen?'

'More prepared – We have to help her. Can't you do something?'

Tamar frowned. Not as such, she thought. Not on my own, it's not as if I can blast the νόθος into atoms, not without Denny's express wish at least. On the other hand – maybe ...

'Yes,' she said decisively, 'I can.'

She stepped out into the light; both men's heads snapped round to look at her, even though neither of them had heard anything. This strange phenomenon can be witnessed in bars clubs and restaurants everywhere. Men just seem to know instinctively when an attractive young woman steps into the vicinity, no matter what they are doing – it's a thing.

Tamar had changed; it was subtle, but she now looked like the most unlikely hooker since Julia Roberts in 'Pretty Woman'

'Hello boys,' she cooed. Not the most original start, but the best she could come up with off the cuff. She smiled maliciously, 'Why don't you pick on someone your own size.'

The nervous one swung the gun round towards her. 'Cop!' he yelled. She dismissed him; he was young and had evidently been led into this against his will, and had now got more than he bargained for. (Whether she would have dismissed him so lightly had she not been immortal is an open question, on the one hand, he did have a gun pointed at her, on the other he looked like a rotten shot.)

'Hold it,' said the other one. He was older, and mean looking, with a thin weaselly face and hard, flinty eyes. 'Don't shoot her yet, looks like we have a real woman here. Might be we could have some fun with her.'

He got up, letting the girl scramble to the corner of the alley.

'Watch her,' he said, gesturing to the terrified looking girl. The younger one obediently swung his gun down towards her, looking sick.

The mean one advanced on Tamar grinning wolfishly, showing yellowing teeth.

Yuck.

From the shadows, Denny watched in horror as Tamar clamped a hand firmly around the man's neck.

'What the ...' The man struggled violently as Tamar pressed her mouth firmly to his, but she clearly had him in an iron grip. As Denny watched the man slowly stopped struggling and then went limp.

Tamar let him go and he dropped to the ground, eyes open, staring at nothing. She gave him a kick and then apparently satisfied; she turned to the other one who was waving the gun at her in a trembling hand. He was working his mouth, but no sound came out. She moved toward him, and he fired off two shots. When they passed right through her, he dropped the gun and ran.

'Let him go.' Denny was right behind her.

She shrugged and turned. They both looked at the man on the ground.

'What did you do to him?' said Denny, hoarsely.

'I guess I killed him – I didn't mean to.' But even as she said it, she knew she was lying. Hadn't the scumbag deserved it?

'I guess I misjudged it,' she said. 'He must have been weaker than you.'

'Weaker ...? You mean that could have happened to me? When you – When we – That's why I passed out?'

'Of course, I thought you knew. I thought you'd realized.'

'Why?' said Denny, apparently apropos of nothing? But Tamar understood.

'I'm not human,' she explained. 'I may look it, but a Djinn is composed almost entirely of pure, magical energy. Everything you see is just an illusion. See this?' She placed his hand on her arm. 'That's not real flesh, it's a manifestation. And when a human is exposed too closely to that kind of raw energy it sort of – shrivels them up, burns then up from the inside they – you just can't handle it.'

'So, that's why you never did it again. I thought maybe ...'

'I wouldn't want to hurt you. I never meant to ...'

'But you're saying that I could have ...?' He gestured to the body on the ground.

She nodded. 'Any longer, and you would have been catatonic, probably permanently. Another few seconds after that and, yes I could have killed you. I didn't know though. You have to believe me; I would never hurt you.'

He had a strange look on his face. Tamar felt panicky. 'Don't...' she began.

'I have to just ... I 'm just going to walk for a minute.' He said. 'I just need to ... Just leave me alone for a minute.'

And so saying he walked away, his head a maelstrom of conflicting emotions, leaving Tamar alone.

'*Oh hell!*'

No, not alone, the girl they had rescued was getting to her feet. Tamar turned and froze – literally, she could not move; it had her. The same fear that she had felt in the water gripped her.

'It's you,' she gasped, terror rising in her throat. 'What are you?' The girl was advancing; her face was familiar, not like someone she had met before. It was more like a face she had seen in a dream. It gave her an eerie feeling. She tried to remember.

'What are you?' she repeated. 'You're not Djinn, are you? What do you want with me?'

'I catch up with everyone in the end,' said the girl. 'There is no escape.'

A long blade appeared in the girls raised hand, the other hand gripped Tamar's shoulder. She was paralysed. I'm going to die, she thought frantically. This time, I'm really going to die.

Vaguely she heard footsteps behind her. '*Denny*,' she thought – hoped. She cried out. 'Denny – help.'

The girl slashed wildly at her and then Denny caught her as the girl vanished.

'It was him, or it, again – from the water,' she sobbed.

'I shouldn't have left you alone,' he said remorsefully.

'But I've been alone lots of times since the last time – you couldn't have known.'

'No excuse,' said Denny. 'Don't the rules say, never leave the damsel alone in a dark, scary alley. It's just asking for trouble.'

'I'm all right.'

'You're bleeding again.'

She nodded. 'It's not Askphrit,' she said. 'It's not a Djinn at all. I don't know what it is. It said it catches up with everybody in the end – what does that mean?'

'What does it want with you?'

'It wants to kill me.'

'Why?'

'I don't know.' She started to sob again. Denny put his arms around her and after a few minutes she calmed down.

'Hey, I'm touching you. How come I'm okay?'

'It's drained out most of my power,' she said. 'Like it did last time, that's how you could carry me back to the hotel.' Denny looked at her in silence and then drew her towards him and kissed her.

She pulled away from him. 'It's no use,' she said, 'I'll be back to normal again soon – and then ...'

'I know,' he said, 'I'll take what I can get.'

'So,' he said after a short silence, 'I guess we're stuck here until normal service is resumed.'

'Where is here?'

'New York I think. So I suppose we'd better find a hotel or something.'

'We haven't got any money or anything.'

'Let's just start walking, we'll think of something. Find a park or something – come on.'

'It's two O'clock in the morning – oh all right.' They walked back to the street in silence. Tamar stopped suddenly. Denny turned. 'What's up?'

'Oh, oh nothing.' She caught up with him.

But it was not nothing; Tamar had just remembered where she had seen the girl's face before. It had been a long, long time ago – several thousand years. The last time she had seen *that* face, had been in a mirror.

~ Chapter Eleven ~

THE "PINK PARROT" had proved thus far to be a far worse clue than the cigarette. There were a total of seventeen "Pink Parrot's" in America alone. Tamar felt that she should have expected this. Denny had suggested that since they were in New York, then it must be there. But, as it turned out, there was no "Pink Parrot" in New York. This was not surprising in one way. "I knew it couldn't be that easy" – but very surprising in another.

But the search for the "Pink Parrot" was, in fact, the least of their problems. A rift had formed between them since the incident in the alley. Denny was not sure how to handle the fact that Tamar had killed a man. He knew in his heart, despite what she had said, that she *had* meant to do it, and he did not know how to feel about that. On the other hand, he had discovered at the same time that her suspected feelings for him were, apparently, real, while simultaneously finding out that she was effectively debarred from him forever, literally on pain of death.

He was also worried about the other incident – two now – when Tamar had almost been killed. It was clear that something was after her, and, despite his mixed feelings he did know that he did not want her to die.

Tamar was also worried about this. In the alley, she had been certain that whatever it was, it was not a Djinn, but Denny was not so sure.

'How do you know it wasn't Askphrit? How do you know what he became after you set him free? He's had a long time and only his own wishes to consult, he might have become anything.' Tamar had to concede that he had a point. She thought about the face of the girl. Who else – who was still hanging around – had ever seen that face? Only Askphrit – the νόθος', and yet she had always felt sure that she would know him again, no matter what form he took; although, she had to admit, she had no solid base for this assumption.

The other thing that had occurred to them both was that if Askphrit was her stalker then the whole plan might well be a bust. So all things considered neither of them was trying particularly hard to find the "Pink Parrot"

So, life had gone back to what passed for normal. Denny had gone back to work at "Disc – Harmony" *

The manager, a tall, lanky, bearded man who dressed like a refugee from the summer of love and never wore shoes (to keep contact with the earth's magnetic fields) and was somewhat inevitably called Bo – real name unknown – had not even noticed Denny's absence. Denny was not even sure that he knew his name.

Had Bo, Denny wondered, ever felt like this? He felt an insane urge to confide in him, to seek advice from a fellow human being. (Or, as Tamar had said on first meeting him – 'a close approximation.) That was typical of her – she could be

---

* Clearly, the proprietor had not thought this one through – this is the sort of "witty" play on words that a certain type of thinker comes up with at four a.m. after a few spliffs. He had obviously never noticed the phonetic irony – and he wondered why he never had many customers.

cruel. It had seemed funny at the time; he wished he could stop thinking about her – well, maybe not "wished".

The truth was he was having second thoughts about the plan. Yes, she needed his help and yes, it was not fair that she had been tricked into slavery, Denny had strong opinions on that kind of thing – but ... She would have such a lot of power if she were free. Did he really want to be responsible for unleashing her on an unsuspecting world? Would that be fair on the world? Who knew what she might do? Oh, she said she wanted to save the world, and he believed her, but how would she go about it? It was as she had said; she might look human, but she was not, she was an ancient and powerful Djinn with an altogether different set of values and morals to humans – that fact had been made apparent to him in the alley. She clearly had no problem at all with vigilante justice. Imagine vigilante justice on a worldwide scale.

All this thinking was giving him a headache, so he decided to slope off home, Bo would never notice.

'Hey man – where you goin'?'

Rats! 'I – um – I – Just nipping out for a few minutes – okay?'

'Yeah man, I guess – hey, how's that chick of yours doin'? That's a fine lookin' woman,' Bo always talked like this (what's in a name? – indeed!)

'Oh – she's um – fine – you know?'

'Fine uh? – sounds bad, you guys having trouble?' This was, by the way, the longest conversation Denny could ever remember having with Bo, who usually seemed to inhabit another plane of existence peculiar to record shop owners.

'No,' said Denny. 'Well, yeah a bit.'

'Just follow your heart man, you can't go wrong. The heart knows what you want even when the brain don't. Yeah follow your heart man.'

* * *

Denny stalked home in a fury, "follow your heart" indeed. What the hell was that supposed to mean? Typical! Load of hippie claptrap. Still, he was not to know. It was not his fault.

He just did not know what was at stake. It just was not that simple.

When he got home, Denny got the shock of his life. The room was back to its original state, peeling wallpaper, stained carpet *et al*, and there was no sign of Tamar or her bottle; she was gone.

He sat down on the bed (unmade) staggered. Where the hell was she? Where had she gone? How? Why? *How* had she gone? He wanted her back. Now that she was gone, he realized that he needed her, perhaps because she was the only person in his life who had ever needed *him*. He should have known she had come into his life for a reason, all his doubts melted away. He had to find her; she would not be safe on her own with whatever it was out there still after her. Oh God! What if ... what if that was what had happened, what if "it" had got her?

'Oh you're home,' said a voice behind him. Denny jumped three feet in the air.

There she stood, large as life and quite clearly un-eviscerated. Anger took over.

'Where the hell were you?'

She held up a bag. 'Peking Duck,' she said mysteriously.

'What?' Denny was nonplussed.

'Peking Duck – your favourite – from Peking. You said you didn't like magical food, so I ...'

'I thought you'd gone.'

'Gone? – gone where?'

'Just gone, you know – for good.'

'Don't be silly – where could I go where *you* couldn't find me? I can't. I told you that, didn't I? – All you have to do is call.'

'But – but – the room,' he gestured wildly around him, 'and you took the bottle.'

'No I didn't – it's there,' she pointed under the bed. 'And I always leave the room like this if I go out.'

'Why?'

'Because you told me to.'

'I did?'

'Yes, because of the landlord.'

'Oh – yes.'

She put her hands on her hips. 'What the hell is wrong with you?'

'I – I – well,' Denny faltered. 'I thought you'd left me, and I felt so bad because – because I've let you down. I said I'd help you and I haven't been – not lately anyway because I wasn't sure and I thought you'd gone because of that. But I am sure now; I have to help you, because I said I would, and you need me to.' He stopped finally, only because he had run out of breath.

'*Why* weren't you sure?' Tamar had an uncomfortable knack of homing in points like this.

'Because – it doesn't matter now – I got distracted that's all.'

She sat down next to him and after a long time finally asked. 'Why *are* you doing this?'

He thought for a moment. 'Look,' he said, 'it's like this. I was worried I guess; I mean you ... you're cruel sometimes and you can be vain. I mean I don't believe for one second, that that's what you really look like. And you're a murderer, but – oh yes you are – but it doesn't matter. None of it matters; I thought it did, but it doesn't. It doesn't change what I have to do. And – and I – well you – you're important to me now I mean ...'

'You and I, we can't. I mean ...'

'I know, and that doesn't matter either. It doesn't change anything. I want to do this; it's the right thing – I think.'

Naturally, after this embarrassing speech they avoided each other for a while.

Denny did not even have the excuse of being drunk when he had made it. *

---

* All women know that if a man has had more than ten pints, then he is quite likely to ring her up at one in the morning or even turn up on her doorstep, spouting drivel about how wonderful she is and what a rat he is not to appreciate her. This is accepted as behaviour that comes under an amnesty agreement and is treated accordingly.

He was wishing that he had never made it at all and was even tempted to make it an official wish. Much more staring at the floor and muttering excuses about needing to go out for teabags, (they had quite a mountain of teabags now – it put a whole new spin on the phrase "pyramid teabag") and he would do it, and to hell with the consequences.

Apart from the mortification, it was business as usual – that is – total and utter bewilderment. They were (separately) cudgelling their brains fruitlessly on the second clue, pausing occasionally to scream in frustration (Denny) or to blow something up (Tamar) most notably Denny's guitar. He had formed the irritating habit of picking out tuneless dirges on it to help him think, he said, and it was driving Tamar to distraction. It had been carbonised six times now, and Tamar only wished that it could stay that way; she had never liked it at the best of times. At least there had been no more attempts on her life, although she was beginning to miss them, any distraction would be welcome – even death – at this point. At least it would be a way out of what was becoming an impossible situation.

Of course, all this could have been avoided if Denny had just wished Tamar free, but he did not because he did not know that he could and Tamar wasn't about to tell him, because – (a) Rule seventeen prohibited it (but so what?) but mainly – (b) despite the fact that she was probably facing death, even being dead, she felt, was better than being mortal. No, she was not that desperate yet.

They had tried the obvious solutions first – to get them out of the way and without much hope. But as Tamar said 'If we don't, it's bound to be one of them.'

A real pink parrot – a rare – or, let's face it, unique breed. The nearest they could come up with was a flamingo – too many of these. An anagram produced a whole lot of nothing (try it if you have nothing better to do – Tamar and Denny wished they had not bothered). Then they tried phonetic variations, on the basis that they had misheard. This was not encouraging. They even wondered if it was the ill-advised moniker of some shadowy underworld Godfather like figure, but even if it were, they would be no further forward.

'Does it have to be *this* particular sorceress?' asked Denny eventually.

'Well I suppose not. Why, do you know any? – Why didn't you say? You get on the phone, and I'll put the kettle on.'

'Okay, okay, but there must be others out there, easier to find. I just feel like I'm in the middle of some cosmic game show. All things considered I'd rather be in Milton Keynes.'

'Don't *ever* say that,' said Tamar in mock horror.

'I was only kidding. I promise – on my life, never to go to Milton Keynes – even if it had the only source of oxygen left in the world.' They both laughed, and weeks of constraint fell away from them.

'Okay, seriously, though, you do have a point,' said Tamar eventually. 'I do feel like a pawn on a chessboard, as if the gods are laughing at us. Or they would be if there were any gods left.'

'So, maybe we should start from scratch?'

'I could. I have nothing but time. But you ... Besides, all sorcerers put up barriers. We'd probably just end up back where we are now, in the end.'

'Okay, I give in – I'll wish.'

'Wish? Wish for what?'

'For Askphrit of course; to be here. It's only one wish it'll be okay. Come on let's cut to the chase.'

'Are you sure?'

'Positive. I should have known it would come to this. I should never have tried to get around it.'

'You want to do it now?'

'No time like the present.'

'Okay, then.'

He took a deep breath. 'Here goes nothing.' They were both grinning.

'I wish,' he winked, 'that Askphrit were here in this room right now.'

They were caught unprepared as a huge, black faced, overdressed Djinn with a booming scary voice, entirely failed to materialise.

'What went wrong?' asked Denny after a while, and they had ascertained that he definitely was not coming. Tamar was floating cross-legged with her head in her hands, a bad habit when things went wrong. She was saying – over and over. 'No, no, no, no, no.'

'Tamar, TAMAR!'

Since slapping or shaking her was out of the question, he just had to wait until she was calmer before he asked again. 'What went wrong? Why didn't it work?'

'It *did* work,' she was laughing hysterically now.

'No it didn't.'

'Yes it did. Oh, I should have known; I should have seen it. There's always a catch.' And she collapsed into a fit of maniacal giggling.

'Tamar stop it, it's not funny.'

'Oh it is, it is,' she gasped and then started to sob. 'Oh Denny, don't you get it? It's me.'

'What is?'

'I am,' she said cryptically.

'Oh for God's sake, I'm going out; I'll come back when you feel like being sensible.'

She looked up seriously. 'Think about it,' she said. Then suddenly the small denomination coin hit the floor.

'Oh.'

She nodded.

'You mean ...?'

She nodded again – like a nervous witch.

'Okay, so how's that then?'

'The short version? I'm Askphrit now because I replaced him.'

Denny nodded. 'I got that, but I didn't ask for the Djinn, I asked for him by name, I was pretty specific.'

'Yes, but look, I'm still me, but I'm also him – because I took his place. I filled the void that he left when he became –

something else. All he had to do was change his name to become someone else entirely. He's fallen out of the matrix, become an anomaly. He's not Askphrit anymore because I am – in a way. He doesn't exist at all anymore. Well I mean he does but ... do you understand? Anyway, I'm a fool because I should have known. I *did* know – sort of.'

'So if we do find him, will the plan still work?'

Tamar thought about it. 'Yes,' she pronounced eventually. 'It'll still work if we word it right. No, it's finding the bugger that'll be the problem.'

'Is this sorceress still our best shot?'

'Yes, unfortunately, but I might have another idea.'

'What?'

Tamar smiled. 'You'll see.'

* * *

Tamar was running for her life. Her heart ready to burst, sweat running down her whole body, terror threatening to engulf her. Behind her was a large building of some sort, glowering darkly against the skyline. The terror was coming from there; inside that building was some horror that she had to escape. She didn't know what, and she didn't know how she had got here, but coming here had been a tremendously bad idea. Why was she running? She could not remember; she only knew that if she stopped it would be bad. She made herself go on, forcing her legs to keep pumping. Don't stop, don't look back. Ahead was a barbed wire fence fizzing in the rain, if she could just get over it somehow, but it did not seem to be getting any nearer. 'Please,' she gasped desperately. 'Please.'

The dogs howled – it's always dogs. Despite her terror, a little corner of Tamar's mind wondered about this. I mean, she thought, why not lions or tigers or bears – Oh My! Or better still, a dragon. That could barbecue you from twenty feet away – no problem.

Against all odds, she sped up. But they were gaining on her; she brushed the sopping wet hair out of her eyes, lost her rhythm and stumbled. 'NO!' she panicked. But it was not too late – not yet, she was up again, the dogs were brushing her heels snapping. They almost had her, but she was at the fence, her breathing was ragged, she was exhausted, almost spent. She reached for the fence and started to climb. The fence let out a pulse of electricity, which threw her off in a shower of sparks. She landed, stunned in the midst of the pack of baying dogs. They leapt as one at her throat; she could feel their hot stinking breath on her face. She screamed and woke up – still screaming.

Half an hour later she was still shaking, not so much from the nightmare itself as from the fact that she had had it at all.

'I though Djinn didn't dream,' Denny was disgruntled at being woken up at four am for a mere dream, and once he had ascertained that Tamar was not being torn limb from limb, thought that she was making a prodigious girly fuss.

'W – we d – don't,' her teeth were chattering. 'It was here – I felt it. Haven't you noticed? Every time it shows up I become more ... more human – mortal I mean. I lose my powers, become more vulnerable – I can be hurt, you can touch me, and now ... now I'm dreaming – *dreaming* for God's sake.

'Is it still here?'

'No, you turn up, and it disappears. Why the hell is that? What is it?'

'You're asking me? What does it feel like?'

'Like ... like a great black hole, a vast, sucking void pulling me into it, and a huge weight crushing me down. If it gets me, there'll be nothing left.'

'Sounds like life. You know – nobody gets out alive.'

'Huh?'

'Nothing, sorry ignore me, I'm just tired.'

'Go back to bed then, I'm all right now. I'll stay up; I don't really need to sleep. You do, and we have a big day tomorrow.'

'You know, you still haven't told me where we're going.'

'Ah, it's a surprise, put it this way, even if it doesn't turn anything up it'll be fun. But not so much if you're knackered, so go back to bed.'

'It's almost morning.'

'GO!'

'Oh all right. Another day off work, I'm going to get fired.'

~ Chapter Twelve ~

'WE'RE IN the park.' So far, Denny was disappointed with his surprise. 'The kid's park round the corner from where I live. Look – swings over there, a slide. What are we going to do? Ride the roundabout? See if getting dizzy gives us any inspiration, or no, I know, there's a magic land at the top of the climbing frame.' Denny was being a prat and he knew it. But Tamar, unusually, was taking it well.

She smiled secretively. 'Close,' was all she said. She was squinting over the top of some feeble looking – well you had to call them trees because they were too big to be weeds and too small to be Triffids, and they were tastefully adorned with modern art – C Luvs P 4 ever, etc. These were sharing soil (and I use the word loosely) with the lesser-known beer can shrub and crisp packet plant.

'What time is it?' she asked.

'Almost twelve – why?'

'What time is it precisely?'

'Eleven fifty eight – what is going on?'

'Wait,' they waited. Two minutes passed, and Tamar said. 'Your watch must be wrong,' she scanned the skyline. 'Ah,' then she stepped sideways and vanished.

'What?' said Denny. Her head reappeared as if she were looking round an invisible door. It looked creepy, hanging in space like that. A hand appeared. 'Come on,' she said, pulling him.

Then he saw her, standing in front of the trees, only they were not the same trees. The view blended seamlessly with the surrounding parkland, but he could see that it was not the same place at all.

'Hurry up.'

He hurried as he stepped forward the traffic noise ceased and the sounds of playing kids faded away. He turned around quickly, but the park had vanished, and he was standing in a forest listening to the birdsong.

Tamar was gleeful. 'Well doubting doofus, what do you think now?'

'Where the hell are we?'

'It's a sort of ... pocket universe. They're all over the place, if you know how to find them. You have to know where to look, and you can only get in at midday or midnight – or out. This is a magic forest – like it?'

'Yeah, it's ... freaky. Hang on a minute though, are you telling me that there are places like this all over?'

'Well, not as many as there used to be, they're fading away. Some have been taken over by evil magic, but most are just gone.'

'Why?'

'The world's getting bigger,' she said cryptically.

Denny was about to ask for a better explanation, when he was distracted by a crowd of ludicrously funny looking creatures scurrying towards them.

'What are those?' he asked, staring in surprise and amusement.

They looked, more than anything, like lumps of dough on short fat legs and with twinkling bright blue or green eyes.

'Brownies,' said Tamar contemptuously. 'Don't encourage them.

'Sod off!' she added as the Brownies started fawning around them, and she gave one of them a kick, which sent it flying. They were chattering excitedly, but it was impossible to work out what they were saying, since they were all talking so fast and all at once.

'Why did you do that?' Denny was mildly shocked at her viciousness. 'They seem harmless enough.'

'Oh they're not dangerous, just annoying. Trust me, one civil word and we'll never get rid of them. All I said was "hello" and I had four of them following me everywhere for seventeen years. They drove me round the bend. Be nasty, it's the only language they understand.'

Denny just stood there; he was prepared to ignore them, but not to kick them. It just seemed too cruel.

The Brownies gave up eventually and disappeared into the undergrowth as suddenly as they had appeared, muttering crossly. Denny could not help laughing; they sounded like a speeded up tape of the Munchkins.

Tamar dusted he hands together; she was dishevelled but composed. 'Lunch?' she said, snapping her fingers and providing the kind of picnic lunch usually only found in E. Nesbit novels.

Denny was used to this by now, but a few minutes later he choked on his pork pie and pointed spluttering.

'That's a – that – there – it's a – a *unicorn*!'

Tamar was amused. 'You live with me – a Djinn, no less – who, by the way, you didn't seem at all surprised to meet, and you're amazed by a flipping unicorn – in a magic forest. Humans – honestly!'

'Sorry.'

'Actually, unicorns are not magical or mythical creatures at all. They're just a variety of horse – with a horn. Magical people always preferred them though – more style I suppose. They're endangered now, like dragons – have been for thousands of years. That's why they're hidden in places like this. Humans used to cull them for the horns, they thought they had magical properties. 'You're a superstitious lot aren't you?'

'You can talk. You *are* a superstition. So, where are the sabre toothed tigers, the woolly mammoths?'

'That's prehistory, no magic back then.'

'Okay, white rhinos, quagga, the dodo?'

'We were too late for some of these species I admit,' said a deep voice from behind them. 'We did not see the danger until it was too late, and now our interference is no longer necessary. Humanity has learned much since the time of the unicorns. They take care of the animals themselves now.'

Denny turned to face a tall, deep chested man who was, unlikely as it seems, wearing a deerskin and antlers (an ironic choice for a conservationist). He was square jawed and handsome with the obligatory cleft chin and rippling muscles and enough matted chest hair to carpet the Albert Hall. You could not imagine him in an Armani suit. He seemed to fill all the available space.

Denny hated him on sight, and on principle. He radiated masculinity in a truly offensive manner. Denny did not want him anywhere near Tamar; he glanced at her, but she seemed supremely unaffected.

'Hi Hank,' she was saying.

'Hank?' said Denny incredulously. 'And who or what is a Hank?'

'And what exactly are you, little man?' said Hank, making Denny wish he was fifty feet tall and could trample cities. He turned red. This was not a becoming colour on him.

'Well, well, well,' Hank was saying, 'Tamar the Black as I live and breathe.' He seemed to find this hugely amusing.

Tamar frowned. 'Shut up Hank,' she said.

'What's so funny about that?'

Hank turned 'Is this guy with you?' he asked Tamar, ''Cause if not ...'

'He's with me,' said Tamar hastily interposing herself between them.

'Aw baby – what are you doing to me? Whaddya see in this insect? Come on, when are you going to come to your senses and come back to me? It was pretty good wasn't it?'

'I'm not, and it wasn't,' said Tamar shortly.

She turned to Denny. 'Hank here is the guardian of the forest.' she explained, 'a sort of god – well demi – hemi – semi god anyway, an anthropomorphic personification of the forest itself. And yes,' she sighed, 'we had a thing, but it was a long time ago and I left him, okay?' She glared at him as if daring him to make something of it.

'And you,' she said turning to Hank. 'This is Denny; he's the master of the bottle and ten times the man you are to boot. And even if he wasn't, I would never come back to you, you're a savage.'

She glanced at them both. 'Any questions?'

They both shook their heads.

'Tough broad,' said Hank, and a look passed between him and Denny as they recognised each other as fellow sufferers. Denny relaxed.

'Good,' said Tamar. 'So, if you've both quite finished hosing down the forest floor with testosterone, can we get down to business? Are you going to help us or not?'

Hank bowed ironically 'At your service Ma'am.'

'Right. So – um well – you have godlike powers don't you?'

'Indeed I do – why?'

'You're all – seeing, yes?'

'Here in the forest I am.'

'Right, but if you left the forest and came with us, could you still ...?'

'I don't know, and it doesn't matter. I stay here; I don't leave the forest – you know that.'

'You can come back.'

'No way babe – sorry.'

'Oh, you haven't changed at all. Don't be so stubborn, it won't be for long. You and your precious forest – it'll still be here when you get back.'

Hank ruminated. 'Look,' he said, 'why don't you explain the problem to me and I'll see if there's anything else I can do – sort of compromise.'

'There isn't.'

'Try me, what have you got to lose?'

'Oh come on,' said Denny. 'He's not going to help us – let's go.'

'You can't leave until midnight,' said Hank. 'So, you might as well tell me all about it.'

* * *

Hank rubbed his massive chin thoughtfully. 'Hmm, that's quite a tale,' he said.

'So, now let's have it. What's *really* going on?' Tamar and Denny sagged.

'That *is* what's going on,' said Denny.

'It's all true,' added Tamar.

'Really? I don't believe it. I've met mortals; they wander in here sometimes. Mortals don't behave like that. Even the brave ones, they takes their wishes and they run – in case the warranty runs out. Even heroes,' and here he cocked an eye at Denny as if to say "And this chump is no hero" 'are only in it for themselves.'

Denny got to his feet. 'I don't have to take this from a ... an anthra – what did you call him?'

'An anthropomorphic personification.'

'Right, it's obvious he can't help us – just like you said. Or he won't – let's go.'

'Okay, you're right, I should have known better than to ask him. He never was any damn use.'

'No, be fair, we shouldn't have expected... I mean look at him, stuck here for years ...'

'Centuries.'

'Centuries, exactly ...'

'Millennia even.'

'The point is,' said Denny, 'he's been stuck here for so long, what could he possibly know about anything? Obvious really.

And you can't blame him for being scared to leave, I mean, all those centuries ...'

'Millennia.'

'Even – in the same place, it's like prison, worse than your bottle really. He's become institutionalised; he couldn't cope in the real world.'

'Not his fault really.'

'No – no, not at all. He can't help it – unfair to expect it.'

Big, dumb, heroic types like the forest god, always fall for this type of baiting. (How do you think they got George to fight the dragon? Three of his mates followed him around for a weekend making clucking noises until he cracked.)

'HEY!' yelled Hank in an offended tone.

Tamar and Denny grinned at each other.

'Who are you calling useless?' he glared. 'Scared am I?'

'It's all right,' soothed Tamar, 'we understand, we shouldn't have asked.'

'Right!' said Hank furiously; he made a motion as if he was pushing up his sleeves – which of course, would have been more effective if he'd been wearing sleeves. He stopped self-consciously. 'What is it you want me to do?'

Tamar and Denny stifled laughter.

They had both been amazed at how easy it had been to bring him round using such blatant reverse psychology as the average twelve year old would not have fallen for, and they did not want to break the mood now.

'Well,' said Tamar, 'what we really want is for you to come out into the real world with us and see if you can find our Djinn – or at least a sorcerer – for us.'

'You guys are serious?'

Tamar pulled a face, which clearly said 'Duh'

Hank looked at Denny. 'You're really serious? That story you told me was the truth?'

Denny nodded. 'Of course, how could you help us if you didn't know the truth?'

Hank looked at Denny with a dawning respect. 'Well I never,' he said, 'a noble mortal.'

He grasped Denny by the hand and shook it vigorously. 'Jolly good show old chap.'

This was a sufficiently un-Hank-like comment that it made Tamar look sharply at him. But he seemed sincere enough. Sarcasm, in any case, was generally above his level of intelligence.

'Well I'm with you,' he said. 'Count me in, a noble and heroic enterprise – but ...' His face fell, and he seemed embarrassed after all his bluster as he admitted awkwardly. 'I don't think I can do what you want. I won't have my powers outside of the forest,' he explained. 'You see, in here, I see all and I know all, but in the real world – I shouldn't think ... well I'm only a spirit. I'm not even sure I can exist in the real world.'

'Oh,' said Denny.

'Still,' said Hank heartily, 'I can but try I suppose. It's for a good cause.' Here he looked at Tamar. 'And who wants to live forever anyway?'

'Maybe you won't have to,' said Denny. 'What about the clue, "Pink Parrot" – mean anything to you?'

'Doesn't ring any bells.'

'Know any sorcerers?'

'No he doesn't, how could he? Stuck in here; and we can't ask him to risk his life – obviously. Well I can show you around at least, while we're here.'

'Let me,' said Hank graciously.

*

They had been wandering around in silence for some hours. Mostly in silence anyway punctuated by gasps of wonder or surprise as Denny saw at intervals Dryads (wood nymphs) emerging from their trees, Naiads (water sprites) and a great flaming bird, which Denny took to be a phoenix, and other strange things.

'They used to live in the real world,' explained Tamar. 'But there's no place for them now. They couldn't adapt. This is like a kind of nature preserve, somewhere they can really be.'

Despite living with a Djinn, having met a god, seen mermaids and walked through a doorway created by a magic cigarette, Denny had not lost his sense of wonder. He wondered if he would ever get used to this sort of thing.

It was getting dark, and Tamar suggested they camp.

Hank was puzzled. 'Camp?'

'Stop and find somewhere to sleep. Mortals need sleep – Oh!' She stopped at the edge of a lake.

'I can last until midnight,' said Denny.

Tamar was not listening; she was staring at the water.

'What?' said two voices.

'I think,' she said eventually, 'that you may be able to help us after all.' She pointed to the lake.

She had found the "Pink Parrot"

* * *

'What are the odds?' Denny said, of us arriving at just at the right moment?' He had a point. The last rays of the sun had lit the water with a rosy glow, and there, reflected in the water, flickering like a faulty neon sign was a constellation in the shape of a parrot. Only just out and faint in the sky but strangely bright in the water.*.

'Are you sure it's a parrot?' said Hank, squinting at it doubtfully, 'it could be a budgie or a puffin.'

'We have to hurry – the sun's almost down, jump.'

'Er – I can't swim,' Denny reminded her.

'I don't think it matters,' said Tamar. 'We want to go down don't we?'

'And if you're wrong?'

'I'm *not* wrong,' she said impatiently. 'Come on.'

'What do you need me for?' asked Hank.

'You have to get us back. This is your land; it'll call you back and you can bring us with you.'

---

* When the gods set signs in the sky or as reflections in icy pools it is expected that it will be something portentous or romantic like a sword or a crown. The sign that Tamar found was, in fact, far more usual. Thus proving that it is not true that the gods have no sense of humour

'I suppose, technically, in there is still his land,' said Denny. 'It's his lake.'

'Good point. See, we're not even leaving the forest, and you're the master here. We may need you, and you did say ...'

'I never said I wouldn't come.'

'Denny?'

'Okay.' I'm not going to be outdone by that macho idiot, he thought.

He took a deep breath. 'Let's go.'

'Hurry up.'

They held hands after some scuffling about to get Tamar in the middle, so that Denny and Hank would not have to hold hands with each other, and jumped.

* * *

The thing about disappointment is that you do not expect it. That is what makes it a disappointment. People who are expecting disappointment, of course, are not disappointed when they get it, because they were expecting it.

There are many different types of disappointment in the human experience. There is the disappointment of standing on the scales after weeks of hellish starvation, living off water biscuits and onion soup – a diet, which can kill you according to experts (you die of loneliness) only to discover that you have gained three pounds.

There's hairdresser disappointment. You go in with a picture of Jennifer Aniston and come out looking like Simon Cowell.

Then there's mail order disappointment. Your item is the wrong colour/size/model. There's no plug and the instructions are in Cantonese. Or you get a notice three months later (after hours of frustration – listening to Greensleeves down the phone) saying 'OUT OF STOCK'. And it's not fair, because you desperately wanted that combination toilet roll recycler / barbecue, or whatever.

There can, however, be few disappointments more crushing than leaping dramatically into a (clearly) enchanted lake and finding nothing more than wet feet. After all, it is an enchanted lake, isn't it? With a sign on its surface full of portent (not to mention luminous tackiness). What should have happened, they all felt, (even Hank – who never read or had adventures and had only a vague idea about how this sort of thing was supposed to work) was a whirling vortex that pulled them down into a mystical chamber tenanted by a wizened sage talking mumbo-jumbo (and asking for a smack in the mouth from Tamar). Or at the very least, a snowy wood tenanted by talking animals. Tamar would have settled for an enormous neon sign saying, "THIS WAY TO THE SORCERESS >>>"

'What went wrong?' asked Denny.

He was, by now, getting fed up with asking this question, but he felt that somebody had to say it.

'Damn!' said Tamar predictably; it was her usual contribution to their run of disasters, and she said it without passion as if it were a reflex. 'It didn't work did it? That's all; I must have got it wrong. And if you two say anything ...' she glared at them both simultaneously, managing to give a whole new meaning to the phrase "two faced"

'Wait a minute,' said Denny. 'Shouldn't we be sinking? – This is a lake – right?'

'Obviously, it's not even a proper lake,' snarled Tamar, 'just a big muddy puddle – it's ...' She broke off because Denny was right.

Although they were only standing in it up to their ankles, below their feet she could see fish swimming about. Deeper down there were shadows moving in unfathomable depths. It was creepy; they were walking on water. Well – not walking, when they tried to trudge back to shore, they found that they were stuck.

'Like quicksand,' observed Denny.

'So,' said Tamar, business -like again, 'this must be the clue – something to do with the nature of the water perhaps or us floating here. Maybe it's symbolic.'

'We're stuck in the middle of a lake,' snapped Denny. 'What's symbolic about that?'

'Well ...'

'And I hope we're not going to be here until we work it out because...' He stopped.

'It's perfectly simple,' Tamar was saying. 'Like you said, we're stuck in the middle of a lake. Which clearly symbolises ...'

Denny tapped her on the shoulder. 'Look.'

Rising gracefully out of the water was a hand. It was a slender, white, female hand, clothed in samite. It barely caused a ripple in the water. It was holding up a jar, a perfectly ordinary jar with a screw top. The label bore the legend. "Mother Hubbard's quality pickled beetroot".

'Anyone hungry?' said Denny, laughing hysterically as Tamar reached out a hand and grabbed the jar. As she did so, the hand vanished, and they all fell in the lake.

* * *

'Not another one,' moaned Denny, as they sat in a circle examining this latest piece on nonsense that the universe had thrown at them.

'Much more of this and I'm going to have to grow a beard and start wearing sandals and a placard saying, "The End is Nigh".' Denny was in a bad mood after being fished out of the lake and slung on the bank like a beached whale. He thought he would rather have drowned.

'It must mean *something*,' said Tamar. 'We'll work it out – or rather, I will, if you'll just shut up and let me think.'

'Huh, what happened to all that "O' My Master" stuff?'

'Okay, *'Master'* you work it out.'

Twenty minutes later Denny said. 'Okay, I give up.'

'Already?' grinned Tamar

Hank was laughing softly. 'It's really very obvious – too easy really.'

'*What*?' said Tamar incredulously. '*You've* worked it out?'

He nodded.

'So come on then – hot shot. What does it mean?' she demanded.

Hank just grinned inanely.

'He doesn't know,' said Denny, 'he's having you on. I mean it's a jar of beetroot for God's sake. It'll take some lateral thinking to get the answer – like the cigarette.'

They both looked at Hank, who was still grinning.

'Sorry,' he said. 'I'm not falling for that again. Think! – It's really very obvious.'

'Stop *saying* that,' said Tamar in frustration.

'Okay' said Hank, 'I'll give you a clue.'

'No more clues,' groaned Denny putting his head in his hands.'

'When is a door not a door?' said Hank.

'*What*?' said Denny, now thoroughly infuriated.

But Tamar was thinking.

After a few minutes, she stood up and, in what Denny understandably took to be a fit of frustration, hurled the jar at a large tree

'NO!' cried Denny, trying to stop her.

The jar smashed against the trunk sending glass and bits of soggy beetroot flying.

'When it's a-jar,' sang Tamar triumphantly, as a door appeared from nowhere in the trunk of the tree.

'Well done,' said Tamar to Hank. 'Who would have thought you had it in you?'

'Well done you,' said Denny to Tamar. 'How did you work it out?'

'Oh it was easy in the end. I just had to wind down my sense of humour a few notches – to about the level of a drunken rugby player.' She jerked a thumb meaningfully at Hank. 'Then it just came to me.'

'Hmm, funny sense of humour this sorceress, whoever she is.'

'Oh it's classic, everything's a pun or a bad joke. You get used to it. I should have been quicker.'

'The cigarette was better. Took us nearly a fortnight to figure that one out.'

'Trust me – from now on it'll get worse.'

'So,' he said looking at the door, 'do we knock, do you think? Or do we just let ourselves in?'

~ Chapter Thirteen ~

IT WAS THE terrible "muzak" that was getting on her nerves. Somebody, either from malice, which would mean they had been expecting her, or by coincidence, had chosen to pick out the theme from 'I dream of Jeannie', (a sixties television program that Tamar had particularly loathed – for reasons that will be apparent to anyone who has ever seen it) apparently with chopsticks banged on the side of wineglasses, and pipe it through non-existent speakers. At least Tamar had not seen any and she had looked, with the intention of ripping them off the wall. Had she been paranoid – and she was – she would have suspected that someone (who?) was trying to psyche her out.

Denny did not need further psyching out. He was huddled in a corner twitching. He suffered from claustrophobia, he had explained before retreating into a panic attack which got worse the lower they got. He evidently could not hear the muzak, nor was he aware of anything else. He seemed to want nothing more than to be left alone to die in peace. And Tamar wondered about this too. It was as if somebody *knew*.

She ignored him as best she could; there did not seem to be anything she could do for him.

How much further? She wondered. Surely if they kept on going they would be in the bowels of Hell, a place about which Tamar had read. A nice place to live apparently – but you would not want to visit.

The lift shuddered to a halt. They had been fairly, but not really very surprised to open the door and find a lift inside. Hank had remained behind on the grounds that there just was not room for him Denny would have preferred a snake pit, but would rather have died than admit it in front of Hank. And the idea of remaining behind with him, particularly after revealing his phobia, was too much for him. (This kind of macho behaviour is what gets most men into situations that they cannot handle.)

As the lift stopped he looked up wild-eyed. He looked like a man who had not eaten or slept for a month (so no change there). He was chattering, not just his teeth, but his whole body. He was rocking back and forth repeating to himself, 'Open the door – open the door – open – door – open.'

The floor opened; this was too much for Denny, and he let out a shriek that would have split the sky, but that was, nevertheless, swallowed up by the sound of a wildly cheering crowd.

Tamar landed ungracefully on the ropes. Denny's shriek was cut off as he landed on the mat winded.

A small, dapper man walked to the centre of the ring holding a microphone, and the noise of the crowd swelled to a deafening roar.

He held up a hand. 'Ladies and Gentlemen,' he cried. 'Welcome to the "Pink Parrot".'

More yelling, 'Get on with it ponce,' and other similar pleasantries.

The little man smiled and waved a hand. 'Tooo- night!' he said. 'For your pleasure – a fight ...' long pause for dramatic emphasis. 'To the death.' The roar of the crowd rose to apocalyptic proportions.

'Gnnng,' said Denny, rousing himself from his disorientation.

'In the red corner – the challengers – fighting for the next clue on their quest. The Djinn – TAMAAAR BLAAACK!!!' He indicated Tamar who was standing in the corner with a look of resignation on her face.

'And also,' the little man continued, 'a special treat – a mere mortal, DE-E-NNY SANGER!!!'

There were some gasps, which quickly degenerated into booing and hissing. Denny was also standing by now and regaining his composure, but he still looked supremely unimposing. Skinny and pale and only of average height, he seemed to be trying to make himself even smaller. He had just enough pride left to stop himself from hiding behind Tamar, but only just.

'What the hell is going on?' he managed, in a strangled hiss.

'Trial by combat,' she hissed back. 'Standard stuff – I should have expected this – sorry.'

Denny groaned.

'They used to do it in a coliseum – with swords. Just ...'

The booing was dying away. 'In the black corner,' the little man was saying, 'we have our reigning champion – the ultimate force of destruction – the deliverer of doom – the evicerator. Your favourite and mine – the incredible the undefeated – SLAMMER LUUUNG!!!'

Climbing into the ring was a gigantic, hulking man, with muscles the size of Volkswagens and wearing headgear that was designed by the same chap who made the mask for "The man in the iron mask". He looked like a movable mountain in a unitard. Tamar had gone white; Denny wondered why.

'That *can't* be his real name,' he said.

'It probably is,' she replied dully. 'He's Djinn.'

'Oh Christ! Are you sure?'

She nodded. 'Pretty sure – I can smell it.'

'Oh, well then – I guess that's our advantage gone then – no chance of you seducing him to death?'

'No.'

'First the lift and now this,' moaned Denny. 'I've got to be the unluckiest bloke in the world. I've probably run over black cats that were luckier than me.'

'Run over?' Denny did not have a car. 'With what, your skateboard?'

'That'd be right, kick a man before he's even down.'

'Now then,' the little man was speaking to the contestants now. 'Let's make it as dirty as possible – for the folks. The only rule is ...'

'That there are no rules?' muttered Denny gloomily.

'No magic can be used inside the cage.'

'Cage?' said Denny, dumfounded. 'What cage?'

As he spoke the little man hopped out of the ring and a large cage clanged into place around them.

'I blame that "Mad Max" film,' said Tamar.

DING, DING – 'Round one'

'Get behind me,' hissed Tamar. 'I'll deal with this.' She squared up to the other Djinn.

'But ...'

'Just do it.'

She stepped in front of Denny as the man-mountain advanced growling menacingly and shaking his head like a dog with fleas.

'I'm gonna crush you like a slug,' the mountainous villain was snarling, 'say goodbye to your intestines.'

'Where's Hank when you really need him?' said Denny to himself. Although this guy would make Hank, look like a brownie by comparison.

The Djinn launched himself at Tamar. 'I'm gonna get you, little girl.' he hissed, 'and your little frog too.'

Tamar leaped gracefully over his head. He grabbed her by the hair as she sailed over him (curse it – too tall) and swung her round his head several times, before catching her and bodyslamming her on the mat. Denny covered his eyes, but she was up again, quick as a cat, before he could pin her.

'Too slow,' she jeered, just before he grabbed her around the neck with one massive arm and started to pummel her with the other.

'What am I doing?' thought Denny, and ran forward to rain blows on the giant's back. He may as well have tried to move a continent. The Djinn swatted him away with his free arm, without loosening his grip on Tamar at all. Denny went flying up to the top of the cage and hung there, stunned. Tamar was going blue.

The bar he was hanging from came loose and pulled out. He dropped with the bar still in his hand, dizzy and disoriented. He jumped to his feet, swaying. Then he charged.

'AAAAGH.' He bashed the giant Djinn in the head.

'Slammer' turned; shaking his head as if trying to get rid of flies. Tamar slid to the floor; Denny backed away waving the bar in front of him like a man swatting mosquitoes. He felt the ropes against his back.

'Uh oh.' He was trapped; he closed his eyes and swung. He missed – when hitting people with iron bars the recommended procedure is to keep your eyes open, that way you can see what you're trying to hit.

Slammer laughed and reached out a massive paw and grabbed Denny by the throat. (He evidently had a limited repertoire of moves – but, since the ones he did have were frighteningly effective why mess with a good system?) Denny naturally dropped the bar. DING, DING!!! The Djinn let go, blindsided by a flying kick to the head from Tamar, he hit the deck.

'Climb,' she croaked, and Denny did not need telling twice. He scrambled awkwardly up the side of the cage. Tamar somersaulted up to the other side, but Slammer had got up and he managed to grab her ankle and drag her back down. He flung her across the ring. Miraculously, she landed on her feet, another leap, and she was close enough to surprise him with an uppercut to his massive chin and a swift boot to the solar plexus – not what she was aiming for but still ... He went down like a giant redwood, and Tamar took her chance. She soared to the top of the cage and clung there like SpiderMan. She looked at Denny, who was almost to the top, and winked out of a blackened eye and thoughtfully spat out a tooth.

'What now?' he mouthed from the other side of the cage and over the top of the well of sound from the audience. Tamar shrugged; a difficult manoeuvre, given her position.

'Look out,' she indicated the infuriated Djinn, climbing up the side of the cage like King Kong, breaking off bars as he went, and grunting incoherently in his fury. If he had stopped to beat his chest, neither Tamar nor Denny would have been surprised.

Denny climbed sideways desperately to the jeers of the crowd. The maddened Djinn had almost reached him when the bar he was standing on gave way and he slid down, bars breaking beneath his feet one after another like a row of falling dominoes. He landed with a grunt and every single bar landed, with perfect comic predictability on his head. He was down but was he out?

*

Ten minutes later, when Slammer was still rattling the cage like a little boy trying to shake conkers out of a tree, they reluctantly had to admit that he was not. Suddenly he backed up, put his head down, and charged like a maddened rhino. The entire cage collapsed like a matchstick house. Technically, they were into round three by the time they climbed out of the wreckage although nobody had paid any attention to the official rounds, and the action had not stopped for the bell. And there was very little chance of scantily clad girls being foolish enough to sashay across the ring holding up placards. Denny was disappointed about this; it had seemed likely enough to be the only thing he had left to look forward to before he died. The only up-side was that Slammer seemed to be in just as sorry shape as they were, having taken the brunt of the falling metal.

They all stood staring dazedly at each other; there was a strange sound which Denny eventually recognised as silence.

The crowd was hushed; obviously nothing like this had ever happened before.

Tamar made a T with her hands for "Time out". The Djinn nodded bemusedly; Denny poured water over his head. He went to hand it to Tamar when he stopped suddenly, what had she told him about the Djinn? – In a pinch...

Slammer was recovering and heading purposefully towards Tamar. Denny nodded towards him. 'Can you hold him down? I only need a few seconds.'

'I'll try,' she said, clearly puzzled.

Denny was surreptitiously ripping a piece off his shirt, increasing her bewilderment. Slammer did not notice him; all his attention was focused on Tamar as the biggest pest currently in his life. Denny did not even rate – big mistake. At least Denny hoped so.

Tamar picked up the biggest bar she could hold, jumped and brought it down on Slammer's head. He staggered and she pounced, driving the bar into his neck and bearing him down, onto the mat.

'Got him,' she called.

Denny thrust the empty water bottle at the Djinn's feet and yelled. 'GET OUT OF THE WAY.'

Tamar made light look sluggish.

'Djinn – home,' said Denny calmly. Slammer roared and struggled, but he was caught, his feet were dissolving, then his legs, torso, head. Within a few seconds, he was gone, Denny made haste to stuff his torn shirt into the neck of the bottle – no lid being to hand. He whooped triumphantly, 'in a pinch' – she had said, 'any bottle will do'.

Tamar punched the air and offered Denny a high five. 'Yes!'

'Way to go Djinn – master. You the man,' she sang.

Denny laughed. 'Back at you – hex kitten.'

The crowd were on their feet chanting. 'KILL – KILL – KILL.'

A crack had opened up in the floor; beyond it was a pit of fire. All she had to do was throw the bottle in...

She lifted the bottle and inspected it, pondering.

'NO,' she shouted. 'We won. It's over. Just give us the clue and let us go.'

'I can't do it,' she said aside to Denny. 'My freedom's not worth his life. He couldn't help it – he was only obeying his master. I'm sorry.'

'Don't be sorry,' said Denny. 'I'm proud of you – you've grown or something.'

'We'll take him with us,' she said. 'Not that it'll stop all this but, well ...'

The little man appeared. 'The rules clearly state that it is a fight to the death,' he said, 'therefore ...'

Denny cut him off. 'I thought you said there were no rules,' he objected. 'You never mentioned that as a rule. I don't think you can hold us to it.'

'It was quite clearly stated ...'

Denny held up a hand. 'You know we could argue about this all night so let's just say that you're right. A fight to the death it is. But you know what? You never stated to *whose* death.' He glared meaningfully at the little man who gulped as he got Denny's meaning.

'After all,' Denny continued calmly. 'I have to ask myself, who's the really guilty party here?' He glanced at Tamar who was staring at him open-mouthed showing a rather unattractive gap in her teeth.

'Wow,' she breathed. 'You would too, wouldn't you?'

'This git?' said Denny. 'No question, I wouldn't have a problem with that at all. After all, he tried to kill us – by proxy anyway.'

'Well now,' said the little man backing away. 'I'm sure we can be reasonable about this, since you have defeated your opponent most thoroughly. And as you say – the rules...'

'Cut the σκουπίδια little man,' snapped Denny,* 'just give us the cursed clue, and let us out of here.'

---

* Tamar's occasional relapses into her original language were starting to rub off on Denny.

'And he goes with us,' added Tamar, jerking a thumb at the bottle.

'Ah well – as to that ...'

'Or else,' threatened Denny.

'Yes, yes – the clue and – your – er – other demands. Yes, agreed.'

The little man suddenly seemed to remember where he was. He took both Denny and Tamar by the hand and raised their arms into the air.

'THE WINNERS,' he cried. The crowd roared.

~ Chapter Fourteen ~

IN A DARK, mysterious chamber, lit with dribbling candles and behind a door of the 'Dread portal' variety, a little man fell on his knees trembling with apparent terror before the imposing figure on the heavily ornamented and stylishly backlit throne.

'Luminous one,' he quavered. 'We have at last discovered who seeks the aid of the powerful one. She is one of the Djinn – Tamar Black is her name.'

The figure on the throne shifted uncomfortably. 'Indeed, and the other one?'

'He is her master.'

'And they survived the combat? How did you allow that to happen, my friend?'

The little man shook.

'Disappointing – disappointing; indeed you have been culpable. They should never have got so far. We will have to do better in the future, will we not? You are my good servant, are you not? I know you will not let me down again.'

The little man let his breath out as he sensed a temporary reprieve. 'I have my best men following them, gracious liege.

We will endeavour to find out what it is that they seek. I could not...'

The figure on the throne waved a hand impatiently, and the little man crumbled into a pile of dust.

'I know what they want,' said Kelon.

~ Chapter Fifteen ~

TAMAR AND DENNY were jubilant. The exhilaration of beating an apparently superior opponent can hardly be overestimated. Slammer had been left in his bottle on a shelf.

'If you release him,' Tamar had cautioned Denny, 'you'll be the master of two Djinn.' And neither of them wanted to be responsible for foisting him on some unsuspecting person and having him undoubtedly wreaking endless havoc on them.

'We'll think of something,' said Tamar. 'And he'll probably be glad of the rest.' And the matter was, to coin a phrase, "shelved".

On the matter of their injuries, Tamar had naturally disposed of hers quite easily. As for Denny, she covered up the damage with a glamour, but he had to live with the pain, since she could do little about it without orders, and he refused to waste a wish on something so trivial.

At least he could go to work, although, had Bo been more observant, he might have wondered why Denny was limping and chugging aspirins every four hours without fail.

The latest clue was as incomprehensible as the others had been, and was accordingly ignored.

'It'll come to us,' said Denny, and Tamar agreed. After their triumph, they felt invincible. They were on a high – the kind of high that makes people jump off tall buildings in the deluded belief that they can fly. The universal result of this belief is pavement splash. Denny and Tamar were headed for a fall.

The clue, for what it's worth, was a child's action figure. Denny took this calmly; he was finally getting used to this sort of thing. He claimed it was an "Action Man" and Tamar did not argue, but continued to refer to it as "ninja doll", which was more or less what it was. Dressed in black up to its eyes and carrying a tiny sword.

But Denny, who had had his fair share of Action Men as a child, objected to this denigration of its character 'It's not a doll,' he insisted, 'it's an action figure.'

'Who cares?' Tamar said, and Denny soon dropped it. The argument was too reminiscent of similar childhood bouts.

But despite all this, there was no discussion of what the "not a doll" might mean, and soon it was almost completely forgotten. There was real danger in their indolence. Tamar did not know it, but she was running out of time.

* * *

'Keep watching them,' said Kelon. The little man, now restored to human form, was fawning at the foot of the throne, quivering with anxiety, he nodded nervously.

'I want to know everything she gets up to,' added Kelon, menacingly.

'If I may, great one, I think that soon, she will cease to trouble you.'

'Indeed? I did not realise that I paid you to think.'

'Er, your greatness, you do not pay me at all.'

'Is that so? Perhaps I should look into that. On the other hand...' There was an ominous silence in which Kelon made a threatening gesture, 'let me down again – and it's the Dustbuster for you.'

'Magnificent one,' grovelled the little man, 'I do not require payment, merely to be in the service of your supreme and wondrous person.'

And if the little man wondered why this powerful creature should be so afraid of being sought by those who only needed help (and one of those a mere mortal) he was wise enough not to ask. He had no desire to spend eternity in a vacuum filter.

'So,' Kelon spoke sharply, 'what have you discovered?'

'Well my liege, they are not attempting to decipher the clue at all – I cannot explain it. But soon it will not matter. "It" is after her.'

'It?' Kelon turned white.

'Yes, luminous one. My men have seen it, soon it will catch up with her; it must.'

'What can she have done to draw it to her?'

'I do not know, but she has, and we both know that once it has you in its grasp, there is no escape.'

'You are sure of this?'

'There can be no doubt.'

'Then she is finished,' said Kelon with horrible satisfaction.

* * *

'So,' Denny was asking, 'what about vampires?'

'What about them?'

'Do they exist?'

'Well, put it this way, I've never seen one. Think about it, walking corpses that feed on the blood of the living and can only be held in their graves by a stake through the heart, it's ludicrous.'

'Well, okay– werewolves then?'

'Nope, that would come under the heading of the un-dead also. Same goes for zombies. Once a human is dead they tend to stay that way. As far as I know they do not rise up from their graves and start wandering about. Probably can't be bothered, after all *you* can't be bothered to get out of bed most days and *you're* alive. What would it take to get you out of a nice, comfy grave, when nobody's expecting you to get up and go to work anymore?'

'Good point. I'd probably get up for you though.'

'Nah, there's not enough magic in the world.'

'Ghosts, what about them?' pursued Denny, 'or other things, the Beast of Bodmin, the Jersey Devil, the Loch Ness Monster?'

It was Sunday afternoon, and they were in the "Press Gang Arms" (for *not* so jolly sailors) having one of those conversations that only occur after several pints of Ecclestons Old Peculiar. (All beer should be called this, by the way, in order to warn patrons of the effect imbibing will have on their brain functions)

Actually, it was only Denny who was three parts drunk, alcohol having no effect on Djinn. (Just another reason to feel sorry for her as far as Denny was concerned). Tamar had spent the last hour nursing the same Gin & Tonic, it being a waste of money – not to mention good booze – to buy her another "Djinn and Tonic", as Denny had inevitably quipped after his third pint. 'I knew I should have ordered vodka.'

But that is beer humour and Tamar was inclined to let it go. She had never experienced drunkenness herself but had witnessed plenty of it. Particularly during her time with "Hogswill the hairy backed" and his band of marauding Viking raiders. Denny was a model of sobriety by comparison and would probably only throw up once.

They were wrapped in a cosy fug of companionship and security. It was them against the world, and the world had better watch out. They were feeling completely invulnerable. Tamar admittedly because, to all intents and purposes, she was, and Denny, because he was experiencing the (entirely imaginary) sense of invincibility engendered by seven pints of beer.

'Ghosts,' she was saying, 'are a manifestation of the subconscious mind of the bereaved or otherwise susceptible mortal investigator. The conscious spirit of the deceased uses the expectations of the living to ...'

Denny stood up, looking slightly unfocussed. 'Needa pee,' he slurred. 'Won' be a minute.' And he lurched off to the Gents.

There was a large man sitting at the table nearest the door of the Gents. As Denny passed him, he called out 'Poof,' probably alluding to Denny's longish hair. This man was of the shaven headed and tattooed variety and undoubtedly possessed less than a quarter of an inch of brain-matter, even when sober. Having more pressing matters on his mind, (not to mention his bladder) Denny ignored him. But once he was relieved of his burden, he decided not to ignore the ape when the remark was repeated as Denny exited the men's room.

'What did you say?' he enquired in what he fondly hoped was a low menacing tone.

The gorilla was unimpressed, but Denny was inhabiting an alcohol induced artificial reality in which he was, in fact, Clint Eastwood, Arnold Schwarzenegger and James Bond all rolled into one, and was, accordingly, very impressed with himself.

The man stood up; he towered over Denny by a good foot and a half, but Denny was leaning nonchalantly against a handy pillar. 'Say that again,' he hissed.

'I called you a poof,' snarled the man, 'and what are you going to do about it?'

'Hey, Tamar,' called Denny. 'This git just called me a poof. What do you think about that?'

'What moron said that?' she enquired lightly.

'I called him a poof,' said the man, 'and now I'm telling you to stay out of it, you little tart.'

Tamar raised an eyebrow. 'Oh really?'

She smiled as Denny brought a chair crashing down on the man's skull. When this had no discernible effect, other than to break the chair, Denny sobered up instantly, and, as the man raised a boulder sized fist he prudently reverted to his normal behaviour during a fight. That is he ducked and covered, he was not strong, but he *was* fast. He dived under a table, which was, unfortunately, occupied, dislodging bottles and glasses as he did so.

Tamar, meanwhile, had risen gracefully, taken the bully by the shoulders and thrown him lazily through the window. The landlord was phoning the police.

The men who had been occupying the table that Denny had crashed into were understandably upset at the interruption of their drinking. They picked up the table, flung it aside and made a grab at Denny. He scrambled, but not fast enough, he was caught by the collar and held up for inspection. Tamar moved fast; seconds later both men were flying across the bar into other tables and Denny was straightening his collar as if nothing had happened. Nobody had had a chance to see exactly what she had done, and nobody cared since everybody was now hitting everybody else with bottles, chairs and glasses or whatever else came to hand.

'I did that,' smiled Tamar, 'with my little hatchet.'

Then the police arrived.

Against all known laws of reason, there had actually been a patrol car in the area that was not too busy chasing down innocent motorists, whose only crime was to be in the driving seat of a moving car whilst under the age of fifty. So they turned up with unprecedented promptitude.

'Leg it!' yelled Tamar. They ran, and the police chased, on the basic assumption that if you run away from the police you must be guilty of something. (Policemen are not often noted for their complex thinking.) They chase because you run, and you run because they are chasing you.

The fight at the pub was left in full swing. No policeman worth his helmet is going to choose to fight over a good chase. They could always come back later and arrest anyone recumbent – if the place was still standing.

Outside were a gleaming motorcycle and a comatose bully. They assessed their options and stole the bike.

'No keys,' said Denny.

'No problem,' said Tamar and clicked her fingers – she really very good at that – and the bike roared to life. The bike, by the way, belonged to the landlord who really was having a lousy day – which is what mortals can usually expect when there is a Djinn in the vicinity.

The police jumped in their car and gave chase.

'Put your foot down,' screamed Denny. Tamar grinned, and they shot away like an overdressed fool out of a cannon. The other vehicles seemed to be going backwards as they passed, the world became a blur, and the G forces pulled painfully at Denny's face.

Abruptly, they screeched to a halt at the end of an alley.

'I think we lost them,' Tamar said, with evident satisfaction.

Denny was furious. 'Put your foot down – does not mean *light speed!*' he raged. 'I think I swallowed a filling.'

'You do look a bit sick,' she said. 'How's your stomach?'

'I'll let you know when it catches up with me.'

Then, to their dismay they saw a police car draw up across the end of the alley.

* * *

'*Speeding*?' said Denny, disgustedly as they sat in the back of a police van, which had turned up after the officer in the car had firstly ascertained that they did not have a license, and then, on radioing the license plate number, discovered that the bike was stolen. This led to his finding out about the fracas in the pub and the officer decided, to his great excitement, that he had stumbled on a pair of dangerous criminals and called for backup.

Tamar had been for teleporting the hell out of there, but of course, Denny would not let her.

'They'd be bound to notice,' he said.

'Ha!' said Tamar. 'Most humans wouldn't notice if I turned into a hippopotamus right in front of them. They'd make up some explanation for it, or pretend it didn't happen. People have some pretty sophisticated shielding in their heads to stop them from seeing what's really going on around them. It's to stop their tiny brains from imploding – no offence.'

'Bound to notice,' repeated Denny, ignoring this, 'then we'd not only have the police after us, but we'd have reporters camping out on the doorstep twenty four hours a day and government types in big shiny cars with blacked out windows, stalking us.'

'It'll never happen I'm telling you. Never,' Tamar frowned. 'You don't even have a doorstep – you live in a flat.'

'Shut up.'

Since her arguments had no effect on Denny, Tamar submitted docilely to being charged with assault, criminal damage and theft, not to mention the speeding charge.

Then it was Denny's turn, and they were carted off to separate cells.

* * *

Tamar felt lonely, which just goes to show how much she had changed. She was also bored – burning graffiti into the walls with her eyes palled after a while. If only Denny were not so stubborn they could have been anywhere by now – what did it matter where?'

Instead, she was kicking her heels in a cold, damp, narrow cell with nothing to do. And no chance of bail either.

The cell door opened, and a burly officer entered. She looked up hopefully, but he closed the door behind him and looked at her, his mean little eyes gleaming with an unmistakable expression. She sighed; she had been half expecting something like this. Many of the policemen had stared at her or given her sidelong glances when she had been brought in; some of them had been openly leering. Oh well, it was nothing she could not handle. Perhaps he had come to offer her a "deal".

She stood up – and froze. Oh no! Not again. The now familiar terror twisted inside her as the "policeman" advanced on her swinging his nightstick and slapping it against his palm. There was no way Denny could rescue her this time, locked, as he was, in another cell. This time she was well and truly caught, and she only had herself to blame. There was no time for self-recrimination. The menacing figure raised the nightstick silently (what no mocking last words?) and brought it down on her head with a sickening crack. Her last thought was that she would never know who or what had killed her, or why. Then everything went black.

* * *

Denny was livid; they had finally released him with a warning and a large fine after questioning him for hours about Tamar's mysterious disappearance. He felt certain that they had let him off so lightly because of this. It was uncanny, they said, and they kept watching him nervously as if they expected him to suddenly vanish in a puff of smoke.

He stalked home, intending to tear strips off her for escaping in such an unorthodox manner, and leaving him to face the music, and when he had expressly told her not to. Just because she had turned out to be right, was no excuse. The police had decided in the end, that there had to be some rational explanation. He watched them gradually convince themselves that she could not have mysteriously disappeared at all. By the time he left, they were all behaving as if the whole thing had never happened.

And the reporters on his doorstep were conspicuously absent, but still ... How could she? Of all the rotten ... words failed him. He marched into the flat and slammed the door – she was not there, and neither was all the swanky furniture she had provided. But this time, this did not surprise Denny. The bottle stood on the mantelpiece; it looked different, no longer opaque and cloudy but perfectly clear – he could see the clock face through it, but he never noticed.

'Out?' he thought. 'She's gone out – swanning about somewhere no doubt. Thinking how clever she is – just wait!'

'TAMAR!' he yelled, 'TAMAR BLACK GET BACK HERE RIGHT NOW.' He was hitting decibels that made dead spiders fall out of the light shade and caused Mr. Whinger, whose real name Denny did not know, to bang on the ceiling of the flat below with what was presumably a mop or broom handle. 'You shut up you little beggar, or I'll get the plod onto you.'

Denny groaned. Anything but that, he thought. But when Tamar did not appear he felt a prickle of fear as he realized what must have happened to her. Of course! He saw now; she would not have just gone off without him, even if she could have – which she could not (how could he have forgotten that?) How could he have thought she would? No, he realized that she *could not* have disobeyed him. Which only left one possibility and it made sense; she had been trapped in that cell – all alone without him. He finally noticed the bottle; it looked different – so ordinary, yet the implication of that was so macabre.

He glanced around the flat; it felt different. He felt a shiver run through him. The flat, the bottle – everything, it was as if she had never existed at all.

* * *

Tamar was – nowhere, literally nowhere. It was not dark because that would have been something, would have meant that she was somewhere, and she was not. There was just nothing, and nobody. She was not afraid because she had no feelings. She was not bored or tired or lonely; she was just there, a tiny sliver of consciousness – fast-slipping away as she ceased to exist. She had no body, no name, no identity, no future and no past, she was almost gone – almost...

* * *

As the full horror of the situation hit Denny, he did, what was probably the most useless thing he could have done, and also the most natural. He lay down on the bed and sobbed.

In normal circumstances, this is the obvious and even healthy thing to do. But these were not normal circumstances, a fact that would not hit Denny until later – perhaps too late, because Denny was forgetting her already. After a while, he sat up sharply and dried his eyes, for a moment he wondered what he was so upset about and he became afraid when he realized what was happening. Soon, he realized, he would forget about her altogether. He could feel it happening already. He clutched desperately at his memories of her, they were fading. The world was healing over; the gap she had filled was closing. He grabbed some paper and a pencil and wrote her name, then watched in horror as it began to fade from the paper. When it was gone, he knew, so would she be – forever. Wiped from existence as if she had never been. Something clicked. She was not gone yet then? Not yet, but soon and what could he do about it? Nothing it seemed. Clapping his hands and declaring 'I do believe in Djinn,' was probably not going to work. Click, went his brain again – that was not it, but it was on the right lines. He concentrated. The Djinn – magic – belief. Oh damn! Think! I wish ... And it came to him. He grabbed the plastic bottle off the shelf, pulled out the rag of shirt. BANG!!!

Slammer appeared dramatically in a puff of smoke. 'O' My Master ... oh it's you. Well you know the drill, what can I do you for?' (It was probably a Djinn who first coined this phrase – if you think about it).

Downstairs, Mr. Whinger was objecting vociferously to the noise again. Denny could not think. Tamar's name had disappeared from the paper.

'I wish ... I wish ...' he said desperately; he knew it was important but ... 'I wish I could remember.'

'Remember what?' asked Slammer courteously.

'I wish I could remember what I was going to wish for,' said Denny lamely. It did not seem important now.

'Your wish is my command,' said Slammer, giving Denny a curious look.

And Denny remembered, but was it too late? Here goes nothing 'I wish that Tamar, AKA Askphrit the Djinn of this bottle,' he held it up, 'were here with me now in this room.' He felt he had to pretty specific or the loophole would get him. 'Alive and well,' he added threateningly to the universe in general and Slammer in particular, as a nasty thought struck him.

'Good job you added that last bit,' said a voice behind him.

'Tamar,' cried Denny, spinning around. 'Thank God – are you all right? Are you ...?'

'I'm fine, full of vigour – so I wouldn't do that if I were you,' she said as he moved to put his arms around her. His face fell, and there was an awkward silence.

'Thank you,' she said, and there was a world of meaning in her voice, it was enough. So it rather spoiled the pathos when she added. 'I wouldn't want to ruin this beautiful moment by accidentally killing you.'

'Ahem,' said Slammer, 'and for your third wish?'

'Later,' said Denny. 'Much later,' he muttered. Slammer retired to his bottle, offended. Neither of them noticed him go.

~ Chapter Sixteen ~

TAMAR DID NOT want to talk about it. Indeed, she said that she could not really remember anything, except that she had almost lost herself and that Denny had somehow found her and pulled her back. She was full of gratitude – wasn't that enough?

But Denny thought it was important. 'We need to figure out what it is,' he said. 'Maybe we can stop it.'

'We need to get on with the quest,' said Tamar. 'I don't know why, but I think the answer's there. We mustn't get distracted anymore. Whatever it is, you can defeat it for some reason, that's all we need to know.'

'And if it happens again? I have a total of three wishes left; it's not enough.'

'Three?'

'Two from you and one from Slammer – remember?'

Tamar considered. 'You could always ...' she stopped, biting her lip.

'Always what?'

'I can't,' she said. 'I'm not allowed... God, for all I know breaking the rules is what set this thing after me in the first place. Old Askphrit – the νόθος' did say it would be bad if I did.'

'What rule?'

Tamar cleared her throat and recited in a pompous manner. 'Rule seventeen – No Djinn may influence the wishes of his/her master/mistress in any way. Not even if: (a) The master/mistress asks for suggestions. (b) The master/mistresses life is endangered or (c) The...'

'Okay, okay I get the idea. But you've already...'

'Exactly.'

'Can't we sort of – cheat? If you've got a good idea then maybe if I try to guess, and you can – oh I don't know – give me a sign if I'm close. Would that work?'

'Tell you what,' she said holding up four fingers. 'I'll give you a clue.'

'Four? – Four what? Oh I get it, four words right?'

Tamar nodded and held up a single finger.

'One word?'

Tamar looked exasperated and held up four fingers again.

'Okay, four words?'

Nod. One finger.

'Ah, *first* word?'

Nod. Then she began to act out the word.

'Um – sounds like – swim?' guessed Denny, 'swimming? And er … gulping? Oh, *fish*? – fish?'

Nod. She tugged her ear to indicate…

'Sounds like, sounds like – yes, don't start swimming again, sound like fish – wish?'

Nod.

'Yes, obviously, um – second word?'

Nod.

'Fourth word? Oh four – Four? – for?' wish for, yes, yes I know that. Wish for what?'

She tugged her ear.

'Sounds like – four again. Um, bore – no sorry obviously not, er – door?'

Shake.

'Law?'

Shake.

'Claw? – saw? – Floor? ... sorry.'

Tamar held up a hand.

'Okay, start again. Third word – counting? No – er, bigger?' He looked down self-consciously for a second, but she was shaking her head furiously.

'Um, what are you doing? Oh – *more*?'

Nod.

'Okay, wish – for – more. Okay, carry on then.'

Unbelievably, Denny still had not got the point. He just did not think the right way. Tamar rolled her eyes and held up four fingers resignedly.

'Okay, fourth word?'

Nod.

'Sounds like – fish, again? No – a longer word, um fishing – fishes?'

Nod.

'Hang on – wish for more *fishes*?' Denny was perplexed.

Tamar gave him a dirty look and tugged her ear sharply.

'Oh yes,' he said apologetically, '*sounds* like. So, wish for more – *wishes*? Wish for more wishes?'

She nodded in relief and collapsed into a seated position, albeit two feet in the air.

Denny ignored this as mere showing off, 'I can *do* that?' he asked.

Tamar nodded again.

'I think you can talk now.'

'Oh – yes. Yes, you can wish for anything.'

'So, let me get this straight, you're saying ...'

'Me? I never said a word.'

'Okay, understood, but – I can? If you need me to, I can wish for as many wishes as I – you – we need? That's handy to know.'

'So, now can we concentrate on the clue?'

'Yeah, dig it out.'

* * *

'Does it do something, do you think?'

'It's just a doll.'

'Action figure.'

'Whatever? It's perfectly ordinary as far as I can tell.'

'No spells or anything? – Don't take its pants off.'

'Why not?' laughed Tamar. 'Look, see it's got less down there than a Boy Band. Pull its head off.'

'Why?'

'Why not? – Oh give it here.' She snatched it and wrenched the head off, which proved absolutely nothing.

'Okay, so maybe it's not the doll itself ...'

'Action figure.'

'Whatever, maybe it symbolises something.'

Denny groaned. 'We've been down this road before.'

'Maybe this time it's the right road.'

'You and your symbolism.'

Tamar ignored this. 'So, it's a ninja doll, right?'

'Action – (sigh) yes – ninja, so?'

'Well, what does that mean to you?'

'Absolutely nothing.'

'You're not even trying. So, ninja – martial arts – silent killers – assassins – um.

'See, it doesn't mean anything to *you* either.'

'It does,' she said, indignantly. 'It means – it means. It means that this damn thing is no damn use at all. Damn, damn, damn!' She flung the toy to the floor. Denny picked it up and looked at it thoughtfully.

'Unless ...'

'Unless what?' she asked hopefully.

'Just – give me a minute,'

Tamar waited.

'Yes, I'm sure,' he said eventually. 'I had one of these – in fact, I think this *is* mine. Or rather it was. Hang on a minute if it is – yes, there it is.' He pointed to his initials scratched into its back, so faint you could hardly see it. 'I lost it, I remember now, when I was ten. It was in Scunthorpe, in this awful hotel – my parents ...'

'What hotel?'

'I can't remember, I was ten.'

'But it might be important.'

'Sorry, I might recognise it if I saw it again, but just wait. Let's not go off all half-cocked, let's think about this. Maybe the clue is me, not the doll – action figure.'

'Or something to do with your past – or just the past in general.'

'Which would bring us back to the hotel where I lost it. I guess that is the connection, in fact, I'm sure of it.'

'Be a bit of a coincidence,' she said doubtfully.

'So, what else could it be?'

'I don't know. But, how likely is it that the next clue is at a hotel that you just happen to have been to before? What about the other people who do this quest thing?'

'Maybe – I don't know. Maybe *they* get a different clue that leads them to the hotel, and it was just luck that I'd already been there.'

'Oh yeah?' She stretched out an arm. 'What am I doing?'

'Reaching,' he said resignedly.

'It's far more likely that the clue is about the past, and that everybody gets a clue that reminds them of the past.'

'That's another possibility,' agreed Denny. 'But we could do this all night. We have to try the hotel first, if only to eliminate it. What have we got to lose?'

'Okay.' Tamar was sullen.

'And if that doesn't turn anything up ...'

'*When* it doesn't turn anything up.'

'...I'll try some regressive therapy or something.'

'I'm right,' she insisted. 'But we'll try it your way.'

'Good,' said Denny. 'Now I won't have to use my Djinn master powers on you. You know what, I bet the quest is different for everybody, sort of tailored to the individual.'

'Which would make *you* right,' she said sneeringly.

'What's the matter with you? What does it matter who's right, so long as we get the answer? Don't be so precious. You worked out the first two clues; it's about time I started pulling my weight in this operation.'

'I'm sorry, you're right. It's just – I don't know what's wrong with me. I'm not used to needing anybody's help, I suppose.'

'Well, I need you too you know, so that's okay.'

Tamar cheered up. 'I'm glad you said that, because, actually, I think you might be right, and that makes it easier to admit it.'

*

'I'm getting sick of this dreary place,' said Tamar grumpily. 'Why did you say your family came here again?'

'It's October,' said Denny. 'What did you expect? Anyway, we couldn't afford the Seychelles.'

'Well, you could now – so to speak,' said Tamar wickedly. 'I could just fancy a day ...'

'Oh no you don't,' he told her sternly. 'Who was it said we mustn't get distracted?'

'We've been here a week, and you haven't recognised a thing yet. I just thought – I mean, you should have some compensation. Much more of this and you *will* get fired.'

'Nah, Bo'll never notice; he never does.'

They sat on a bench and watched the obligatory sweet old couple walking by hand in hand, still in love after all those years.

'I hope I never look that old,' said Tamar.

'Well you won't, will you?' said Denny. 'I will though – if I live that long.'

There was a silence. 'Denny?'

'Yes?'

'Do you ever wish ...' She started again. 'Do you ever ... regret opening my bottle? I mean it's messed up your life really, hasn't it? You know lots of people wish for adventure and end up regretting it. It's never what they hoped for. And you, well you didn't even *ask* for this,' she rushed on. 'You just wanted a quiet life. You never wanted adventure, did you? And then I show up and turn your life upside down. I mean you didn't have to do any of this and I know why you are, but … don't you ever wish it had never happened?'

'No, never,' said Denny, surprising himself. 'Maybe it's been good for me. It's not been easy sometimes, but maybe it's just what I needed. Never a dull moment eh?'

'Really?'

'Yes, really. Maybe I was always a closet thrill seeker.'

'No,' she said thoughtfully, 'I don't think so – maybe I'm not the only one who has changed.'

'Well, maybe you coming along sort of woke me up or something. It's probably destiny or some such bull. Anyway I've never regretted it.'

'Even when Slammer was pounding your head into mush?'

'Don't exaggerate. And yeah, maybe then just for a second or two.'

'The thing is,' he continued, 'that's when I realized that I would rather die with you than live without you.'

There was an embarrassed pause. 'I have *got* to stop saying things like that, haven't I?

'What I mean is,' he continued after a pause, 'I couldn't go back to how my life was before. It was so empty – you have no idea.'

'I think I might have *some* idea.'

'Yes, I suppose you do. The thing is I never realized it, I thought my life was just fine – well okay anyway, well, not terrible at least.'

'What you never had, you never miss,' she said.

'I know.'

'So, we go on?'

'And when we get to the end?'

'We find something else to do.'

~ Chapter Seventeen ~

KELON ALMOST REGRETTED dusting the little man. The other spies might not be as annoying as he, but neither were they as efficient. It had been frustrating to learn of Tamar's close shave and lucky escape, and taking it out on the messenger had been some release. But the truth of it was it had been an excuse to get rid of the little weasel for a while. He would have to be brought back eventually, but not yet – not yet. Kelon baulked at the idea. The guy was just so irritating, and, furthermore, Kelon did not trust him.

While Kelon thus pondered, Tamar and Denny were closing in. And Kelon, without a spy, had no idea.

* * *

'That's it,' said Denny, pointing excitedly. 'That's the hotel.'

'Are you sure?' Tamar asked.

'I remember now, that awful tree swing there at the side; I almost broke my neck on that. And the "No Vacancies" sign, it's still broken. God it really used to piss me off.'

'Why?'

'Because it's broken; it's annoying.'

'You're quite anal aren't you?

'So what do we do now?' she added, when he did not answer this.

'I guess we book a room and take it from there.'

'Okay.'

'They walked into the – well, charitably you would call it the lobby, but actually it was more of an awful hole – with a desk. A thin distracted looking woman with a lot of frizzy hair and a penchant for occult jewellery and embroidered blouses looked up and smiled vaguely.

'Miss Trenchard?' said Denny.

'Yes dearie,' said the woman, burying her face in a lace hanky. Women of this type always call people "dearie". It was a fair bet, Tamar thought, that she threw pots and pressed flowers too.

'Oh, um – double room please.' They had discussed this outside and decided that they could not afford two rooms and also that they should stick together in case of trouble.

The woman raised an eyebrow but only said. 'How many nights dearie?'

Denny looked at Tamar.

'Just one,' she said decisively. 'We can always extend it,' she added to Denny. 'I don't think business is exactly booming.'

'Well it is October.'

'Exactly.'

'Okay, just one night, please.'

The woman looked up for the first time. Tamar met her eyes. '*Euphemia*?'

The woman raised her hanky again.

'Don't bother Euphemia, I know it's you.' Tamar told her, forthrightly.

'Who the hell is Euphemia?' asked Denny.

'An old frie – acquaintance,' said Tamar. 'A witch, in fact, so I guess you were right. The clue led here; I guess it's like you said, different paths – same destination.'

'Clue?' said Euphemia. 'Oh right, it's like that is it? – in that case, right this way.' She parted a beaded a curtain behind her and gestured into the adjoining room.

Denny and Tamar slid awkwardly past the desk and stepped through.

'You're not coming with us?' asked Tamar.

'Oh no dearie, that's just for you – nothing to do with me. I just point the way.'

Tamar noticed a strange look on the woman's face, almost like triumph. They had just gone through when they heard her call. 'So, will you still be wanting that room?'

*

'Do you get the feeling they were expecting us?' said Denny.

'Who's *they*? I don't see anyone,'

'No, but I mean – look at the place.'

'What was that you were saying before about destiny?'

'Destiny?'

'It's just funny that's all. We keep running into people we've met before. And you've been here before, and Euphemia, you recognised her too, because she was here what was it ten…?'

'Fourteen.'

'Fourteen years ago. And you losing your doll ...'

'Action figure,' Denny interjected automatically.

'...here of all places. Then you get it back just in time to lead us back here. It's one hell of a coincidence.'

'Not coincidence – magic. Remember magic? Magic quest, it's supposed to be mysterious – you taught me that. I mean do you think that everybody who walks through these curtains ends up here?'

'No, of course not.'

'So, what's wrong with you? You're thinking like a human – like I used to. All this talk about destiny and coincidence, that's bull, and you know it. Anyway, I don't believe in destiny, load of hogswill. People have free will; they make their own choices. You said it yourself; I didn't have to do any of this; I could have chosen not to.'

'That's true,' admitted Tamar. 'If anybody knows that humans have free will, it's me. And I've seen enough to know that destiny's a myth and that there are no coincidences. Human thinking eh – it must be catching. Soon I'll be thinking that I have free will too.'

'Soon,' said Denny. 'In the meantime, all this,' he waved a hand, 'it's just "standard".' And he smiled wickedly.

It did seem as though they were expected, although it would be difficult to say why exactly. Probably it was because what should have been, through those dingy curtains, a dingy "parlour" was, in fact, a gleaming waiting room such as might be found in a private clinic or a dentist's office. There were just two chairs. 'One each,' as Denny observed, with a sign above saying "Sit Here" and an arrow.

Denny was inclined to take this personally. 'Just as if we were terminally stupid,' he said.

There was an unmanned desk and a potted plant, (it took them some time to work out what was unusual about this – it was not dead) and a table with the obligatory pile of out of date magazines, although these turned out, on closer inspection, to be out of date by up to 4000 years and bore titles such as "Which God?" and "Dragon Breeders Monthly". A sign above the desk read "Thank you for not smoking", 'How do they know we're not going to?' asked Tamar. (She was just like that.)

All in all, it seemed to be a perfectly ordinary waiting room – apart from the magazines and the fact that there were no doors. The entrance had become a smooth wall behind them.

'I don't like it,' Tamar said. 'It's like being in a bottle – no way out, until they let you out.'

'Don't,' pleaded Denny. 'Claustrophobia, remember?'

'So,' he changed the subject, 'are we waiting to see Kelon, do you think?'

'Could be, maybe she's busy.'

'Well I hope it won't be too long.'

* * *

'T,' said Denny.

'Nope.'

'Um – C.'

'Nope – ha, hangman.'

'Okay, so what was it then?'

Tamar filled in the blanks.

'Neighbours?' said Denny disgustedly. 'I should have got that; I had all the vowels and the N and the B.'

'It's always easy when you know the answer,' said Tamar.

'In hangman as it is in life,' he replied, absently.

They had played charades and eye spy (this was a pretty short game since the room was bare and did not even have windows) and had then turned to hangman. Denny being one of those people who always carries a pad and pencil in case he should need it. This was the first time he had ever used it since he was too afraid to ask girls for their phone numbers and fleeing criminals – whose number plates he could take down – had been scarce in his life.

'Your turn,' said Tamar, handing him the pencil. He shook his head.

'Sore loser?' she mocked.

'No, just bored, and I have to pee.'

'Be my guest,' she indicated the plant pot. 'I won't look I promise.'

'Very funny! How much longer?' It had been at least two hours and this was, to Denny's mind, the very worst of the quest experiences. He would far rather have been fighting for his life than sitting here with the blood slowly coagulating in his buttocks.

What was even more irritating was that Tamar seemed perfectly calm and unperturbed as if she could wait here forever, until he realized with a shock that it was because more than half of her very long life had been spent in exactly this manner. At least she had company this time, 'and I can't even sit still for a couple of hours, well not without the TV or something,' he chided himself.

He squirmed in his seat; at least she was not suffering bladder pain. He did not think he could stand it much longer; the plant pot did not seem such a bad option after all, except that he had the uncanny feeling that they were being watched.

Tamar glanced at him. 'What's the matter?' she asked.

'I told you,' he said irritably. 'I need to pee, it's starting to hurt.'

'Oh.' She waved a hand over his – trouser area. The feeling went away.

'Better?'

'Yeah, thanks. How did you...? Second thoughts, I don't think I want to know – do I?'

'Probably not.'

'Okay,' he said, 'my turn, hand me that paper.'

She smiled, and then they both jumped. There was a phone on the desk that neither of them had particularly noticed. Desks have phones on them – it's just the way it is. It had started to ring.

'I suppose we'd better answer it,' said Denny. 'It must be for us.'

'Nobody here but us chickens,' agreed Tamar. She picked up the phone.

* * *

Kelon paced up and down the chamber. 'And you say they now have the last clue?'

'Yes, my gracious liege. But ...'

'Damn!'

Kelon had given in and brought the little man back. It was either that or come out of seclusion and do the watching instead.

'Forgive me, O' shining one,' simpered the little man, 'but I do not understand why ...'

Kelon glared, and the little man subsided.

'I am most powerful, am I not?' said Kelon, almost absently.

'Oh yes indeed.' Agreed the little man obsequiously.

'And yet not more powerful than they – a Djinn and her master, no?'

No answer, but Kelon did not require one.

'So, I must wonder, what can they want from me? Do they really seek my aid, as have so many others? Impossible. I run a good business here – witches, wizards, mermaids, wraiths. And in return for my help with their petty problems they owe me a favour, better than payment yes?'

'It is your way.'

'Hmm.' Kelon frowned at this non-committal answer. *"Irritating man"*. 'So, I wonder, what do they want? And I do not like it, I do not like it at all. I sense trouble, little man.' *

'Liar!' thought the little man, 'trouble indeed? You know very well, I think, what that trouble will be. And you're afraid of it. Well I never ... One more clue – and then the fun starts.'

* * *

'Why are we doing this again?' Denny asked. 'I mean why do we need this sorceress?'

'Because a sorceress, or sorcerer for that matter, is a lot more powerful than a witch or wizard. It's like the difference between a – a ... Well put it this way, witches and wizards learn their craft over many years; they're humans with a natural talent for magic that can be developed. But a sorcerer is a magical creature from birth – not human – not exactly. We can ask this sorceress to do a finding spell on old Askphrit – the νόθος'. It's got a much better chance of working than the one the witches did.'

'And this sorceress, she'll know what to look for?'

'No, that's not the point, she won't look for him. She'll *find* him – without looking; it's quantum.'

Denny did not understand this, so he ignored it. 'How is she supposed to find Askphrit, if he's not Askphrit anymore?'

'That's her problem. Look I never said it was perfect – but if anyone can do it, a sorceress can.'

'*You* couldn't.'

---

* If Kelon had ever bothered to learn the little man's name, it had long since been forgotten.

'That's different.'

'Why?'

'It just is. Look I could do it, if you knew exactly what to wish for. But you don't, and I don't. But a sorceress works differently, her power comes from herself, she's free, the cosmos is her oyster.'

'So, if she can work out the how, then the doing it will be no problem?'

'Oh, she'll probably already know how, and if she doesn't, she'll have ways of figuring it out that I don't because she's her own boss.'

'You hope! I just hope we're not on our way to the Emerald City.'

* * *

The latest clue turned out to be a list of numbers.

'Lucky I brought a pencil and paper,' Denny had said, smugly.

After she had put the phone down, the gleaming waiting room had become the dingy parlour that one might have expected. And then they had walked back through the beaded curtain. It had all been disappointingly ordinary in the end.

'Why did we have to wait for so long, just for that?' Denny wondered.

'I don't know,' she replied. 'Maybe you can ask Kelon, when we find her.'

'*If* we find her.'

'Now, now.'

* * *

As they left the hotel, Euphemia appeared again looking mysterious. She took Denny's arm and leaned in toward him, looking around her suspiciously as if she expected the Gestapo to come bursting in at the door any minute. Then she whispered conspiratorially right in his very private ear 'Under the clock at midnight for the password.' Then nodded happily at Denny's bemused face and jogged away in a satisfied manner, pleased to have passed her message on.

'What was all *that* about?' asked Tamar.

Denny told her. 'What did she mean, do you think?'

'Search me. Maybe she's going senile, perhaps she thinks she's in some old spy movie.'

'We can't afford to ignore it, what if it's part of the clue? I mean she is involved in all this somehow, isn't she?'

'But it's so vague,' objected Tamar.

'And all the other clues have been so clear-cut and obvious,' said Denny sarcastically.

'All right, but what clock, where? And midnight when, tonight, tomorrow night? It's not enough.'

'I expect it'll all become clear, and it won't be like that at all.'

Tamar sighed. 'You're right, it never is.'

~ Chapter Eighteen ~

THEIR FIRST IDEA had been that the numbers might be co-ordinates, but this turned out to be unlikely when following up this idea planted them squarely in the middle of a desert.

'Maybe we have to cross it,' suggested Denny.

'And maybe we'll find "King Solomon's mines" over that way if we do,' said Tamar, sarcastically. 'You can if you want. There's nothing here.'

Despite the fact that Denny had wanted to follow this up further, they decided that they could always come back to it later on, if necessary.

They had then tried turning the numbers into letters by their denomination in the alphabet, a sort of reverse numerology, but if the numbers were a secret code, that was not the way. Tamar even tried it with several different alphabets; but eventually gave up.

They tried it as a telephone number, and after getting a busy signal several times (causing a certain amount of cautious hope) they finally got through to a restaurant in New Delhi*.

'Well, you didn't expect it to be easy, did you?' Denny asked, as Tamar blew up the phone in frustration. 'Fix that, will you?' he added absently. 'You know,' he continued, 'it could have been the right number. And, you know, if you'd said who you were, they'd have rung back or something. And the restaurant thing is a cover, like a secret, covert government operation.'

'Your favourite show is the "X Files" isn't it?' She manifested a drinking straw.'Here's you,' she said, 'clutching.' She mimed the action and dropped the straw as the rebuilt phone rang. They both spun round to stare at it.

'No way,' she breathed.

'Answer it,' he ordered. She tentatively picked up the receiver. 'Hello.' She listened.

'Oh – yes, hi.' The disappointment in her voice was obvious. Denny sagged.

'No, he's – not here. Oh I see, yes. I'll tell him, okay, yes I'm sorry too – bye.' She replaced the receiver.

'Um, that was Bo,' she said. 'I don't know how to tell you this. He says you're fired.

'I'm really sorry,' she said, to fill the silence. 'This is my fault. I could probably fix it if you ...'

Denny started to laugh. 'Don't bother,' he said. 'I hated that job anyway.'

'But ...'

'Who would have thought he had it in him?' said Denny, still laughing. 'I guess he was more on the ball than I gave him credit for. Who the hell's got time to work anyway?' he said, picking up the last clue and waving it under her nose. 'We've got more important things to do.'

'You really don't mind?' she asked. 'I thought you said you needed that job – to keep you grounded in reality.'

---

* This always happens when you ring a wrong number. Either that or you get a generic "Angry Man" or, worse, a person who sounds exactly like the person you wanted to speak to and even has the same name leading to endless confusion and lost tempers. There's probably some kind of secret society behind this

'Reality bites,' said Denny, apparently thinking this very funny.

Tamar stared. 'Does it?' Something had clicked in her brain.

'Yeah, it does,' said Denny, now hysterical with laughter.

'Reality bites?' mused Tamar. 'And maybe sometimes it stabs you, or clubs you to death with a big truncheon.'

Denny stopped laughing, confused by this apparent divergence from accepted sanity. 'What are you talking about?'

'And it always catches up with you in the end.'

'Oh my God.'

'Yes.'

* * *

Every time a child says he does not believe in fairies, (it's always the boys) a fairy drops dead. This is true – fairies are not real (oops another one bites the dust – get clapping) they exist only in the collective belief of children everywhere – and some adults, usually the ones who are waiting to be released into the care of the community. The same goes for gods, spirits, aliens (so be careful what you believe in) and of course, the Djinn. Mostly they do not let it bother them and just get on with their lives – you can't worry about every little thing, or you would never get anything done.

Denny believed fervently in Tamar, (this despite the fact that she had told him many times that she was not real) but Tamar was beginning to lose her belief in herself.

* * *

'But of *course* you're real,' said Denny, perplexed. 'I can see you, talk to you. Don't go all "Scully" on me.'

'Hold that thought,' said Tamar grimly. 'I'm going to need it. The truth is out there – and it has teeth.'

They decided to get back to work on the clue. What else was there to do? It would take their minds off it.

'May as well see it through,' said Denny. 'Anyway, I can't see that you're in much danger as long as I'm here.'

Tamar thought there wasn't much point. 'It's bound to get me in the end,' she said gloomily.

'You don't know that,' argued Denny. 'Maybe this Kelon can help with that too, and anyway it might *not* be that – you've been wrong before. Anyway, I'm the boss, so let's get on with it.'

'Sir, yes sir!' barked Tamar. But she was comforted by the idea, and they set to work.

* * *

'We're going about this all wrong,' said Denny later.

'We always do,' said Tamar. 'We have to go through all the wrong answers before we get to the right one, it's ...'

'*Standard*,' they said together.

'Well it is,' she said. 'You wear your brain out and then the answer comes when you're not looking for it.'

'Well, my brain feels pretty worn out – why don't we try *not* looking for the answer down at the "Pig in a Poke",' he winked.

'That's not funny,' Tamar groaned.

~ Chapter Nineteen ~

IN THE END, they compromised. Denny went down to the local "Off Binns" and got beer, and they ordered a pizza. They let Slammer out to join them, Denny felt sorry for him, and Tamar thought there might be a slim chance that he would be some use with the clue (after all Hank had worked out the jar) but he was not.

He did entertain them, though, by turning himself into Tom Cruise and flamboyantly shaking cocktails for them. Now that he was not trying to kill them, he was pretty decent company, apart from the way he kept trying to trick Denny into making his final wish. But since he did this with all the subtlety of a sledgehammer to the nuts Denny had no problems deflecting these attempts even though he was pretty drunk, and it did not detract from the fun.

They had got to that stage of the evening when it seemed like a good idea (to Denny, at least) to make silly phone calls to complete strangers out of the phone book. Example: -

'Is Mr. Wall there?' Answer, 'No.'

'Is Mrs. Wall there?' Answer, 'No.'

'Well, are there any Walls there?' Answer. 'No.'

'So, what's holding up the roof then?' At which point the caller hangs up the phone to a stream of angry expletives and so on.

Denny also had a nice line in bogus requests to speak to funny named people in pubs, gleaned from years of watching "The Simpsons" (he was also the sort of person who saved the jokes out of crackers). Slammer, having led a sheltered life, found all this hilarious and the party became riotous – in the manner of a four year old's birthday party.

Tamar was inclined to be indifferent to all this; it was better, she felt, than marauding the village, singing rude songs and looking for maidens to abduct (and arousing the wrath of a hound of Hell to haunt your family for generations).

Slammer had joined in this game with immense gusto and had suggested afterwards that he or Tamar magick up a karaoke machine. Denny hailed this idea with enthusiasm and Tamar was nothing loath, she enjoyed hearing him sing. But she soon regretted it. For although Denny's voice was unimpaired by the vast quantities of beer he had consumed, the same could not be said of Slammer and after three rounds of "We Are The Champions" she was about ready to throttle the pair of them. Mr. Whinger downstairs apparently shared her opinion and was making his objections known in his usual manner, which did nothing to accompany the singing. Then Denny wanted to go out and have Tamar hex a cash machine (the morals are always the first thing to go) so that he could pay his rent, but, of course, she would not agree to this.

'Riches beyond the dreams of avarice I can do,' she said, 'but no petty stealing – well, not without a wish anyway.'

'Aha,' said Slammer. 'I can do that – no problem boss. You need money? That's what I'm here for.' And he winked hugely.

'Get back in your bottle you,' said Tamar. 'Denny – tell him.'

'Yesh,' slurred Denny. 'Bock in yer baccle – I mean bockle. Who's the boss 'ere anywhere? Me that's what!' He was stabbing vehemently in the air and swaying alarmingly. 'We could always try computer fraud,' he said before he threw up and passed out.

'My God!' said Tamar.

* * *

Drunkenness produces a lot of those ideas that seem inspired at the time but which turn out to be disastrous in the cold light of day when you wake up in a fountain twenty miles from home with no trousers. Well, searching for pirate gold in downtown Basildon seemed like a good idea at the time. The lack of trousers is just an inevitable consequence of drunken tomfoolery which nobody has ever been able to satisfactorily explain; it's "standard".

Drunken ideas which seem stupid at the time, but which turn out to be inspirational, on the other hand, are much rarer (you try saying "Eureka" when you can barely articulate your own name)

* * *

Denny woke up feeling like he had put his head through a meat grinder. He lurched through the living room with his head in his hands, groaning like Frankenstein's monster and looking like a vampire in the sunlight.

'Oh God,' he moaned. 'I feel like something the cat barfed up.'

'Yuck,' said Tamar. 'Do you *have* to say things like that?'

'Can't you do something?' he pleaded.

'Here,' she said, manifesting a smoking phial of purplish liquid and handing it to him.

'You don't deserve it, but I need you in full working order.'

Denny eyed it dubiously. 'What is it?'

'Hangover cure, beyond that you don't want to know.'

'If I turn into Mr. Hyde or the Incredible Hulk, there's going to be trouble.'

'It couldn't be any worse than how you look now – drink it.'

He closed his eyes and swallowed. He opened his eyes. 'AAAAGH'

'Oops.'

'Oh God, get me a drink – nobody deserves to be this sober.'

Tamar grimaced in sympathy. 'Sorry, I must have overdone the formula a bit. I devised it for the Norsemen; big drinkers the Norsemen – mead makes lager look like Tizer.'

'Drink!' barked Denny like a crazed Irish priest. 'Drink!'

She handed him a bottle of Jack Daniels. 'There's no beer left – just drink a little at a time until you feel normal.'

'I hate this stuff,' he complained, sipping at it like a wino on a building site until he said, 'that's better. What did you do to me?'

'I removed the alcohol from your system – took out too much it seems.'

'God, it was terrible. I didn't know the world was so awful.'

'Now you know how I feel all the time.'

Denny winced. 'Really?'

'Never mind, I'm used to it – hungry?'

'Now you mention it, I'm starving. I could eat a scabby horse between two rusty bread vans.'

'Well, if that's what you really want ...'

'Er, how about a steak sandwich. No, on second thoughts, cheese.'

'Can do.'

Denny scanned the room. 'A traffic cone?' he said. 'What the hell? And what's that?'

'Policeman's helmet.'

Denny actually scratched his head. 'But – I didn't go out last night – did I? Or did I?'

Tamar grinned slyly; she had not been able to resist it. Denny shook his head and turned his attention to the food. He looked up with his mouth full. 'What are you doing with that computer?' He said through a mouthful of sandwich (you know you have to wonder sometimes what she saw in him).

'Transferring funds into your account.'

'*What*?' he spluttered, spraying crumbs all over the table.

'Like you said last night – computer fraud.'

'I never.'

'Oh yes you did, Slammer heard you too. Want me to go and wake him up?'

'I would never ...'

'You did actually, but you can relax, I'm only kidding, I knew you didn't mean it. But it gave me an idea.'

'It's not illegal is it?'

'No, I'm looking for something.'

'On the Internet?'

'No, not exactly, on the Aethernet actually.'

'The what?' Denny got up and looked at the screen. 'What is this? I've never seen anything like this before.'

'Virtual reality files – archives.'

'Archives?'

'I'm looking for disused files.'

'Disused files?'

'Are you going to repeat everything I say, or are you going to make yourself useful?'

'Useful?'

Tamar narrowed her eyes (just like mother used to do). 'Are you doing this on purpose?'

'On purpose?' said Denny, predictably.

For answer, Tamar manifested another smoking phial. It was, if anything, even more toxic looking than the other one.

'Do you need sobering up again?'

'No, no, I'm sorry. What are we doing? What do computer files have to do with anything?'

As Tamar explained, Denny was stunned.

'Well, where did you think virtual reality came from?' she asked 'Did you think *humans* invented it?'

'Er, yes.'

'Well, I suppose so, in a way, but we came up with it first. Only we call it magic.'

'So, you're telling me that magic comes from computers?'

'Not originally. Look, I suppose you could say that everything in the universe is created from computer code – of a sort. All life, natural and supernatural, although that's a massive oversimplification, but it'll do. And everything and everybody has its place in the matrix, okay? Right, now you could say that there are two main divisions – reality, that's here, that's you, and virtual reality, that's me – magic, okay? Okay, well, when humans invented computers they inadvertently accessed the universal matrix because they unconsciously mimicked it. So now we can make use of it too... no, go back a bit. Everything that exists, real or unreal, has a file.'

'In a computer?'

'No, we just use a computer to access it. Anyway, some files become disused, when things cease to exist. But the space they inhabited is still there, and you can use it; it's just sitting there.'

'Cool – I think. So, is there a dinosaur file?'

'In the archives – what we're looking for are deleted files, stuff that never happened – so to speak.'

'But – if the files are deleted ...?'

'The stuff that was in the files is deleted; the actual files are still there.'

'Okay, and *why* do we want to find these files?'

'Oh, didn't I say? I think these numbers are a file number. I think Kelon's hiding in a deleted file.'

'So, you're hacking the universe?'

'No, you are, I'm no good at this stuff.'

'Oh? I see, and you just assume that I am? Just because I'm boring and physically unimpressive and I have no friends, I must be a computer geek. Is that it?'

'Aren't you?'

'Well, yes, I mean no, but I can probably do it. Move over, give me the numbers and get me a coffee. Then leave me alone.'

'Okay, and – Denny.'

'Yes?'

'I don't think you're boring, I think you're very clever.'

'Tamar.'

'Yes?'

'Coffee.'

'Okay.'

Denny stared at the screen. It looked weird, as if it was alive. There was a pentagram spinning in the middle of the screen. 'Magic files,' he thought, 'wow!'

'Hey!' he looked up, struck with a thought. 'So, you *do* think that I'm weedy, unimpressive and unpopular then?'

'Yes, but so what?'

'Oh – I suppose it doesn't matter.'

'No – it doesn't. That's just surface stuff, look at me, totally gorgeous, extremely powerful – everybody loves me, and I'm a horrible person.'

'Not anymore.'

'No?'

'Just mildly unpleasant – but getting better.'

Tamar threw a cushion at him – not entirely lightheartedly.

'Look,' she said, 'I've met plenty of big, handsome men who had ugly little souls. I like you the way you are.'

'Still, do you think I should start working out or something?'

'Only if you want to. I thought vanity was *my* thing.'

'Oh, it is, along with ...' He caught her eye and subsided. 'Where's that coffee? I'd better get on.'

Denny was so absorbed by the time the coffee arrived, that he never noticed it; it went cold, so did the next one. The hot dog she got him at one went stiff at the edges, and the mustard congealed.

At three-seventeen, he yelled. 'I'm in.'

'Stop and eat something.'

'No, I have to find the files. I thought I could just type it in, but I can't – I have to search for the deleted files first. I don't think you're supposed to find them. She doesn't mean to be found, does she?'

At five-twenty-two, he said. 'Got them – deleted files. You know I was wondering – could Askphrit be hiding in one of these?'

'Yes, it's possible, but I doubt it, and even if he was, we wouldn't know which one.'

'Damn, I have to scroll through ... oh no I don't though. Search engine, okay.' He typed in the number.

'Now we just have to wait.' He leaned back. 'Christ, I'm starving.'

Tamar pointed wryly to the desiccated hot dog.

'Okay, maybe I'm not *that* hungry.'

'How long will this take?'

'How can I know? It's a pretty unusual system; it could take until yesterday for all I know.'

'Well, come and have some proper food, and a drink.'

'Beer?' said Denny, hopefully. Tamar pursed her lips.

'Okay, okay, coke then, you're not my mother you know.' He stood up stiffly. 'You know, I never thought I'd say this, but I could use some exercise.'

'Food,' ordered Tamar.

They turned away from the screen, and the computer beeped. They both snapped their heads round; the screen was flashing.

<< FILE FOUND>>

'This is it,' breathed Denny.

'Not yet,' Tamar said.

'We just have to press "Enter" to access the file,'

'I can't,' she told him bluntly. 'I'm not ready, and neither are you. Eat something, have a drink. It'll still be there in half an hour.'

Denny protested, but Tamar won – for a short while, anyway. All too soon Denny was fed and watered, and they were standing in front of the screen.

'Ready?'

'Not really.' She was pale and twitchy.

'Too bad,' he said callously and he hit "Enter" as Tamar watched with a feeling of foreboding that she could not have explained.

<<PASSWORD PLEASE>> flashed up on the screen.

Denny and Tamar stared at each other.

~ Chapter Twenty ~

DENNY WAS DOING a pretty fair imitation of a man at the end of his tether. 'Under the clock, under the clock,' he muttered as he paced the floor. 'You were right, it's impossible, what clock? I mean, how many billions of sodding clocks are there in the world?' And we might already be too late.' He stopped pacing suddenly with a skid and collapsed into a chair. 'I give up,' he said, 'it's too hard.'

Tamar bit her lip and said nothing. He looked utterly defeated. It frightened her a little.

He suddenly leapt out of the chair and started pacing again. 'I mean, we're so close,' he ranted. 'I'm such a fool. I should have been concentrating. She gave me that clue, and what was I doing at midnight? I was damned well drunk wasn't I?' he answered his own question.

Tamar relaxed a little; he was clearly working up to something. A stroke probably, but she'd rather have him like this. 'You're right,' she said soothingly, 'it's too hard, even if you'd been thinking about it, and I wasn't either, it doesn't mean anything, it wasn't your fault.'

This well-meaning speech only seemed to infuriate Denny further. 'If I'd been thinking about it, maybe I'd have worked it out. There's no excuse.'

'There may still be time'

Denny ignored this. 'Anyway,' he ranted on, 'if there's a password, why couldn't they just give it to us, why all this bleeding mystery, it's bleeding ridiculous. And you know what? You know *what*?'

'I'm sure you're going to tell me' murmured Tamar. 'I'm on the edge of my seat,' she drawled more audibly.

Denny spun. 'You were right,' he announced. 'It's impossible; there's no way to solve it.' He sank back down in the chair. He ran his hands through his hair in a gesture of weary resignation. 'What time is it?' he asked suddenly, apropos of nothing.

Tamar was startled. 'Um,' she glanced at the clock on the mantel, 'half past five.'

'Right, so that's – six and a half hours till midnight,' he grinned. 'We'd better get on with it.'

'What? But you just said… oh okay.'

'Just because it's impossible is no excuse for not doing something,' said Denny. 'The impossible I can do. The possible may take a little longer.'

* * *

'I just don't know where to start,' said Denny hopelessly.

'Well, in those old movies it was usually the clock in a railway station, wasn't it?'

'How does that help us?'

'Well…' Tamar shrugged.

'Anyway,' he continued, 'going off past events, I think that's a little too obvious. I mean it's more likely to be a play on words or something, isn't it? If I could just figure out what it means…'

'"Under the clock",' she said, 'what else could it mean? It's not exactly ambiguous is it?'

'We've got to stop asking each other useless questions.'

'Huh?'

'Okay,' Denny gritted his teeth, 'let's just get on with it. We start looking for large clocks that a person can stand under. I mean, even if it's wrong, well, everything we've done so far has been wrong hasn't it? You said it yourself; we have to go through all the wrong solutions to get to the right one.'

'But…'

'No buts – come on.'

'Hmm, we seem to be against the clock, no pun intended, on this one. And like you said, we might already be too late.'

'Well, in that case it doesn't matter does it?' he said, shortly. 'Now start with the most obvious. What's the most famous clock in the world?'

'Er, Big Ben?'

'Okay, and…'

'I think it is anyway,' she said thoughtfully, 'I mean, I don't know. I expect there are people in Muntab who've never heard of it.'

'No, but it's the first one *you* happened to think of. This is *our* quest after all. It'll do for a start.'

'But we won't know if it's the right one until midnight, and if it isn't it'll be too late,' objected Tamar.

'Until midnight tomorrow, there's always another midnight. As long as we're working on the assumption that we're not too late now, then we can assume that it's never going to be too late.'

Tamar thought about this. 'I think you're right,' she said, after a minute, 'after all, it's probably midnight already in Muntab. It's always midnight somewhere.'

'Exactly, it's probably midnight *yesterday*, somewhere. It's not the same time everywhere, so I'm guessing that any midnight will do, once we've found the right clock.'

'I hope you're right.'

'Okay, so there's that. And also we ought to work on the assumption that we're totally wrong and "under the clock" is some obscure play on words, like a cryptic crossword clue. You can work on that; you have a twisted mind you ought to be good at that. Besides, you understand how these people think better than I do.'

Tamar let that one go – for now, and merely asked. 'So, what are you going to do?'

'I'm going on the Internet. I'm going to check out time zones and famous large clocks

'And spy movies,' he added after a moment's thought.

'Why, spy movies?'

'To see which clock the spies met under of course.'

'Oh, of course. Wait a minute, though, if you do that, you'll lose the file.' She gestured to the computer screen still flashing >>PASSWORD PLEASE…

'Good point, well, zap me up a laptop, you can do that, right?'

'I'm not supposed to be doing all this really,' Tamar grumbled. 'You're supposed to wish for stuff like this.'

Denny raised an eyebrow. He thought it made him look like Mr. Spock. It did not.

'What's the matter with your eye? You seem to have a tic.'

'Ahem, now we have just under six hours before we have to check out Big Ben, so let's get on with it, shall we?'

* * *

It was 11.30 when Denny finally said, 'I think that's all for now, how are you getting on?'

'Not so great, I don't think crosswords are my forte.'

'Well, what have you come up with?'

'Well…' she looked at the pile of paper in front of her, all covered in scribbled out writing.

'Nothing, actually.'

Denny took this calmly. 'Okay,' he said, then there's probably nothing to find that way. It was worth a try.'

'You never expected it to work did you?'

'Not really. I don't expect what I've been doing to work either, but we have to work the problem. I think I'm getting the hang of this stuff now you see. What always happens?'

He answered his own question. 'We fool around for hours or days or whatever, getting nowhere, until the answer just pops up out of nowhere. But it only works if we try.'

'Maybe we've just been lucky up to now.'

'No such thing as luck,' said Denny dismissively. 'Anyway, I reckon we try out Big Ben tonight, and then all the railway stations in England next, one by one. And then if that still hasn't worked we move on to Europe. I've got a list and the time zones for the major cities for a start.'

'Oh my God.'

'I know, I know. If you've got any better ideas…' he held his hands out.

Tamar shrugged.

'You know, you might try and be a bit more enthusiastic. I'm not doing all this for the good of my health, you know.'

'I know; I'm sorry.'

'What did you say?

'I said I'm sorry.'

'Blimey! Wonders will never cease. You're sorry, *you're* sorry, *you*?'

'Very funny,' she said dryly. 'Shall we get on with it then? What time is it now?'

* * *

Kelon paced the chamber agitatedly. 'They are getting too close. I blame you for this, little man. How did they get this far? They should never have got this far. Do you realise that if they find the password, they will be upon me?'

Since this was clearly a rhetorical question, the little man did not bother to venture a reply. He was more concerned with how the hell Kelon had found out how far they had got without his help.

'How could you let this happen? Never mind, they will not find the password. Ha! Even now, they are standing under Big Ben in the pouring rain. Fools, they have no understanding.'

Kelon must have another spy in the ranks, one at least as efficient as himself. This was a disturbing thought.

Kelon seemed to read his mind. 'You should have told me how far they had got, it is as well that others are not so slack as you seem to have become.'

'My liege…'

'No matter, no matter,' said Kelon expansively. 'What's done is done, they will get no further; they have no idea how to reach the password, that it evident. And soon, if your information is correct, they will run out of time. "It" will get her, and all my problems will be over.'

Another disturbing thought. Kelon was right. The little man bit his lip anxiously; it was all going wrong.

Kelon was now convinced into a better mood and sat down, smiling in a satisfied manner. 'Soon, it will all be over, and we can go back to normal, heh, my friend?'

'I'm not your friend, you overgrown, bumptious, larcenous fraud,' thought the little man, but he kept this thought to himself, naturally.

* * *

'Strike one,' was all Denny could be drawn into saying, before throwing himself into bed, fully dressed and still soaking wet.

Tamar stared moodily at the computer screen; so near and yet so far. Damn!

She sat down at the table and pulled the papers that she had been working on toward her. 'Okay, under, under – beneath, below? Well they meant the same thing didn't they? She pulled out a dictionary. So – "under"? – okay there was "subordinate to, less than" in other words, "less than the clock"? Nope. What about "clock"? Well, it was slang for a speedometer – no. Also, a person's face – even worse. A dandelion clock?' Tamar swept the paper off the table in frustration. She realized that she was getting ridiculous "Dandelion clocks" indeed, as if there were not millions of them.

Less than a clock could mean a watch she supposed, but it still did not tell her what it meant. 'Hmm, a watch.' The white rabbit carried a watch, and he took it underground – down a hole in a field, which could, conceivably be full of dandelion clocks. 'Oh for God's sake!' she thought, 'I'm cracking up, I must be getting tired.' Tamar completely missed the significance of this observation, well, she *was* tired. She fell asleep.

She was awoken by the sound of Denny banging his watch on the table.

'Stopped,' he said laconically in answer to her interrogative look.

'What? Oh sorry, I was thinking of something else.' She shook her head to clear it. For one surreal moment, Denny had taken on the appearance of a large white rabbit.

'Maybe it'll be okay,' she thought, 'it might be nice to be insane – peaceful,'

Denny sat down at the laptop. 'Might as well get on with it,' he said, but he did not sound as if he meant it.

'No, leave it. We've got enough to be going on with. You'll drive yourself mad.

'Or me,' she added silently.

There was a loud banging. In their disoriented state, it took them a few minutes to realise there was somebody at the door. They looked at each other and shrugged. Denny almost never had visitors.

He went to the door; as he opened it flew back and smacked him in the face, breaking his nose and sending him flying down the passage. 'Wha'd the hell?' he spluttered. Whoever was towering above him was in shadow and, therefore, not instantly recognisable.

'Hello Denny,' said a familiar deep voice, causing Denny to cover his kneecaps protectively. It was Barry.

'We haven't seen you for a while,' Barry observed. 'Not been avoiding us have you? I'd be *very* hurt to think that. Very upset, after all, we're friends, aren't we? You wouldn't avoid your friends now would you?'

'Do, do, ob course dot, just beed a bit busy dat's all.'

'You seem to be bleeding all over your carpet,' observed Barry, in menacingly courteous tones, proffering a large, dirty handkerchief.

'Thagyoo,' said Denny obsequiously.

Tamar appeared in the doorway. 'What the hell is going on?'

Barry looked up. 'Ah,' he said, as if he suddenly understood something, 'busy is it? I see.' He reached down to help Denny up. 'Sorry about that mate,' he said, grinning, 'didn't realise. No hard feelings eh?'

'Who the hell is this?' asked Tamar, and the look on her face was not pleasant.

'Old friend,' Denny explained.

'He *hit* you,'

'Yes, he did, didn't he?' said Denny thoughtfully. 'Just sort him out will you? Not fatally,' he added as an afterthought.

Tamar grinned. 'Okey dokey,' she said perkily. This perkiness did not bode well for Barry.

Denny left the room, whistling as well as a broken nose would allow him to. He'd finally solved the Barry problem once and for all. Whatever Tamar did to him (and he didn't want to know) Barry was certain never to be bothering him again, and would probably end up a reformed character.

* * *

Tamar returned in a much better mood. 'I needed that,' she said. 'How's your nose?'

'Find,'

Tamar waved a hand over it. '*Now* it's fine,' she said.

'I thought you weren't supposed to do that,' said Denny, fingering his restored nose gingerly.

Tamar waved a dismissive hand. 'Whatever. Sod the rules, I've had enough. What's the time?' she added, just for the fun of seeing him look at his broken watch. Wreaking mayhem always put her in a playful mood.

Denny, however, glanced at the screen of the small laptop. 'A quarter past eleven,' he said.

Then a peculiar look came over his face. 'I don't believe it,' he exclaimed. 'It can't be!'

Tamar was disappointed that her joke had failed and asked a little sulkily, 'What?'

'The computer,' yelled Denny, excitedly. 'I'm sure I'm right. Yes, look.'

He pointed at the screen of the large computer that they had used to access the files of the so called Aethernet. In the corner of the screen was a small digital clock, just like on the laptop. The difference was this clock read 0.00.

'I knew it,' crowed Denny triumphantly. 'Oh, I'm so thick; I can't believe I didn't think of it before. I knew that this clock read midnight all the time. I noticed it before, when I was working on the file. I just didn't think anything of it. I mean, zero hundred hours; you know. We were thinking of it in terms of midnight. I just didn't make the connection. "The clock at midnight", it meant the clock that is *set* at midnight, see?'

'And the "under" part?'

'Look.' He pointed to a small icon underneath the clock. When he put the cursor on it, it flagged up the words "Go To"

Denny glanced at Tamar, his finger poised on the mouse. He was grinning. 'Ready?'

Tamar gulped; she had that queasy feeling again. 'No,' she said.

'Too bad,' said Denny and clicked it.

Tamar had that horrible feeling of destiny again as she felt her body dissolve.

'Beam me up Scotty',' Denny quipped, as they dematerialised.

~ Chapter Twenty One ~

'WHERE THE hell are we?' Denny did not seriously expect an answer to this.

'I don't know.'

'Why are we in black and white?'

'I think it's just the moonlight.'

'No, I don't think so; we're definitely in black and white.'

'You're imagining it.'

Denny changed tack. 'Is this the file?'

'No, this is – something else. I don't know what it is.' Tamar was feeling unaccountably relieved. This place was not so bad. Although, she had a feeling that it was only a temporary reprieve.

Suddenly the air was split by the sound of a loud clock chiming. Denny and Tamar jumped. They were in an empty plaza. The rain sparkled on the cobbles in the hazy glow of a street light. There were shops and cafés, all closed. There was no clock.

They counted the chimes; there were twelve. They would have been disappointed if there had not been. Then they heard the sound of swift footsteps.

'Behind you,' said a deep, throaty voice. They spun round. They saw a tall man wearing a trench coat and a trilby pulled low over his face. Unnecessarily in Tamar's opinion, since the man, whoever he was, was completely in shadow anyway. The shadow, they now saw, of a large clock tower. Denny and Tamar looked at each other and raised their eyebrows.

'It took you long enough to get here,' the man growled. 'Ages I've been waiting, *and* it's pissing down. I have got better things to do you know, well actually I haven't, but at least I could be not doing them in the comfort of my own home, if you know what I mean.

'Anyway, here goes.' The man lowered his voice to a conspiratorial whisper. 'Go to the café Maurice,' he told them. 'The password is "Swordfish".'

Denny groaned. 'It would be. *I* could have thought of that.'

The man clicked his heels and was gone as swiftly as he came.

'Okay,' said Denny when he had recovered from this affront to all common sense. 'Café Maurice it is then.'

It was directly across the plaza from them. They wandered desultorily over toward it, Tamar dragging her heels every step of the way. Denny did not appear to notice.

'So, will this get us into the file then?' he asked.

'Undoubtedly,' she answered.

'Good.' There did not seem much else to say.

Denny knocked on the door and a small hatch opened at eye level. They could not see a face, but a voice said peremptorily, 'Password?'

'Swordfish,' said Denny a trifle wearily. The door vanished, in fact, the whole plaza vanished, and they found themselves standing on a grassy heath in, what was apparently the middle of nowhere, it was wreathed in mist and blowing a gale. All that was missing was Heathcliff.

'Oh no!' Tamar croaked.

'What?'

'It's the place from my dream – from my nightmare.'

'It can't be.'

'Well it feels like it; and listen – dogs, getting closer.'

'Okay, it may *look* the same, but it won't be. I'm here this time and the dogs won't bother us, we're not running for the fence. I mean we want to go to the castle, don't we.'

'Castle? Looks more like a high security prison to me.'

'Really? It looks kind of like "The Enchanted Castle" to me.'

'Enchanted *what*? Try Alcatraz.'

'I don't think we're seeing the same building. Why are you afraid of it?'

'I don't know, there's something in there – something scary.' She was shaking.

'That was just in your dream.'

'Yeah, well it feels the same.'

'It's okay; I'm here. You'll be all right. Besides we *have* to go.'

'Face your fears, you mean, and all that?'

'You already did that. I meant because we have to find Kelon.'

'Oh – yes, of course.' The dogs howled.

Suddenly, Tamar metamorphosed into the calm, strong-minded person that Denny knew. She squared her shoulders as if she were shrugging off her fear.

'Let's go.'

They trudged off in the direction of the castle/prison. It started to rain, typical.

* * *

'A moat?'

'Probably shark infested,' said Tamar gloomily. 'Or alligators, or sharks *and* alligators – *and* piranhas.'

'Don't be silly. It's only a few feet deep. Even *I'm* not scared of *that*.'

'It's fathoms, and full of sharp rocks.'

'No it's not. Look, you'll just have to trust me; it's perfectly harmless. It's just the fear talking, besides, there's a drawbridge.'

'It'll probably disappear into the wall just as we get halfway across.'

'It'd have to be quick; it's only two or three steps at most.'

'It's at least thirty feet. Okay, okay, I'll take your word for it.' She closed her eyes and stepped onto the drawbridge. 'If I fall in, it'll be your fault.'

'Even if you did, you'd only be up to your knees.'

'No, that's what would happen to *you* if *you* fell in there. If *I* fall in, I'll be swept away by raging white water, and eaten by croco-sharks.'

'You seriously believe that, don't you?'

'Are you willing to risk it? Just don't let me fall.'

'I won't.'

'You can open your eyes now.' It had taken about thirty seconds.

'What?' She opened her eyes and saw... 'It's just a stream.'

'Yes, with trout.'

They could both see the portcullis, but only Tamar could see the dried blood and the skulls hanging from the gateposts. It looked, however, equally impenetrable to both of them.

It was Tamar who found the lever. Well, this mode of entry was relatively uncommon in modern England, but Tamar had seen her fair share of castles over the centuries, and the design never varied much. The portcullis creaked ominously as it was slowly and torturously raised.

Denny laughed. 'It must have taken years to get that creak just right.'

Tamar looked at him sourly. 'You're enjoying this, aren't you?'

'Oh please,' he said. 'This place is practically a caricature of a scary castle. It'll be bats flying out of the battlements next.'

* * *

'You *had* to say it didn't you?' seethed Tamar, wiping bat shit out of her hair. 'Just shut up.'

They had found themselves in a large, echoing, stone courtyard.

'Wow!' said Denny, 'I feel like "Indiana Jones". Bring on the skeletal warriors.'

'That's Sinbad, and don't *say* things like that.'

'Sorry.'

'There's the inner gate,' she pointed. 'I suppose we go on.' She sounded resigned.

'At least we're alone – see, the bats weren't my fault.'

The gate swung open easily, and there was a complete lack of burly guards demanding passwords and waving swords menacingly. Tamar found it eerie, Denny, on the other hand, found it. 'Disappointing – it's too easy; you'd expect it to be better guarded.'

'It *is* guarded,' she said, shivering, 'by fear, I don't know why you can't feel it. And there's no such thing as "*too* easy". I like easy, easy suits me just fine.'

They were now in the inner courtyard, which was smaller – naturally, and beautifully kept, with an ornamental fountain, trees and pillars. The fountain was running and was lit up in some way that they could not see. The trees waved gently in the breeze, and the pillars were inlaid with gold and ivory. There were tigers chained to them, asleep and Marrakech lanterns in ivory hung from brackets on the walls, highlighting the hanging baskets beside them. Night blooming jasmine wafted a sweet, heady scent over them.

'Wow!' said Denny again. 'Sinbad indeed! It's like the "Arabian nights" in here.'

A faint, tinkling music floated over the night air, and Denny thought he had never seen such bright stars.

'Seductive,' agreed Tamar sourly. All in all, she thought she would rather be hanging over a scorpion pit surrounded by broken glass, with a candle burning through the rope. Imminent and horrible death, after all, is imminent and horrible death. You may not be looking forward to it, but at least there is not any kind of mystery about it.

Then the Houris appeared, and Tamar felt on familiar ground again. There were three of them. *'Bad things always come in threes,'* she thought as they descended on Denny, ignoring her entirely.

Denny stood there, bewildered and stupefied. They had his shirt off in seconds and were fawning over him, giggling. Houris are even worse than mermaids. They stroked his chest and ran their fingers through his hair, offering him cherries and steaming gold goblets of something, almost certainly not wine. Denny just stood there looking dazed. Only Tamar could see that their hair was infested with snakes, the talons on their fingers and their blank, dead eyes. They were dragging him to the ground; he offered no resistance. It was as if he was in a trance. Their talons raked his chest and face drawing blood. Tamar cried out and ran into them, kicking them aside. They hissed and struck out at her. She grabbed Denny and hauled him to the doors; large ebony doors inlaid with gold in a pattern that she found strangely disturbing and familiar. She wrenched the doors open and dragged him through.

~ Chapter Twenty Two ~

ON THE OTHER side of the door was a large corridor, the stone walls were painted in a black and white chequered pattern, which nevertheless, looked surprisingly dingy. The pattern was carried on, on the floor and the ceiling. This in itself would have been nasty enough, but the perspective looked wrong. It was subtle, but each square was just a little off from the corner of the next, and just slightly the wrong size. Tamar tried not to look at it. It was frustrating, intentionally so, she realized. The corridor ran to a point of infinity, and yet, it did not, not quite, you could drive yourself mad trying to make sense of it.

Denny had come round. 'What happened?' he looked down. 'I'm bleeding, and where's my shirt?'

'Houris,' said Tamar, laconically.

'What?'

'Don't you remember them?'

'No, we were in a courtyard, and then we were here.' He looked around. 'Have you been sobering me up again?'

'It's an optical illusion.'

'It's giving me a headache.'

'Don't look at it then, and keep still, you're losing blood.'

'I'm fine. What did you say about Houris?'

'I'm guessing, but I think they appeared because you weren't afraid. They decided to try – something else on *you*.'

'Something...? Oh, sorry.'

'It's okay; I'm not upset. They hexed you.'

'So, how do we get out of here?'

'There's probably a door.'

'No kidding.' He looked around, 'Where is it?'

After they had walked up and down the corridor twice, feeling the walls – whilst trying not to look at them, Tamar conceded. 'Okay, so, maybe not a door.'

'Trapdoor?' suggested Denny, pointing at the ceiling.'

'I doubt it.'

They tried it anyway, with Tamar jumping up and down like a demented cheerleader.

'You know, 'said Denny,'I'm getting fed up with being stuck in rooms without any doors.'

But he seemed perfectly calm. Tamar, on the other hand, was getting decidedly panicky.

'It'll be something obvious,' said Denny. 'You'll see.'

'It's always obvious when you know the answer,' she said, sinking down on the floor with her head in her hands.

'Don't give up,' said Denny, sitting beside her.

'I'm not, I'm thinking. I just don't want to be distracted by that awful paint job.'

She glanced up; Denny's cuts had dried. She removed her jacket and started to unbutton her shirt.

'Um, not that I don't appreciate it, but what are you doing?'

'Put it on.' She handed him the shirt.

'Oh – right.'

She slipped her jacket back on. It tells us a lot about Denny's physique, that apart from being a little too short in the arms and very slightly snug across the shoulders, the shirt fitted him pretty well.

'I just thank God it's not embroidered.'

'As if,' said Tamar, scornfully; she was a jeans and black leather girl. 'Actually, it's the smartest I've ever seen you.'

All Denny's clothes came from charity shops and market stalls; he dressed with the savoir-faire of the average scarecrow. Tamar was only surprised that he did not own a Parker.

They sat in gloomy silence for a while, and then Denny said slowly. 'What was it, I said before?'

'That you were glad my shirt isn't embroidered?'

'No, before that, about being trapped in a room with no doors.'

'What about it?'

'Well, we're not, are we?'

'Yes we are.'

'So, what are we leaning against?'

They turned round. 'But that's the door we came in by.'

'So? It's the only door in here; it has to be the way out. I mean you can't say that you're trapped in a room, when there's a flaming door right there.'

Tamar actually smacked her head. 'Of course! Oh, I am so stupid, it's so obvious; it's a trick.'

She wrenched open the door. It now led, not into the courtyard, but into a large ballroom.

Denny was triumphant. 'You see, I bet the corridor spins round to this room, once you're inside. Lateral thinking you see.'

He took in his surroundings. 'Good God!' he exclaimed. The ballroom was furnished in the most surreal manner. Like a turn of the century funfair, bathed in the sepia tones of a hundred flickering candles.

The centrepiece was a carousel, the candy coloured horses staring eerily in the gloom. The other "amusements" included a puppet show, dodgem cars, some small rowing boats standing in dry dock in a corner and here and there, waxworks in period clothes. All were standing about in various attitudes among the rides like patrons, silent and still, like a scene, frozen in time.

'What the hell is all this?' said Denny. 'I think we're dealing with a sick mind here. Do you think this guy moonlights as a pop star?'

The only other door was beside the rifle range at the back of the room. The sign above it, framed in lights, bore the legend 'HALL OF MIRRORS'.

'I'm not going in there,' announced Tamar decisively. 'God knows what'll happen.' And she swung round and opened the door again. The chequered corridor was still there.

'You didn't think it would work twice, did you?' said Denny. 'Right, hall of mirrors it is then.

'How bad could it be?' he added with ghastly cheerfulness. 'Mirrors. Right up your street I would have thought.'

'I hate you.'

'No you don't,' he grinned. Then his face fell and he turned the colour of putty and his stomach lurched as they both heard – 'ha ha ha ha - ha ha ha ha – ha ha ha ha.' It was sickening, unnatural laughter, repetitive and sinister.

'I don't *think* so,' said Tamar, picking up an oar. She stalked over to the glass case, smashed it and beat the laughing policeman therein, until the sound wound down like a broken tape recorder. 'I'm not putting up with that!' she announced. 'I hate those things. Some people,' she said to the air, 'have no imagination.'

She looked defiantly at Denny. 'All right, hall of mirrors then – got any cigarettes?'

* * *

They picked their way, gingerly through the dusty amusements. 'Watch out for these waxworks,' said Tamar.

'Oh yes, I'm really worried about Shirley Temple here,' said Denny, indicating a wax figure of a small child with golden curls, carrying a large lollipop. It could have been either a girl or a boy.

'Clown.'

'No need to be insulting.'

'No. CLOWN! On your right.'

Advancing on them was the largest clown Denny had ever seen. He may well have been crying on the inside, as the saying goes, but he was just damn scary on the outside.

Denny had never had a scary clown experience at a birthday party, and of course, the last time Tamar had had a birthday party, clowns, as we know them, had not yet been invented. But they had both seen Steven King's "It" (Tamar, while it was in pre-production, but that is another story) and the symbolism was not lost on them. Besides, the thing was immense and brandishing a large dagger.

Denny sensibly backed away, but Tamar was frozen to the spot. She had lost her powers the moment Denny had hit "Enter", as she had feared she would, and now had no idea what to do without them.

"Pennyfarthing" or whatever its name was, raised the dagger with the mechanical slowness of the terminally brainwashed. Denny darted forward and bore her to the ground, and they both went careering into the rifle range.

It was raining rifles; Denny grabbed one, cocked it expertly, and started firing with surprising accuracy. The clown staggered; a dark red stain appeared on its colourful tunic. Real bullets? Well why not? He fired again. The clown went down like a punctured balloon and lay still. Denny dropped the gun as if it was red hot.

'Nice shootin' Tex,' said Tamar, with studied casualness, she had been taken aback by this impressive display of heroism; taken aback and seriously impressed. In fact, her heart was threatening to start fluttering again, but she was determined not to show it.

'Well, I was always pretty decent at 'Space Invaders',' said Denny, modestly. 'After you,' he added, indicating the door. 'Or – no, I don't suppose that's very chivalrous under the circumstances. Second thoughts, stay behind me.'

* * *

The hall of mirrors was not quite what they were expecting. For one thing, it was not so much a hall as a gallery, really. And the mirrors were not of the full-length distorting funfair variety but hung on the walls in ornate frames like a row of blank portraits. Their reflections in them looked perfectly ordinary. No two mirrors were facing each other.

'Well, I don't get it,' said Denny.

'Whoever designed this, missed the point I think,' she replied. 'I guess they never saw a hall of mirrors, which suggests that they've been in this file for a long time.'

'How does that help us?'

'It doesn't; I was just sneering.'

'Oh.'

At the end of the room was a heavy red velvet curtain hanging from a gilt pole, with a tasselled pull cord of the type you usually find a plaque behind. The obvious thing to do was to pull the cord, so they did.

Behind the curtain were two more mirrors. Plain, unframed and apparently also perfectly ordinary.

Tamar stared at her reflection. There was something... It looked almost too real, as if it were not so much a reflection, as an exact duplicate of herself on the other side of an empty frame, mimicking her every move. She felt like a cartoon character; as she twisted and turned and pulled faces, trying to catch it out.

'What are you doing?' asked Denny clearly wondering if she had lost her mind.

'I'm trying to – aha. There. I knew it.' She faced her reflection. 'Okay, the game's up, who are you? What's going on?' Her reflection shrugged, although she had not moved. Denny gaped. 'What?'

'Don't ask me,' the reflection said. 'I just work here.'

Denny turned to his reflection. 'What about you?' he asked, feeling slightly foolish, as if he had been caught talking to himself.

His reflection smiled at him; it was profoundly unnerving. 'We are the guardians of the portals,' it said. 'You have to decide which one to go through – we're here to help you.'

Tamar's reflection cut in. 'It's very simple; one portal leads to your desire and the other leads to certain death. As for which one is which, well ...'

Denny's reflection took up the thread. 'You can only ask one question, and you should know that one of us always lies and the other always tells the truth, and I'm not telling you which is which. You couldn't be sure that I'd tell you the truth anyway, so ...'

'That old saw,' snorted Tamar, a world of contempt in her voice. She turned to Denny. 'Didn't I say? No imagination.'

'Wait,' said Denny, 'I know this one.' He turned to his reflection 'If I were to ask the other one which portal leads to certain death, which one would she say?'

His reflection grinned. 'Oh, she'd tell you that it was this one. She's a terrible liar.'

'Or you are,' Denny pointed out. 'Either way it doesn't matter, because if it's you who's lying, then she wouldn't say that, because she tells the truth. On the other hand, if you tell the truth, then she would say that, because she's a liar. Either way, it's not the truth, so,' he paused for breath. 'This portal *isn't* the one that leads to certain death – we go this way.' He grinned at Tamar, who was looking at him in exasperated pity.

'All this time,' she said. 'And you haven't learned a damn thing, have you?'

Denny was hurt. 'What do you mean?' he said indignantly. 'I got it right, I know I did.'

'I wouldn't know,' she said. 'But I do know that these people don't play by the rules. You should know that by now. What's to prevent *both* these jokers from being liars?'

'Oh,' Denny was crestfallen. 'I see what you mean.' There was no arguing with this logic. He tried anyway. 'But it's a riddle, if you're right, then what *do* we do?' He was almost wailing.

'I think a mallet would be handy right now,' she said.' But failing that ...' She pulled down the curtain pole. 'Okay, tell us the right portal, or I smash you to smithereens.

The reflections tried to look at each other, but naturally they could not. They both shrugged, and Tamar's reflection said, 'They both lead to the same place, so it doesn't really matter.'

Tamar lowered the pole. 'And where is that?'

'We don't know,' said Denny's likeness. 'Honestly.' It added, as Tamar lifted the pole threateningly. She lowered it again.

'How did you know?' Denny asked.

'Simple – look at them. They're us – sort of. *That's* the point! You have to face up to who you really are and admit the truth about yourself to get past them. I figured they were lying because that's what I would do. And you, well you're not as bad as I am, but can you honestly say that you've never told a lie in your whole life? Of course not. They know us; they knew exactly how to play us. That puzzle stuff, you live for that stuff. But *I* knew that neither of us would rather die than give up the truth.'

'Brilliant.'

Tamar bowed.

'So,' said Denny. 'Let's see what's behind door number one.'

The mirrors slid up to reveal open doorways, which led apparently nowhere.

'One each?' suggested Denny.

Tamar shrugged. 'Okay.'

~ Chapter Twenty Three ~

IT WAS FUNNY, Denny thought, how from one side of the doorway it looked completely dark and yet once he had walked though he found himself squinting in the bright sunshine.

He was not altogether surprised to realise that Tamar was not with him. He had half expected it. She undoubtedly had too. The portal guardians had lied about everything else, so it had been only sensible to assume that they had lied about that too, and only prudent, therefore, to take a passage each. That way, at least one of them might reach their goal. It was the "might" that was bothering him. He was wondering where Tamar had ended up. Since he did not appear to be facing certain death, he could only hope that she was not either. On the other hand, there seemed to be a shortage of reticent sorceresses in the vicinity too. A shortage of everything, in fact, except for sand, sea and palm trees. Actually, certain death seemed a distinct possibility, now that he thought about it. He had evidently been cast away on a desert island.

The doorway through which he had come had naturally vanished the moment he had stepped through.

It was obviously an illusion. For one thing, he was in a castle wasn't he? And, for another, it was too perfect, the sky was too blue, the sand too soft – not a pebble or shell anywhere – and the palm trees too symmetrical. But for all that, it was enticingly convincing. He wondered how it was done.

Denny was annoyed. He yelled to no one in particular, but he was sure someone could hear him. 'I didn't come all this way to play "Robinson Crusoe" you know.'

His voice echoed slightly, which in the absence of cliffs, gave him the eerie feeling of being in a bubble. 'So, this is what it feels like to be on reality TV,' he thought.

The beach seemed to stretch for miles in every direction, and it was desolately empty except for one thing, far ahead of him, stood a large cheval mirror. Well, why not?

Denny, by now, would not have been all that surprised to have seen a nuclear reactor away in the distance. On the other hand, it did seem a singularly useless thing to leave there. It stirred his curiosity. Feeling like a laboratory rat, Denny was now certain he was being watched, he approached it cautiously. When he got close enough to see his reflection he found, to his intense relief, that it did not reflect himself at all. He had had enough of himself today. The thought of any more conversations with his reflected image was more than he thought he could put up with.

Instead of a reflection, the surface of the mirror, if indeed it was a mirror, showed a spinning logo. Round and round and up and down it spun, sometimes backwards, sometimes forwards, sometimes it turned round on itself so that the lettering was in reverse. It did this very fast, and it was a few minutes before Denny was able to read it. When he did, he realized two things. One, that it was indeed a mirror. And two, he had heard about this before, although he could not remember where. The spinning logo read "THE MIRROR OF FUTURES".

His spine prickled. He reached out to touch it, but then drew his hand away. 'I'm not playing,' he said evenly, 'do you hear me?' he turned to walk away, then hesitated, turned back, turned away again, took a few steps, then finally gave in. He touched the mirror. The screen changed.

He saw himself; at first it seemed a normal reflection. He was just looking at himself, looking in the mirror. Then he saw himself walking away from the mirror. 'Pretty obvious,' he thought, 'even I could have predicted that!'

Then the images started to change rapidly in a montage of views that went by too quickly to follow. 'Slow down,' he begged. The images slowed down, and he saw...

The future. His future, many futures it seemed, conflicting futures. All possibilities – as yet unfulfilled. He remembered Tamar's warning about knowing the future. "Knowing the future will make you afraid". He understood now. How do you make a decision, knowing that it could end up like that? Or how do you know how to make the right decision to avoid it? How do you know that you will not cause the very thing you want to avoid, by *trying* to avoid it?

He saw himself in a strange room bending over Tamar; she appeared to be dead.

He saw the world darken and the faces of people he had not yet met. All were grim and tired and hopeless. He saw himself fighting dark shadows in dark places. The future seemed full of faceless monsters.

He saw a grim old house that he did not recognise. It was shrouded in darkness.

And the face of a man he had never seen before, grinning at him in a knowing fashion and wielding a knife.

He saw himself... but no, he would never do that.

Finally, he saw his own death. It was gruesome. He still looked very young.

He turned away, shuddering. The whole thing was obviously a cheat. What he had seen before his own death was clearly impossible. Clearly – impossible!

'So, you didn't like my mirror then?' said a voice behind him. 'Well, it takes some people like that; everybody actually.'

'Kelon?'

'No.' The voice lilted with laughter.

Denny looked round about in vain; there was no one to be seen.

'Where are you?'

'Everywhere.'

But Denny had not spent so much time in Tamar's company for nothing. He snorted derisively. 'Cut the bull,' he snapped in Tamar's best scathing manner. 'Show yourself or bugger off.'

'Well!' said the girl appearing from out of nowhere. 'There's no need for that I'm sure.' She smoothed down her short pinstriped skirt and fluffed her hair. 'You only had to ask,' she added.

Denny took in her appearance without much surprise. Blonde, smartly dressed, glasses and a briefcase.

'Don't tell me,' he said, 'Girl Friday?'

'Quaite,' she agreed. In a voice that Denny would have described as "hoity toity"

'And that's your mirror is it?'

'Well, I'm in charge of it, you might say.'

'Really?' said Denny without much enthusiasm.

'You didn't like what it showed you, did you?'

Denny didn't answer. The girl did not seem to mind. She carried on. 'Of course you didn't, who would? But of course, it doesn't have to be that way.' She waited for a moment to let him speak, before carrying on. 'You see, those futures are predicted on where you are now, do you see?'

Denny shrugged. He had an idea where this was going, and he did not like it.

'If you carry on down this path, one of those futures is inevitable and they were all pretty nasty weren't they?'

'If they were even true,' Denny said, 'which I don't believe they were. I bet that's not the whole story.'

'Oh, they're true all right,' the girl giggled. 'And the thing is, I don't think it can be avoided now, whatever you do. You're not the sort of person to just give up on a thing like this, are you?'

'NO,' said Denny vehemently. 'So, why are we even talking about this?'

'She's in a lot of trouble right now,' said the girl, apparently changing tack. 'You saw what could happen to her?'

'How do you know all this?'

'It doesn't have to be this way,' said the girl softly. 'Wouldn't it have been better if none of this had ever happened? If you'd never opened the bottle at all? The future would be very different then, you know, and you'd never know the difference, none of this would ever have happened. You'd be safe; she'd be safe.'

'Well, I *did* open it,' Denny said. 'It's too late to change that now.'

'Not necessarily.'

For a moment, Denny was tempted; then he remembered where he was. These people, whoever they were, could not possibly have the power to do what the girl was suggesting. If even the Djinn did not have the power to turn back time, (and he had it on the very best authority that they did not) then he was sure that a mere sorceress did not. Besides, he could not betray Tamar like that. And, even if he could, he would not want to go back to his old life, not really. If those horrible futures were real, so what? If he was destined to die young, so what? And even if they were real, that did not mean that it would all be bad, did it? Or even that it would be the way it looked; it might not be the way it seemed. It was a trick probably. Like a photo album, you see the pictures, but that's not the whole story. Grandma's birthday party might look like a nice family occasion, but what the photos do not show is Uncle Bert getting drunk and insulting everyone or Auntie Ruth coming out of the closet and causing a furore and cousin Luke being sick on mum's best rug. He felt he was getting into a complicated metaphysical area here. Anyway, he decided that he would rather take his chances on the future as it was. Come to think of it, he did not have a choice did he? There was no going back. The only question now was why was this person trying to convince him that there was? Answer – to get him out of the way. Or was it some kind of test?

The girl was watching him, waiting for his answer; he disappointed her.

'I need to think about this,' he told her.

*

The problem, he decided, was simply this. Where would she actually send him if he agreed, assuming that it would not, in fact, be the past? Would she send him to Tamar? Unlikely, if it was a test, then he would have failed, obviously. And, if not, then they were trying to get rid of him. Although, if that were true, then presumably they were also trying to get rid of Tamar too, which meant he might end up wherever she was. But that might not necessarily be a good thing. They might both end up trapped together somewhere. It did not help that he had no idea where she was. Okay, so this was not so simple as he had thought. In fact, it was giving him a headache.

Okay, so, if they were trying to get rid of him, why not just leave him here? As far as he knew, there was no way out, was there? Perhaps there was. Actually there must be, if the mirror told the truth, because he had seen…

Suddenly he knew what to do.

~ Chapter Twenty Four ~

'I TAKE IT BACK, I take it back,' whimpered Tamar. Suddenly, when faced with the reality of hanging upside down fifty feet over a scorpion pit, the Houris did not seem so dreadful after all. She glanced over to the candle that was burning through the rope; she reckoned that she had two minutes at the most left before she fell.

Now, a scorpion pit should not hold too many terrors to a powerful Djinn, and the fifty foot drop? A mere bagatelle, surely? But when you are no longer a powerful Djinn but only a girl (and Tamar was beginning to fully realise that that was what she was in this place) a scorpion pit takes on a whole new aspect of dread.

Even so, she had wasted the last few minutes trying to use her powers to get her out of this mess; some habits are too deeply ingrained. Her mind knew the score, but her instincts had yet to catch up.

She tried to think through it. What would a normal person do in this situation? She wondered. But of course, normal people did not find themselves in this kind of situation very often, except on Japanese game shows. This line of thought was not terribly helpful.

What would James Bond do? No, wrong way. The correct question, right now, was what would Denny do? He was the closest thing to a normal person that she knew. She did not know. Well, he would not just hang here; he would try *something*. 'Maybe if I could haul myself upwards and climb the rope. Damn, I wish I'd thought of that sooner, it's going to break any second.'

She scanned the area. Was there a ledge she could grab? No, the pit was at the bottom of a sheer rock face, the sides of which climbed up far beyond the point at which she was hanging. It was too dark to see just how far. The only light was a dull red glow; she could not see where it came from, but it flickered as if it came from a distant fire. The whole effect was like being trapped in the bottom of a volcano.

She wondered idly what the point was. Surely the scorpions were surplus to requirements; the drop alone would kill anyone, wouldn't it? She was about to find out, the rope burned through, and she fell.

About three feet from the ground she stopped in mid-air, hanging horizontally like a cat burglar above a priceless diamond in a glass case.

She was trapped there, caught by the wrists and ankles by fine but strong threads that she had not even noticed before. Her first instinct was to try to get down, but since she could not manage it, this gave her time to reflect on the fact that this would probably be a lousy idea given the amount of scorpion activity going on immediately beneath her nose.

From the spider's web into the scorpion pit, hmm tough decision. Of course, she knew that the decision was not really hers. Sooner or later she would drop. And then the scorpions would get her.

She decided to try to get it over with; apart from anything else, just hanging here was humiliating. She tugged her right arm; the thread stretched like elastic and bounced back making her bob up and down like a puppet on a string. She came dangerously close to the scorpions at this point. The scorpions scuttled around her curiously, but she settled just out of reach again. She froze. However, this gave her an idea. It would be dangerous, but since she was going to die anyway...

She gently pulled her arm back towards her back pocket. The strings twanged and again she bobbed dangerously close to the ground. The scorpions gathered. She tried to ignore them, as she reached slowly but surely into her pocket. She was now hanging at a most peculiar angle with her feet higher than her head and her body twisted in mid –air. But it was working; she very slowly and carefully eased out of her back pocket, a nail file.

All women carry nail files whether they need them or not. Not many women ever think they are going to need them to escape from a deadly trap in a sorceress's castle, however...

She allowed herself to settle into position again, forcing herself to wait until she was still and out of reach. No point in rushing it or taking risks; there was plenty of time.

She noticed a scorpion on her arm and thrashed suddenly to get it off, sending her into a frantic spin, which removed the offending arachnid, but put her in a position to be assailed by two more. Okay, don't do that again, she froze. Once she had stopped moving she concentrated on trying to use the nail file to free her legs, ignoring the feeling on her head, that told her that there was definitely a third one nestling in her hair, urrrgh.

It was extraordinarily difficult to reach her own ankles, while tied up by the wrists. Eventually, she flipped herself over, so that she was facing upwards, twisting the threads around her legs as she did so. She immediately found that she did not like being in this position at all. Not being able to see the ground was far worse than being able to see it, considering what was scurrying about on it. She tried not to think about it and eased herself, by means of pulling herself along her trouser legs, into a sitting position. This took a tedious amount of time, because the slightest movement, sent her bouncing and spinning around. But she stuck at it. Now she could reach her ankles to cut them free. A nail file is not the sharpest tool; even a pair of nail scissors would have been better, but she stuck at it, sawing away diligently, until eventually, her right foot came free with a twang. What the hell she thought she was going to do once she got all of her free is anybody's guess. She was not thinking that far ahead. She pulled her dangling foot up out of reach, hanging grimly on to her tethered left foot to stop herself from being pulled backwards by the threads still attached to her wrists. She then gingerly lifted her right foot and rested it on top of her left one. When she managed to free her left foot, both legs dropped to the ground; she was standing, tethered by her wrists. Within seconds, scorpions swarmed up her legs.

Without even thinking about it, Tamar grabbed the threads around her wrists and hauled herself up as far as she could. She swarmed up the thread with difficulty since she was still attached to it, and managed to pull herself out of just reach, before she could not get any further without being hopelessly tangled up. Worse, in her scramble, she had dropped the nail file.

Still, she was safe for now, and was pretending, quite convincingly, to herself, that this was what she had intended to do all along. And was trying, fairly successfully, to ignore the fact that she was, in fact, no better off than she had been before all the aerial gymnastics. If anything, the situation was worse, she was now hanging from only two threads instead of four, and was, therefore, likely to fall that much sooner. The threads gave a creak as if to reinforce this detail.

After the longest minute and a half of her life (and that is saying something when you are talking about a person who has had to sit through one of Denny's songs) she decided to try and get down. Maybe if she landed with a thump, and started kicking, the scorpions would scatter and give her chance to find a way out. She would head toward the fiery glow. Animals did not like fire she seemed to remember.

This was patently the most ludicrous plan since some fool said, "pet crocodiles, what a marvellous idea". And, deep down, she was aware of this fact, but she chose to ignore it. After all, what else was there to do?

The only problem was how to get down. Of course, Sir Isaac Newton had solved this particular problem for her. If she just waited long enough, it would come into operation; problem solved. As if to remind her of this, the thread creaked threateningly again.

Then she fell. The scorpions scattered; this was a heartening development. She leapt to her feet and started kicking, but there were too many of them, and now she was making them angry.

She ran. Out of the corner of her eye, she spotted a small, shiny object on the ground. Denny's lighter. One of the many things he carried about with him (but never used) on the principle that it "might come in handy". It would never come in handier than now, she thought, if she could only get hold of it.

She kicked and stomped her way to it, then took a deep breath and plunged her hand into the fray of outraged creatures and grabbed it.

The floor was littered, rather chillingly, with large bones; she grabbed one of these and tore her shirt off to wrap around the end to make an impromptu torch. Fuel, what did she have for fuel? She patted her pockets frantically and found nothing but a small bottle of hugely expensive and rather pungent perfume. Well, it was better than nothing – a can of lighter fluid was probably too much to ask for.

She was backed against the wall of the pit by this time with scores of infuriated scorpions crowding around her ankles. It was something of a miracle, she thought, that she had not been stung yet. But every time she kicked them away, they seemed to lose their minds and turn on each other. There were a number of dead bodies lying around the floor of the pit already. Not the most co-operative of God's creatures obviously. On the other hand, there were hundreds of them; she could not rely on them killing each other off before at least one of them got her. Hundreds of them, and only one of her, it was just about the arithmetic really.

She poured a little of the perfume onto the rags of her shirt and held the lighter to it. It went up with a satisfying "whump!", so far, so good.

She waved the torch in front of her, low to the ground and cleared a space in front of her and walked cautiously forward crying, 'back, back!' like a crazed lion tamer.

In this way, she managed to get several feet into the centre of the pit. She was trying to edge her way toward the glow, where she guessed, or rather, fervently hoped there was an opening which was letting the light in. The scorpions would not follow her in there she was certain. Probably for the same reason that it would not be a brilliant idea for her to go in either – the fact that the cavern beyond was on fire. Still it was the only way out, so she was disappointed when she was forced to turn back by the intense heat. Disappointed, but not really surprised.

She gritted her teeth; she had gone too far now to give up. She made her way back to the centre of the cavern and looked up at the threads still hanging there. The ones that had been around her legs still hung low enough to reach, maybe she could climb up to the ledge around the top, and swing herself onto it. It was worth a try surely.

As she swung herself up with the torch held precariously between her teeth, she did not want to think where it had been, she dropped the bottle of perfume; it smashed spilling a positive flood of perfume onto the ground below. The scorpions scattered. 'No taste,' she thought. 'That's expensive stuff that is.' Then she thought, 'oh what the hell,' and dropped the torch before the perfume seeped away into the earth. The ground was as dry as tinder and littered with dry sticks and old bones, and it went up like a bonfire immediately. Tamar laughed to see the panicking scorpions flee as the fire spread.

'Die, suckers,' she crowed. Within seconds, the whole floor of the pit was a raging inferno. '*Oh hell,*' she began to climb frenetically, as the flames leapt higher.

Once she was high enough to feel safe she was exultant. She had done it, all by herself, without magic. She had never done anything brave without her magic. She had never, therefore, really done anything brave at all. She felt giddy with triumph. It was a real accomplishment for her. She did not even think about the string of astonishing co-incidences that had allowed her to achieve it.

She looked up. If there was a roof to which this thread was attached, it was too far up to be seen. She climbed a little further up, and just dangled for a while, watching the flames consume everything in sight.

Then she started to climb.

~ Chapter Twenty Five~

DENNY SURVEYED his new surroundings with a certain amount of complacency. It had been all too easy in the end. He was sure he could work out the next step. It had been a stroke of pure genius, he smugly felt, to go back to the mirror and see what the future held in regard to his escape from the desert island, and then just make sure that the future he had seen came true.

This challenge, he felt, would be easy by comparison.

It had been ludicrously simple in the end. So simple, that he was sure he would have thought of it in the end. Which when you think about it, had to be the case because if he never would have thought of it, then it could not have been in his future. In fact, what he actually did had to do with his decision to look in the mirror again in the first place. When he slowed down the images, he saw himself using the mirror as a portal into the future. So that is what he did. Confused? Denny was. Whenever he tried to work out how it had worked it sent his brain spinning. (But it had worked, that was the main thing.) He had a sneaking suspicion that it really should not have worked. He just could not get his head round it. Surely you could not just step into a future that had not been created yet, without first taking the steps to create that future? If there was a point in the future where he had arrived in this place, then surely there had to have been steps taken in order to arrive at that point. Somehow he had taken a shortcut. This was hard to think about, but it had been easy to do.

Be that as it may, and he would leave all this conundrum solving to a more convenient moment, he was now standing in a large circular room, with doors all around it. The walls were stone and the doors were typical castle doors, in heavy oak with large black studs hammered into them. Between each door was a large flaming torch in a wall bracket. The floor was made up of large, uneven flags. So, apart from the multiplicity of doors, it was a typical castle room. Denny suspected that this room was the staging area for the rotating hallway trick he and Tamar had been treated to earlier. The hub of the whole operation. He was getting close; he could feel it. And that meant that there was a strong probability that Tamar was behind one of those doors. Well, since he had no way of knowing which one, he would just have to take them in turn. There were around fifty doors, and since the room was circular with no distinguishing features anywhere and the doors were all alike and unmarked. Denny decided that he would have to mark each door himself as he tried them. The torches would come in handy for that. He opened the first door. It opened onto an empty room. Denny had not been prepared for that. He closed the door, and then, on a whim, opened it again. It was as he had thought. This time it opened to the outside air, some sort of turret at the top of a tower. There were armed soldiers leaning on their halberds and having a quiet smoke. Damn. He closed the door hurriedly before they spotted him. Damn, damn, DAMN. He opened it again, this time it was a garden. Denny sighed. This was going to take a lot longer than he had first thought.

* * *

Tamar had decided to give up and accept her fate. She was never going to get out of here. She had climbed up the twanging threads with immense difficulty. She was hot and sweaty and tired. She was fed up and discouraged, but she had kept on going for an hour or more, riding a wave of victory. This feeling had been slowly ebbing away as her strength grew less. And now, just when the ledge was finally in sight, she had almost fallen, and when she tried to save herself, she got herself so hopelessly tangled up in the threads that she was now pretty much immobilized, and was now hanging there, like a bag of washing. It was over. She gave up.

She had been hanging around for about half an hour more, when she saw a yellow shaft of light appear off to the left of her. She swung herself round, bobbing and swaying to see where it had come from. There, in the side of the cliff, was an open doorway, how was it that she had not noticed it before? She squinted into the light and made out a shadowy figure standing in the doorway. It was shaking. As her eyes grew used to the light, she could make out a face. She fixed the figure with a baleful eye. 'You took your bloody time, didn't you?' she said.

It was Denny, and he was shaking with laughter.

~ Chapter Twenty six ~

'IT WAS AMAZING,' Tamar was saying, excitedly. 'I mean I was afraid, really afraid, you know, but I did it anyway, just like you would have. I mean I think I know now, a little bit, anyway, what it must be like to be you – to be human. You know I've seen humans do things that they must have been terrified to do, now that I come to think about it. I've seen you do stuff, you know, that you must have… anyway, I never knew what it felt like to be afraid before. It's terrible, really terrible; well you know that, obviously. I'll tell you something; I'll never take my magic for granted again. I mean, my God… are you listening?'

'Of course, I was just wondering where we go from here.' He was gazing distractedly at the doors that surrounded them.

'Oh – well, anyway, I was never so glad to see anyone in my whole life as when I saw you.'

'You could have fooled me.'

'Oh, yes, well. You *were* laughing at me. How did you find me anyway, where were you?'

Denny told her what had happened to him.

'It took me ages to find the right door,' he finished. 'And now, I'm wondering which door our sorceress is hiding behind, if any.'

* * *

When Denny had found her, Tamar had been perilously close to falling, although she had not been aware of it. The thread above her was just about ready to snap. Denny had not wasted any time. Since he was not actually carrying a length of rope in his pockets, their supply of convenient coincidences having apparently run out for the time being, he had to improvise. Keeping the tone light, so as not to alarm her, he had suggested, casually that she might try swinging toward him, while praying that the thread did not snap under the pressure. He carefully did not mention this concern to Tamar, but instead made jokes about how Lara Croft never found herself in situations like this. He then kept her occupied by explaining who Lara Croft actually was. By the time she understood, and had voiced the opinion that she sounded like a truly awful fabrication, Tamar had managed to swing herself more or less into Denny's waiting grasp. It was the "less" part that almost caused the fatality when the thread finally gave up and snapped. Fortunately, due to the elasticity of the threads, she was bouncing slightly as she swung; just enough to throw her clear of the chasm and land her with a thump on top of Denny in a classic comedy finish.

They were now both feeling bruised and tired. But, whereas Denny was also feeling disgruntled, Tamar was exuberant.

'Well,' she said now, 'what kind of negative attitude is that? Of course, she's behind one of them. She has to be. I thought you said this room led everywhere in this place.'

'In theory,' Denny corrected her. 'Only in theory. I mean I don't really know, do I?'

'Oh,' Tamar was briefly subdued by this information. 'Well, never mind,' she brightened up. 'We should just pick a door and see where it takes us. Get back in the game, so to speak, don't you think?'

'Hmm,' Denny was dubious. 'I think that might be a bit dangerous, and will you please stop dancing around like a mad pixie, I'm trying to think.'

'Oh don't be so grumpy; what's the *matter* with you?'

Denny debated telling her about seeing her lying cold and still in the "Mirror of Futures". It was preying on his mind.

'Nothing,' he said, eventually. I just want to get this over with.' There was no point worrying her, he decided.

'Is it something you saw in that mirror?' she said, shrewdly.

'No, no, nothing like that,' he lied.

Fortunately, at that moment, Tamar was distracted. 'Look at that,' she said.

'What?'

'That door, there,' she pointed. 'Is it me, or does it look different from the others?'

Denny peered. 'You, know, I think you're right,' he said, after a minute.

The difference was subtle; the door just looked slightly larger and deeper set than the others. Somehow, perhaps because it was deeper in shadow than the others, it looked more sinister than the others, more dreadful in some undefined but yet definite way. The more they looked at it, the more certain they became that it was different from the other doors in the room. That it hid something significant. Or someone. They looked at each other with raised eyebrows.

Tamar voiced the thought. 'In there, then?'

'After you,' said Denny, and this time he meant it.

~ Chapter Twenty Seven ~

THEY FOUND themselves in a plush study. There was a monumental fireplace with a fire blazing away like a small sun, miles and miles of bookshelves, two leather sofas and a large imposing desk, behind which sat a large, imposing man in a dark suit, backlit by a vast, striking window.

'Well done,' he said, standing up. 'I hardly expected you to get this far – Guards.' He snapped his fingers. Denny spun round and found himself face to face with five more men. These were dressed in black pyjamas and hoods and were wielding large swords.

'Ninjas?' he said.

'Appropriate I thought,' said the man. 'Kill them,' he added to the guards.

He addressed himself to Tamar. 'I'm afraid, my dear that as you will have already discovered, your magic is of no use to you here. You'll have to rely on *him*.' He threw a contemptuous glance at Denny.

Often, when you are dreaming, you will find yourself doing things that you would normally never even contemplate. What happened next, Denny later said, was a bit like that.

Denny, mysteriously enough, was grinning. 'You have to feel sorry for them really,' he said, twisting the sword out of the hand of the nearest "ninja" and kicking him out of the way with surprising dexterity.

'I mean, the odds are against them, aren't they?'

'Are you out of your mind?' screeched Tamar. 'Or didn't you ever learn to count? There's five of them.'

'Four,' said Denny, nodding briefly at the one who was whimpering on the floor.

He spun the sword. 'Anyway, that's what I mean. Come on, five trained guards attack one unarmed man. They're gonna get creamed, everybody knows that.'

The guards were hanging back uncertainly. 'Am I right boys?' He nodded to them.

They looked at each other nervously, as if they did indeed know this to be true. Two of them dropped their sword arms.

'I bet no one ever asked them if they wanted to – did they boys?'

They shook their heads vehemently.

'Still, you haven't really got a choice, have you? So come on guys, let's dance.' He thrust out the sword, fighting stance. Two of the guards moved tentatively towards him.

'Three – two – one,' muttered Denny under his breath.

'KILL HIM,' shouted the man.

'Ah,' said Denny, 'there it is.'

'He's just one weedy boy. What are you good for? He's just trying to confuse you.'

The "ninjas" charged.

'Uh oh,' said Tamar and averted her face.

'That's,' (thrust) 'the,' (parry) 'point,' said Denny, dispatching the first one with a well-placed thrust under the ribs.

'One.' He moved into position, to take on the next one.

'The,' (slice) 'weedier the,' (kick) 'better.' He sent the sword whirling out of the hand of the second one, and moved like greased lightning around to face the other two.

'Had enough yet?' he taunted. He was not even out of breath.

Tamar was staring now, open-mouthed. The guards submitted to the inevitable and charged. Denny somersaulted gracefully over their heads. As he rolled, he picked up the discarded sword and bounced to his feet. He advanced on the guards twirling a sword in each hand, wearing the kind of smile usually seen beneath a fin slicing through the water.

The guards did not move a muscle; behind Denny, "ninja" two was up again. He aimed a slash at Denny's head, which Denny parried, behind his back without even looking round. "Ninja" two dropped the sword wringing his hand, Denny thrust backward in a smooth motion, keeping his eyes on "ninjas" three and four. "Ninja" two dropped to the floor making bubbling noises.

'Two,' said Denny. 'Feeling lucky?'

"Ninja" three sliced at his legs, he jumped, and the sword passed harmlessly under his feet. "Ninja" four thrust at him, and he turned the jump into a backward somersault.

Tamar had a childish urge to catcall, 'Nyah nah nah nyah nah.'

Denny spun and sliced at "ninja" three, who was coming at him from the side and took his head off. He came out of the spin pointing the sword at "ninja" fours throat, "ninja" four raised his sword just as Tamar brought a vase crashing down on his head; he slumped. "Ninja" five, the first to go down, stirred and Tamar kicked him in the head.

Denny smiled; Tamar shrugged ruefully. 'I thought it was about time I did something.'

The man behind the desk was clapping slowly in his best sarcastic manner. 'Well done,' he drawled.

Denny dropped the sword with a clatter, and shook his hand as if there was something sticky on it. He had gone a little pale.

Tamar turned on the man behind the desk. 'You're not Kelon. We ...'

'No,' said the man. 'I am just the – ahem welcoming party you might say.'

'You might,' agreed Denny, 'if English wasn't your first language.' He turned to Tamar. 'Do you get the feeling this Kelon character's not too keen on visitors? I wonder if everybody has to go through this?'

'Somehow I doubt it,' she replied dryly.

'You are correct,' said the man. 'You may not see Kelon.'

'The hell you say,' exploded Denny. 'Who's going to stop us? – You?' He picked up the discarded sword and waved it threateningly.

'Yeah,' Tamar joined in. 'We didn't go through all this just to turn round and go home. Thanks for a pleasant visit and all that.'

The man appeared to consider. After all, a man with a sword is a man with a sword, and this one had just polished off five of his best trained guards. There was probably some destiny at work here. In any case, sometimes you just had to say 'I don't get paid enough for this stuff.'

He shrugged. 'That way,' he said, pointing to a door off to the left of him. 'Third door on the right – go through the magic mirror.' Denny lowered the sword. 'That's more like it.'

* * *

'How did you do that?' asked Tamar, as they made their way down a corridor that was dimly lit with candles.

'The fighting, you mean?'

'Obviously.'

'I don't know, it just seemed to happen. I just knew I could do it; it was like I was following a script.'

'So, no fencing lessons aged twelve that you forgot to mention?'

'Who, me? You forget I'm a nerd. Not to mention a tremendous physical coward.'

'You haven't been afraid once since we got here.'

Denny pondered. 'You know, you're right. It's like I'm a different person in here.'

'Well I for one am glad of it. I didn't realise how much I'd come to rely on my magic. I guess I never thought I'd have to do without it. I'm not making a very good show am I?'

'You're doing okay. You got me away from the Houris, and you survived the scorpion pit.'

'Just barely, and only thanks to you in the end.

'You did really well to get as far as you did, in there.'

'You're still you after all,' she said, 'kind.' And she gave him a smile that was almost shy.

He blushed. 'Er, okay. Tamar?'

'Yes.'

'Why did you bring that with you?'

'What, this?' Tamar said demurely, glancing at the sword that Denny had left behind. She had gone back for it at the last minute.

'I just thought it might come in handy.'

'You know how to sword fight?'

'No, but you apparently do.'

'I don't think…' they both turned as they heard the sound of many running feet behind them. 'Oh damn it'

'That swine!' screeched Tamar. 'He's sent more of them after us.' She tossed the sword to Denny. 'One for you, I think.'

This time there were about ten of them, and they did not seem too keen to approach. They stopped short about ten feet away from Denny's swinging sword. It soon became apparent why. This time, they were going for a different approach. Without warning one of them hurled a throwing star at Denny. The twist was that it caught fire in the air. Denny fielded it with the sword and it hurtled back toward the guards. One of them, not the one who had thrown it, caught it. He caught it, unfortunately for him, full in the chest. After letting out a thin wail, he unexpectedly exploded.

'One down,' muttered Tamar.

'Here we go again,' sighed Denny. 'Look out, it's about to get worse.'

He was right. The remaining guards all took aim. Denny backed away, but there was nowhere to go. The guards seemed to have an unlimited supply of the damn things which all burst into flame when they hit a certain velocity. Suddenly the air was filled with blazing throwing stars. Denny raised the sword and swung. He fielded every one, despite the fact that this was patently impossible, and sent them back at the guards with pinpoint accuracy. Each time he hit one, the poor guy immediately exploded. Every time this happened, the remaining men howled with rage and redoubled their attack. And there were more, coming up behind them, as Denny could dimly see through the smoke.

The sword was moving so fast now; it was little more than a blur. Right up until the moment that it was moving so fast that it too, caught fire. Evidently it shared this facility with the other weapons that the guards used, although, Denny was not to figure this out until later. He never even flinched.

'Now that's what I'm talking about,' he shouted triumphantly, and whacked another flaming missile, which exploded as it hit the sword in a huge ball of flame. 'Oops.'

Denny considered his options for a thirtieth of a second; then he held the flaming sword out in front of him, and charged through the smoking acrid air.

The guards took one look at him and ran.

'See,' said Tamar smugly.

* * *

The sword went out, and Denny dropped it.

'We should keep that,' Tamar said. 'A flaming sword, what couldn't we do with that?'

Denny considered arguing, but found that he could not be bothered. Anyway, she had a point. She had been right to bring it along in the first place after all.

'Okay,' he said, handing her the now extinguished sword. 'But you can carry it.'

'Okay.' Tamar looked pleased. 'I wonder what makes it do that.'

'I've no idea, does it matter?'

'Well, I think it's brilliant.'

'I gathered,' Denny responded dryly.

'We look like a witch's coven,' giggled Tamar suddenly, apropos of nothing. 'You look like a devil looming through the smoke.

'Devil yourself,' said Denny amiably, ruffling her hair. 'Come on you, the door's that way, I think.'

'Denny?'

'Yes?'

'You do know that your hair is on fire?'

* * *

'It's in here,' said Denny. They pushed open the door; the room beyond was bare except for a full-length mirror in a gilt frame fastened to the wall and two flickering candles in sconces on either side of it.

'More magic mirrors,' said Tamar. 'Wicked Queen complex, do you think? I'm beginning to feel like Snow White.'

'So, who does that make me?'

'Dunno, is there a dwarf called Scruffy?'

'And they do seem to go in for the flickering candles here don't they?' said Denny, ignoring this. 'They seem to prefer them to putting in windows. Who lives here for God's sake – Dracula?'

'Well, this is it,' she said. 'Finally!'

They grasped hands and stepped forward. A trapdoor in the floor opened up beneath them, and they went shooting down a tunnel and landed on a heap of straw in what appeared to be a dungeon.

'You've got to be kidding,' wailed Denny.

~ Chapter Twenty Eight ~

'WHERE'S THE old man?' asked Denny after scanning their prison.

'*What* old man?' asked Tamar, perplexed.

'The one who's been down here for decades, patiently digging his way to freedom with a soup spoon. And now, because he's on his last legs he hands on his spoon to us – along with the treasure map.'

'Oh, *that* old man. I don't think there is one.'

'There's *always* an old man in a dungeon. It's in the brochure.'

'I think we're on our own this time.'

'When aren't we?'

The heap of straw stirred. 'Ooof,' it said.

Denny and Tamar jumped up, and out of the straw struggled an old man with a straggly beard dressed in rags. He was wheezing hard.

'What do you mean by it?' he complained, 'landing on me like a herd of buffalo. I was asleep.'

'I'll be damned,' said Denny.

'Language,' snapped the old man.

'Sorry,' said Denny. 'Um, you haven't, by any chance, been digging a tunnel out of here for the last thirty years or so, have you?'

'Tunnel?' said the old man. 'No, why would I dig a tunnel?' His eyes were twinkling.

'Figures,' said Denny gloomily.

'What do I need a tunnel for?' continued the old man, 'when I can use the door?'

'Door?' said Denny and Tamar together. Two pairs of eyes scanned the walls fruitlessly – there was no door.

'Mad!' said Tamar. 'Poor old thing. Being down here, it's turned his mind.'

'Mad, am I?' snapped the old man.

'Nothing wrong with his hearing anyway.' said Denny, 'Pardon us,' he added, 'but what door?'

'What?' said the old man, cupping his hand behind his ear, 'speak up.'

He laughed at Denny's exasperated expression. 'Ah, I'm jest funnin' with ye.' He said. 'I'm no' sure I wants to tell ye. Ev'ry time ah shows people the door, they nev'r comes back. It gits lonely down here.'

'We have something important we have to do,' said Denny. 'How would it be if we promise to come back and visit you? Would you show us the door then?'

'You won't,' said the old man stubbornly. 'They always says that, but they nev'r comes back – no nev'r.' He looked at them out of rheumy eyes.

Tamar pulled Denny to her. 'Why are you humouring him?' she whispered. 'If there was a door, why would he still be here? It's ridiculous; he's obviously crackers.'

'Why does it have to make sense?' objected Denny. 'Since when are *you* so literal? Besides, it's our only chance. There's no window, the grate's too high and we have no tools strong enough to dig through a stone wall – a stone – wall ...' He broke off.

'What?' she followed his gaze. 'What *is* he doing?'

'He appears to be drawing a door on the wall,' said Denny, clearly perplexed. And indeed the man was drawing a door on the wall with a shaky hand, using a small stone.

'I told you,' said Tamar. 'Crackers.'

'I create,' said the old man proudly.

Tamar and Denny looked at each other and shrugged. Tamar shook her head.

'Software,' said the old man, obscurely as far as Denny was concerned.

But for Tamar the flashbulb popped. 'Of course,' she said. 'That's how *everything* in here is created. They took an empty file and created new software. In theory, we can too.' She looked questioningly at the old man. He nodded gleefully. 'Yes, yes, I create – see,' he pointed at the door, no longer a shaky chalk outline, but a proper door.

'Amazing,' breathed Denny.

The old man tugged at the door. 'Sticks a bit,' he muttered. 'There.' The door opened into a tunnel, which climbed upwards. 'Off you go then,' he said. 'Crazy old man, eh? I showed you, didn't I? Heh, heh, heh.'

Denny and Tamar scrambled for the door. 'Thank you,' said Denny, poking his head back round the door. 'Sure you won't come with us?'

'No, thanks, I just ate,' said the old man obscurely. Denny shook his head.

* * *

The old man's parting remark was explained when after climbing for what seemed an eternity they came out of the tunnel into a large kitchen.

'I guess if you're going to create a tunnel out of a dungeon, it may as well be to somewhere useful,' Tamar observed.

'About that,' said Denny. 'Could we have been doing that all along, making doorways and stuff?'

'I suppose so, I never thought of it. I kept thinking of this as a real place; you have to admit it's pretty convincing.'

'It might have come in handy that's all. It might explain a few things too.' He looked thoughtful.

The staff of the kitchen ignored them as they passed through, and the green baize door opened out onto the same dim corridor that they had passed through already.

'That's convenient,' said Denny. Somebody had to say it, and it was Denny who did.

'Maybe it's not a very long program,' said Tamar.

* * *

They found the room again easily enough. The trapdoor still gaped open in the floor, and they skirted warily around it and stood in front of the mirror. It seemed absurdly easy after all the trials they had passed through.

'Oh no!' wailed Tamar.

'What?' said Denny, alarmed.

'Just look at me. I look like Courtney Love.'

She did indeed look pretty dishevelled. Her clothes were torn and dirty, and so was her face. She had a cut over one eye and all her nails were broken. But the biggest torment to her mind was... 'My hair!' she wailed, 'look at it.' Birds would have disdained to nest in it. She looked like the bride of Frankenstein after a nasty encounter with a combine harvester, all this nor helped by the extra adornment of clumps of straw sticking out at odd angles, making her look like a crazed hillbilly.

'What?' Denny was annoyed. 'That's it? Honestly, I ask you, is this the time?' He softened. 'Look, I don't look any better.' He gestured to his own torn clothes and tangled hair.

'I can't see any difference,' she said.

'Concentrate,' he snapped, offended. 'Magic mirror – *not* for admiring yourself in. What do we do?'

'It doesn't look magic,' she forced herself back to the matter in hand. 'It's not shimmering or anything.' She touched it. 'Seems solid enough. Perfectly ordinary, hmm.' She closed her eyes and walked into it. 'Ouch!'

'Denny tried not to laugh, unsuccessfully. They stood and looked at it. They looked at it some more. It completely failed to do anything magic at all.

'It's not a flaming magic mirror at all!' said Denny. 'I should have known; the whole point of sending us to this room was that,' he pointed to the trapdoor.

The logic of this seemed indisputable.

'Let's go back and beat it out of him,' suggested Tamar, now thoroughly back on form. Denny nodded; they turned to go, and then Tamar snapped her fingers. 'Wait,' she said. She pushed the mirror hard on one side of the gilt frame. The whole thing spun like a revolving door.

'How did you know?'

'I didn't, I just thought, that trapdoor had to be protecting *something,* and if it wasn't a magic mirror, then perhaps it was just a hokey old hidden door. I used to watch "Scooby Doo" a lot,' she added, as if this was some kind of explanation.

They walked into a dark chamber, stepping carefully over a large pile of dust; somehow it just felt wrong to walk on it. Facing them was a large ornate throne and sitting on it was a tall, imposing woman who looked, for some reason, extremely nervous. Kelon at last.

~ Chapter Twenty Nine ~

DENNY COULD NOT think of anything to say. Probably because, on some level, he had never expected to get this far, and it wasn't nearly over yet. Suddenly he felt tired; he just wanted to sleep for a week. He thought about where he was; the whole thing was ludicrous. Here he was, standing in a mystic chamber, in a castle, in a deleted file of the universe! With a dishevelled Djinn, a sorceress and a pile of dust that he could have sworn was looking at him. How in the hell had he got here?

Tamar, on the other hand, was suddenly animated. She was glaring at Kelon with a disbelieving look on her face. 'Nice outfit,' she said sneeringly. Her face was just inches from that of the sorceress. She strolled around to the back of the throne and put her hands on the woman's shoulders and leaned over to speak in her ear. 'I'm not sure it's really you though.' She slid round to face her again. 'I suppose I shouldn't be narrow-minded.' She took the woman's chin in her hand. 'But I didn't know you swung that way.'

'Hello Tamar,' sighed the sorceress. 'I suppose I should have known you would catch up with me in the end.'

'I can't believe you thought this "disguise" would fool me.'

Denny had a sense of time rushing by, a feeling that they had suddenly jumped to the end, and he had missed some steps. He tried to catch up. 'Who ...?' he started. 'Do you know each other?'

Tamar smiled. 'This,' she said, jerking a thumb at the sorceress, 'is Askphrit – the νόθος' She turned to Askphrit 'I always knew I'd know you again, no matter what you looked like. Although I have to admit, I never expected to find you "*en travesti*".'

'I knew you would too,' said Askphrit resignedly, 'Why do you think I tried so hard to keep you away?'

'Yeah? Well you lose.'

'It was inevitable I suppose. What I did, well … you were never just going to let it go, were you? I should have known there was no point trying to hide from you. But I had to try all the same.'

'So, why the drag? – And for God's sake, *change*. We've found you now.'

Askphrit changed back into himself. 'The "drag" as you call it, was to confuse the trail in case you ever came looking for me. I must confess. I never anticipated that you would come looking for *Kelon*. A miscalculation it would seem.'

Denny suddenly found his voice. 'You tried to kill us,' he exploded.

'It was you or me,' said Askphrit mildly. 'That was how I saw it.'

'Will your magic work in here?' Denny asked Tamar.

'A wish will,' said Tamar grimly. 'Why else would he try so hard to keep us away? A wish is technically *your* power you see. Well, your will anyway. He can't block that; no matter how much he wants to.'

They looked at each other and nodded.

'Okay,' said Denny. 'Let's do it.'

'Know what to say?' she asked. 'Denny nodded shortly. The air was thick with destiny; it felt as if time had slowed down – stopped – reversed. The room vanished, and they were caught up in a vortex, a tornado of time. Destiny likes to do things properly. They were back at the beginning – Tamar's bedroom – Ancient Greece. For some reason, Denny did not need to be told. It seemed fitting. When his head had stopped spinning, Denny took a deep breath.

'I wish,' he said. 'That Kelon here, the sorceress, formerly known as Askphrit the Djinn was a human – a mere mortal – there.' He breathed out and looked questioningly at Tamar, who nodded and smiled. It was done.

'It worked?' asked Denny anxiously.

'Of course – hey shall we just kill him? – only joking.'

Askphrit looked resigned. 'All right, so I'm human. I get it; I'm you and you're me – so what?'

'Denny?' she smiled. 'This is it, last wish.'

Askphrit looked worried, as light dawned. '*Last* wish?'

'Got the bottle?' Denny asked.

'Right here.' She waved it threateningly at Askphrit, who cringed.

'I think I'd rather you just killed me,' he said.

'Yes,' she agreed. 'I expect you would.'

'It won't work,' said Askphrit desperately.

'Then why are you sweating?' asked Tamar wickedly. Then, abruptly, she froze.

'Oh no – not now!'

Denny did not even have to ask. 'Where? How? How can it be here? *I'm* here.'

A dark cloud had gathered and was advancing on Tamar. Askphrit laughed.

'Just do it!' she croaked. 'If it kills me, it'll be too late.'

'I wish Askphrit was a Djinn again,' shouted Denny. And so he was. He howled with rage as the shackles appeared on his wrists. Denny thrust out the bottle, and Askphrit started to dissolve. Denny ignored him.

'Tamar!' The cloud had enveloped her and she was held floating in the air, helpless. It started to sparkle; it would have looked pretty if it had not been so menacing. Then, suddenly it vanished; she dropped to the ground. Denny ran to her and lifted her head into his lap. It was just as he had seen it. 'Please don't be dead.'

She opened her eyes. 'Okay, if you insist.'

'Oh, thank God – it let you go?'

Tamar had other things on her mind. 'You got him?'

Denny pointed to the bottle 'Safe and sound.'

'That explains it,' she said. 'I'm human again.'

Denny gaped, not for the first time he was lost for words. Of all the possible outcomes, this was the last thing he had expected.

He found his voice. 'How? What? Are you sure?'

'Pretty sure.'

'But – you look exactly the same.'

'I do?' She was unreasonably pleased about this. 'I suppose it's like my mother said. If you make a face – you'll stick like it.' *

'But – why are you human at all? I don't understand.'

'Neither do I?'

'The natural order has been restored.' As neither of them had said this, they spun round (as they tended to do rather a lot). The voice appeared to have come from a large pile of dust.

'...?'

'Oh, sorry,' said the pile of dust, and it formed into a small spiralling dust-cloud that became a dapper little man standing there brushing off his sleeves as if it were the most natural thing in the world. He looked vaguely familiar.

'Perhaps I should explain,' he said. 'Pick up that bottle and we'll go back.' He produced a laptop from his briefcase.

Back in the chamber of the now former sorceress Denny asked. 'Why were you a pile of dust?'

---

* Yes, mothers really have been saying things like this since the dawn of time

'Hmm, yes she, I mean he, did that a lot. Nasty temper.'

'And you let him? I mean you obviously ...'

'I couldn't let him know who I really was, or what I was up to.'

'And who *are* you? And what *were* you up to?'

'Righting a wrong,' said the little man. 'Took me long enough too. Finding you,' he pointed at Denny, 'was the hardest part. Or rather waiting for you to be born.'

'ME? But I'm just ... you could look me up in "Who's nobody".'

'On the contrary,' said the little man. 'You are a direct descendent of Hector of Troy a great hero and an inveterate meddler and do-gooder, well the whole family were really, you may have heard of a more recent member of the family "Sir Ector?" Very big in medieval times, no? Well heroics are in the blood.'

'I *knew* it,' said Tamar. 'Well, not about your antecedents but...'

Denny was shaking his head. 'My family ...' he began. Then he changed his mind.

'Why is Tamar human again?'

'I think I'd better tell you the whole story,' said the little man. 'Sit down, sit down.'

They sat.

'First of all, my name is Clive, and I am a – well a sort of clerk I suppose, I keep the files in order, I'm not the only one of course. There are hundreds nay, thousands of us.

'Anyway, when this reprobate,' here he indicated the bottle. 'Pulled his little stunt, well, you've no idea of the chaos, I was exceedingly angry about it. It took us ages to sort it all out. Of course, we did it in the end, and that should have been the end of it, but I was still very upset. It wasn't really right anyway; things were still out of order, and the longer he was roaming around free, the more things went wrong, oh the extra work it caused... Well, I decided to put it right you see? It was a complicated business of course; finding him was easy enough. I just followed the trail of destruction in the fabric of reality, but persuading him to set up in a disused file, that was harder. The becoming female thing was all his idea, but perhaps it was to be expected. I did play on his fears rather strongly to get him to do it.

'So, then I changed my appearance and offered my services, I suggested the quest, since he was going to need magical associates, helping those who could later help him was a convenient way to make a living; a tried and tested method, and I knew it would appeal to him. And, in time, I took over the handling of the clues. Once I'd done all that, I set out to bring you here, and for that, I needed him.' He indicated Denny. 'Of course, it was a gamble – you were right young man, about free will; you could have done nothing, but I had a feeling about you. You heroic types are all so predictable. – You know,' he mused. 'I thought you'd be taller.' He shook himself. 'So, where was I? Yes, I set up the plan, guided you if you will. Then, when the time was ripe I brought you together and kept my fingers crossed.

'Wait a minute,' interrupted Denny. 'I know you; you were the announcer at the wrestling match.'

'Yes indeed. You have both met me many times. Coincidence indeed!' he snorted at Tamar. 'By the way, sorry about the beetroot, I was out of pickles.'

'That was you?' said Tamar, stunned.

'Yes, indeed, also – ' he counted off on his fingers, 'the young witch in Basingstoke, who gave you Kelon's name. And before that the talkative mermaid who led you to the witches, the stag who first led you into Hank's little forest that was a long time ago. And, let's see if you remember this one. "Need a room dearie?".'

'Miss Trenchard? 'Euphemia?' they both said together

'The little man laughed. 'Oh, yes – a cast of thousands, in fact.'

'And I bet you were that old man in New York too, weren't you?' said Denny.

'Old men,' he winked, 'are my specialty. 'They nev'r comes back sonny– no nev'r – heh, heh, heh. Well I had to get you out of that dungeon somehow. *You* weren't coming up with anything. By the way,' he turned to Denny, 'you're not actually fired. I made that phone call. Sorry about that, but you were so close, you had to start focusing on the job, no distractions.'

'So, it was you who took my doll?' said Denny.

'Action figure,' said Tamar, automatically.

'You weren't the man who set the ninjas on us were you?'

'No, no, I was masquerading as a pile of dust at the time. Incidentally, that's also why it took me so long to phone you with the last clue.'

'But why go to so much trouble?' asked Denny. 'Why not just bring us to him?'

'I couldn't do that. You had to do it yourselves. There are rules you know, about free will and so on. All I could do was guide you. Anyway, where was I? Oh, yes, well, how well the plan worked you can see for yourselves. Tamar Black is no longer Djinn; she is human again, as she always should have been. But ...' He grinned. 'The wish you made still stands you know. Old Askphrit – the νόθος' may have twisted it to suit his own ends, and that has been undone. But a wish is a wish. It can't be undone. So now, you are a human with the powers of a Djinn. The best of both worlds you might say. What do you think of that?' If he expected an answer, he did not get one. He got a question instead, from Denny.

'So, is she safe now, from the, from ...?'

'The reality? Yes, quite safe, it already got her as you saw, it was always meant to of course. You see, making the wish was what caused it to take her. Reality caught up with her just as she became human again and she became human because reality caught up with her. A photo finish, you might say.'

'It got her before that,' said Denny angrily.

Clive looked grave. 'I know; I was a bit worried about that. I'm not entirely sure why it came after her so soon; it was probably after you formed the intention to wish Askphrit back into his bottle. As soon as you did that, the die was cast. If you succeeded you were bound to become human again, you see? You even started acting more human, depending on another, feeling hope and fear, falling in love.'

Denny glanced at Tamar. She blushed. She was human now, after all.

'So, I think that's all, unless you have any questions.'

'Why was I so afraid of this place when Denny wasn't?'

'He had nothing to fear. But for you, reality awaited. I'm sure that you knew that on some level, sensed it maybe. Anyway, your fear was instinctive.'

'I have a question,' said Denny. 'How do we get out of here?'

'Wait,' said Tamar suddenly. She turned to Clive. 'you certainly did go to a lot of trouble over this,' she said, I mean, surely … you said the other clerks would have been happy to let it lie – I'm not trying to sound ungrateful but …'

Clive sighed. 'Well, the fact is, it was our fault too; I just couldn't live with that. Askphrit told you that the Djinn were enslaved yes?'

Tamar nodded, it had been a long time ago, but that was one thing she would never forget.

'That was us; we amended the files, the Djinn files in mainframe I mean, but somehow… the file for him was, well it was not done properly, we left him a loophole, that he should never have had.'

'It was you, wasn't it?' said Tamar shrewdly, but not unkindly. 'That was why you took it so personally?'

Clive nodded. 'Yes, Askphrit was my fault. I was the one who … we were so busy in those days, I got distracted, forgot to run the program to test the results, and ended up leaving out some of the protocols that should have been added in his case. I am sorry my dear, but on the other hand, the loophole I accidentally left for him, has now worked in your favour.'

Tamar grinned. 'I suppose it has,' she said.

'Still, it was good of you to go to all this trouble,' said Denny. 'We are grateful, you know.'

Clive smiled expansively. 'It was my responsibility,' he said, 'that was how I saw it. Besides, it's been an experience;

I've enjoyed it all in way. I never knew humans could be so interesting, but it's time to go home now, for all of us,'

'Yes,' said Denny, 'about that …?'

'Well, there's the long answer,' said Clive. 'Or you could just ask superwoman here.'

'Of course,' said Tamar. 'No problem.' She jerked a thumb at the bottle. 'What do we do with him?'

'That's up to you.'

Tamar picked up the bottle and took Denny by the hand.

'Well ... then,' There was an awkward silence. ' … um, thank you – Clive – er, I suppose we should be going. – Er, what will you do now?'

'Oh, back to the filing, you know?'

'Oh – well, good luck with that. Goodbye.'

'Goodbye to you my dear and good luck to you both. Use your power responsibly, I think you're ready.'

'Goodbye,' said Denny. 'And – you know – thanks – for everything.'

'My pleasure – goodbye.'

Tamar snapped her fingers, and they were back. They arrived outside Denny's flat. Pinned to the door was a note. It read. "NOTICE OF EVICTION".

~ Chapter Thirty ~

'HAVE YOU EVER thought about red?' asked Denny.

Tamar looked at him curiously 'Red?' she queried.

'Red hair,' he explained, 'I always liked red hair.'

'Do you *want* me to have red hair?'

'Not if you don't like. I mean I don't want to come over all chauvinistic about it. I mean if you absolutely hate the idea ...'

'No, I don't, not at all. Actually, I spent most of the middle-ages as a redhead. And part of the renaissance too. It was very popular then.'

'Ha, so you were a Djinn-ja?'

Tamar groaned theatrically and threw cushions.

'You know what?' Denny mused. 'I still can't get used to it when you talk about history like that; like you were there.'

'I *was* there.'

'That's what I mean, it's weird. Although, I could have used you when I was at school, I was terrible at history.'

'Hmm, I don't know that I would have been much of a help really. I had a somewhat unique perspective. A lot of what I saw never made it into the history books, all I could have told you is what happened, and that's not the same thing at all. Besides, I missed a lot, living in a bottle. – So, you don't like my hair then?'

'It's beautiful,' he said hastily. 'I didn't mean ... I'm sorry, am I being a sexist pig?'

'In what way?'

'Well, you know – change this or change that. My father was like that. I didn't mean it to sound like an order.'

'It didn't.'

'All right, but now you're thinking about it, just because I suggested it. And you don't really want to; otherwise you'd have done it already, wouldn't you? I was only wondering if you could – if you might...'

'You know what, it's been a while, maybe ...' She shook her hair out. 'Whaddya think?'

'Wow!'

'You like?'

'Yes, but ...'

'But?'

'You look different; I don't know. I'm not sure.'

'Well, I think I look fabulous actually. I'm going to keep it. You got a problem with that?'

'I think I should have just kept my mouth shut.'

'Probably.'

Denny mused for a moment at the transformation and asked 'Why black?'

'Huh?'

'I mean, if you can do that with your hair, why have it black? I mean to say I would have thought, with your personality, you would have gone for blonde. More eye catching.'

Tamar laughed. Hah, says you, the only blonde in the room.'

'I'm not blonde, I'm mousy.'

'Only because you never wash it, you filthy bugger.'

'Well, you haven't answered my question, why not be blonde?'

'It's inverted vanity I suppose,' she said.

'Explain.'

'I have noticed that almost anyone can look prettier with blonde hair, unless they're a real monster. Like you said, it's eye catching. But it takes a real stunner...'

'Like you?'

'Thank you,' said Tamar without a trace of irony. Denny grinned to himself but said nothing.

'A real stunner,' she reiterated, 'to get away with dark hair and still turn heads. You see I'm being completely honest. I'm vain, get used to it.'

'Oh, I don't mind. As long as you don't mind that I'm not. Well, I've got nothing to be vain about, let's face it.'

'You're *not* ugly.'

'That's not what you *used* to think.'

'Shut up.'

Tamar sighed. 'I wish...'

Denny cut her off. 'Don't,' he warned, jerking a thumb at the bottles that sat side by side on the mantel. 'There are still two active Djinn in the house.'

'I know, it's okay.'

'Well, you're human now, you have to be careful.'

'Yes that's the problem.'

'What?'

'Well, I thought it meant that we... that you and I, well you know?'

'I know, but you still have all that power it's too dangerous.'

'I wish – no I *will* say it, I want to say it and to hell with the consequences. I wish I didn't. So we could be together – properly.'

They waited, and Tamar shrugged. 'I don't feel any different.' She shook her hair out to its original midnight black.

'I guess it didn't work,' said Denny. 'Do you have to let him out first?'

'No, how do you think people managed to get us back into the bottle. Once you have the bottle. You have the Djinn, no matter where he is.'

'Then I guess it's not our destiny to be together.'

Tamar snorted. 'Destiny be damned. It should have *worked*.'

'Well it didn't. Maybe if I tried it.' But they both knew it would not make any difference. Tamar had wished for the power, and a wish cannot be undone. These were the consequences.

There was a short silence before Tamar changed the subject. 'We're just putting it off, aren't we?' she said.

'What?'

'You know what.' She jerked a thumb at the plastic bottle on the mantel. 'What are we going to do about *him*?'

* * *

Slammer was furious. 'What did you want to go and do that for?' he raged. 'What am I supposed to do now?'

Tamar shrugged. 'Tidy yourself up – for God's sake, change your name. And get yourself a job.'

'A job? A job?' howled Slammer. 'I *had* a job. Why did you do it to me?'

'Because, the Djinn are a damned plague and a rotten nuisance whose time is over. We're going to get rid of all of you – except one.' She picked up Askphrit's bottle. 'I think a few thousand years in here to think about his sins will do him good.'

'A fitting punishment,' agreed Denny.

'But what about me?' wailed Slammer.

'Well, I guess we're stuck with you, until you get on your feet anyway,' said Tamar.* 'In the meantime, we're going Djinn hunting.'

---

* Slammer lung, after bumming off Tamar and Denny for a while, eventually got sick of them, and – without changing his name – joined the pro – wrestling circuit. And so you could say he lived happily ever.

'Do you think we should?' asked Denny. 'What about the files and all that? Maybe we shouldn't have even done this.' He gestured to Slammer.

'No, you damn well shouldn't,' interjected Slammer, heatedly.

Denny ignored him. 'I mean we don't want Clive coming after us.'

'He won't,' said Tamar calmly. 'It's time, and he knows it too. The Djinn are an anachronism; they don't belong in the world anymore. So, we free them; they become human; they live, they die and they go to the archives.'

'All these Djinn we release, are they all going to be like him?' asked Denny. 'Are we going to end up babysitting all of them?'

Tamar smiled. Virtue is its own punishment,' she said serenely. 'You know the score by now. There are always consequences.

~ EPILOGUE ~

ONE YEAR LATER...

Tamar was lurking, something she had got exceptionally skilled at over the last year.

A different Tamar this, her beauty was still remarkable by human standards, but that was just it, she was now only human. The pale luminosity of her skin had become pallor, and the drama of her presence was reduced. Older, she seemed somehow, and grimmer; not physically exactly, to a casual or loving eye, she looked exactly the same; there was just something about the dark hollowness of her eyes. Being human had taken a toll; the price of freedom is constant vigilance.

She and Denny had tried hard, over the last year, to save the world, one person at a time. Not with grand futile gestures, no world peace, nor the eradication of all evil. Just the saving of lost souls, protecting the innocent and helping ordinary people in trouble like "Amelie" with bite, making only a small difference in the world perhaps, but a big difference in the lives of individuals. They were adding their light to the sum of light; it was the only way.

She wondered why she was skulking in this alleyway, since Denny was several thousand miles away, and did not know where she was anyway. Guilt probably; she should not be doing this, and he would have stopped her if he had known. That was why she was here. She would just do it and then confess later. He would be angry, but it would be too late by then.

The alley was silent; Tamar lifted the bottle out of her bag and pulled out the cork. BANG!!! Curse it.

She looked around furtively. 'Don't be ridiculous,' she told herself. Denny was miles away, and anyone else in earshot would tell themselves that it was a car backfiring. Didn't she know all about the lies people told themselves? She controlled herself,

Askphrit was grinning hugely. 'O' My Mistress... Oh it's you! Well it's about time you let me out.'

'Shut up,' said Tamar, she faltered, why was she doing this? Oh yes. She took a deep breath. 'I wish ...'

Askphrit smiled. Some people never learned.

Next for Tamar and Denny

Reality Bites

Ran-Kur was growing, thirty feet – forty, fifty. Tamar stood her ground and did nothing, except watch silently. Ran-Kur reached down and plucked her off the ground.

The spectators were watching in terrified horror. This was more than they had bargained for.

Tamar was lifted high into the air; Ran-Kur continued to grow.

Denny was panicked. 'She's stuck,' he said. 'Her arms are pinned; she can't reach the dagger.'

Ran-Kur was now seventy feet tall at least. He held Tamar out in front of him on his palm, as he brought her closer to look at her.

'I am the mighty Ran-Kur,' he said. 'That you, puny mortal have dared to summon, now you shall pay the price. My name, it means "ill feeling", and "spite".'

'Yes, I know.'

Ran-Kur lapsed into normal speech for a second. 'Oh, you speak Demon then?' he asked interestedly.

'No, it means the same thing in human.'

'Does it now? Well there's a thing.'

She saw her chance. She crossed her fingers; the dagger seemed awfully small now, and leapt, sliding down the robes, and plunged the dagger into the chest as far as it would go. As she did so, she felt all the strength ebb out of her. She let go of the robes as Ran-Kur gave a shudder and fell.

As she hurtled through the air, powerlessly, she thought, 'at least it worked.'

* * *

The world is overrun with vampires, and finding out where they came from is secondary only to finding out what they want. And who exactly sent them.

Who is the mysterious "Master", and what is happening to Denny is it possible that he has gone over to the dark side?

With both gods and vampires, not to mention a dizzy witch and an extremely suspicious policeman to deal with, can Tamar discover the truth before the whole world goes to hell and she loses everything she ever cared about?

About the Author

Nicola Rhodes often can't remember where she lives so she lives inside her own head most of the time, where even if you do get lost, it's still okay.

She has met many interesting people inside her own head and eventually decided to introduce the rest of the world to them, in the hopes that they would stop bothering her and let her sleep.

She has been doing this for ten years now but they still won't leave her alone.

She wrote this book for fun and does not care if you take away a moral lesson from it or not.

You have her full permission to read whatever you wish into this work of fiction. As she says herself:

"Just because I wrote this book, doesn't mean I know anything about it."